# A Devious Secret

## Gentlemen of London

# Laura Beers

# Chapter One

England, 1813

Mr. Stephen Wycomb had the terrible misfortune of being alive. He should have died alongside his crew on his ship, but instead he was forced to relive the agony of his past failures, over and over. He had no peace, only wretched torment.

He reached for his drink and brought the glass up to his lips. When it was quiet like this, he could practically hear the sounds of the cannons' blasts as they bombarded his ship and the panicked screams of his men as they were boarded. His crew had trusted him with their lives, and he had let them down. He couldn't save them all, despite his best efforts.

Placing the glass down onto the table, he reached into his waistcoat pocket and pulled out a folded piece of paper. He unfolded it and read the names on it. These were the officers that had died on his ship, and he felt it was his duty to speak to their families and to offer his condolences. He had visited all of the families on the list but one. His first lieutenant, his friend. He knew this visit would be the most difficult of all.

Stephen returned the paper to his pocket and reached for

his drink, hoping to numb his pain. He couldn't abide being left alone with his own thoughts. They were unrelenting, causing him to take every piece of joy that he possessed.

He had been so distracted in his misery that he had failed to notice his brother-in-law, Lord Hugh, and Lord Hawthorne until they came to a stop at his table.

Hugh smiled and it grated on his nerves. "I thought I might find you at the club," he said.

There was a time that just the thought of Hugh would make his blood boil, but now he found the man to be somewhat tolerable. He seemed to make his sister, Marielle, very happy. But that didn't mean he had to be nice to the man.

Stephen lowered his glass to the table, not bothering to look up. "It is too early to be dealing with the likes of you," he grumbled.

Hugh didn't appear bothered by his lackluster response. "I see that you are in a pleasant enough mood," he joked as he pulled out a chair. "My brother and I couldn't help but notice that you were sitting alone, and we wanted to keep you company."

"I prefer to be alone. It is much easier that way." Stephen tipped his head at Lord Hawthorne. "My lord," he greeted.

Hawthorne pulled out a chair and sat down. "I do believe I asked you to call me Hawthorne and forego formalities between us." He caught the eye of a passing servant and indicated they wanted drinks.

Hugh leaned forward in his seat. "I wish you would come to live at our townhouse for the duration of the Season and leave that ramshackle place that you call home."

"There is nothing wrong with the place that I rented," Stephen defended. "It is in Westminster and is perfectly respectable."

"Marielle would rather have you close," Hugh attempted.

At the mention of his sister's name, Stephen's tone softened. "I visit her nearly every day. Is that not sufficient enough for her?"

Hugh glanced over his shoulder before he lowered his voice. "She is worried about you."

"There is no reason to be worried about me," Stephen said, dismissing the man's concern. It was warranted on his sister's part, but she couldn't help him. No one could help him now. His misery was too deep.

"I don't think that to be true," Hugh responded. "You have seemed rather despondent as of late, and I know it must have been hard on you when Haddington married Evie."

Stephen stiffened at the mention of Evie's name. "Lady Haddington made her choice, and I have no choice but to respect it. Besides, I do believe it was a fool's errand to try to court her anyways. She was clearly in love with Lord Haddington the entire time. I was just too blind, or stupid, to see that."

Hawthorne spoke up. "There is no shame in following the dictates of your heart."

"I said nothing about love," Stephen said. "I cared for her, deeply, but that is a far cry from love."

"Yet you offered for her?" Hawthorne asked.

"I did, because I knew I could grow to love her," Stephen explained. "She was unlike any woman I have ever known, and she intrigued me."

A server placed two drinks onto the table and asked, "Will there be anything else?"

Hugh shook his head. "Not at this time," he replied, reaching for one of the drinks. "But do keep them coming."

The server acknowledged his words before walking away.

After Hugh took a sip of his drink, he lowered it to the table and asked, "Do you intend to stay for the duration of the Season?"

"I do," Stephen replied. "I am staying for Marielle's sake, nothing more."

Hugh nodded his approval. "She is most grateful for that."

"I need to ensure that Marielle is happily settled before I can return to Brightlingsea," Stephen said.

"You do not need to worry about that since I see to Marielle's happiness now," Hugh remarked.

Stephen held Hugh's gaze. "I will always worry about my sister, especially since she is the only family that I have left."

Hugh gave him an amused look. "Ah, but you forget that you now can count me as family."

"Don't remind me," Stephen muttered. "I would have preferred if Marielle had married anyone else but you."

"Regardless, we must learn to get along for Marielle's sake," Hugh said.

"I agree, but I don't have to like it."

Hugh chuckled. "Who would have thought that we would end up as brothers when we were fighting with each other at Eton?"

"Brothers-in-law," Stephen corrected. "There is a distinction."

Hawthorne interjected, "My mother was hoping you would join us for dinner this evening."

"I would be honored, but you don't need to keep feeding me," Stephen said. "I do employ a cook."

"Yes, that also acts as a housekeeper," Hawthorne remarked. "You need to hire more household staff."

"The staff is sufficient for my needs," Stephen assured him.

Hawthorne gave him a look that implied he didn't believe him. "Do you even employ a valet?"

"There is no need. I have managed to dress myself for many years on my ship," Stephen replied. "You learn to make do with what you have when you are on the high seas for months on end."

"But you are not at sea anymore," Hugh said. "You are attempting to navigate the trappings of high Society."

"I don't know why I bother since the *ton* will never accept me as one of their own. I just own a shipyard," Stephen said.

"A very successful shipyard which has made you a very rich man," Hugh pointed out.

"That it has, but I detest the pomp that comes with interacting with the *ton*," Stephen griped.

"That, my friend, goes along with it," Hugh said.

Stephen swirled the drink in his hand. "We are not friends."

"Yet," Hugh corrected.

"No, not ever," Stephen said. "We both can tolerate one another's existence for Marielle's sake, but we do not have anything in common."

Lord Grenton approached the table and pulled out a chair. "Good afternoon, gentlemen," he greeted.

Stephen knew that he should count himself fortunate that Hugh's friends had embraced him so willingly, but he was more than happy to be alone. Although, he did find Grenton to be an interesting fellow. He allowed his wife to spend most of her time at an orphanage in the rookeries. It was very progressive of him.

With a tip of his head, he acknowledged Lord Grenton. "Grenton," he said.

Grenton leaned to the side as a server placed new drinks into the center of the table. "Did I interrupt something?" he asked, glancing between Hugh and Stephen.

Hugh grinned. "Stephen was just telling me that we will never be friends."

"I wouldn't catch Marielle hearing you say that," Grenton teased, turning his attention towards Stephen. "She is adamant that you get along with Hugh."

"And I will," Stephen said, "when she is around."

Grenton smirked. "Is it so awful to be Hugh's friend?"

"You seem to forget that Hugh used to line the inside of my trousers with honey," Stephen replied.

Hugh shrugged nonchalantly. "That was only because you would pour jam into the pockets of my jackets."

"I do believe that was in retaliation for you dumping a bucket of water onto my feather mattress," Stephen remarked. "It always stunk after that."

"Maybe you shouldn't have put worms in my bed," Hugh said.

Stephen opened his mouth, but Hawthorne spoke first. "That was in the past, and you two need to accept that you will now be in each other's lives."

Grenton shifted in his seat towards Hugh and said, "I had forgotten that he put worms in your bed."

"They were no regular worms either. They were big and fat." Hugh shuddered. "It was dark when I pulled back my sheets and I didn't notice them until I crawled into bed."

Stephen tossed back his drink before saying, "I will admit that was rather a cruel trick to play on you."

"It was no less than what I deserved," Hugh replied. "Our antics did get out of hand, and I do question the headmaster making us sleep in the same room."

"That was some faulty logic on his part," Stephen said. "It didn't bring us together. Frankly, it only made us hate each other even more."

"That it did," Hugh agreed.

Stephen pushed his empty glass away from him. "I should be going. I have a meeting with my solicitor."

Hawthorne met his gaze and shared, "I would be remiss if I did not inform you that my cousin, Lady Hawkinge, will be joining us for dinner this evening."

"Duly noted," Stephen said.

"Her husband died over a year and a half ago and my mother invited her for the remainder of the Season now that her mourning period is over," Hugh shared.

"I do not know why this is any of my concern," Stephen

said. "With any luck, she will dismiss me as unimportant and will avoid me altogether."

Hawthorne grew solemn. "My cousin has had a rough go of it, and she will need our support."

Rising, Stephen remarked, "I have no intention of being mean to the woman, if that is what you are implying. I am, after all, a gentleman."

"What my brother is trying to say," Hugh started, "is for you to change everything about yourself before dinner. You are far too boorish and might frighten my cousin with the resting scowl on your face."

"I do not scowl," Stephen said.

Grenton gave him a knowing look. "You are a scowler, but there is no shame in that. I was the same way before I met Georgie," he said. "It will all change when you meet the right woman."

Stephen blanched. "I have no desire to get married at this time."

"I do believe we all said something similar, and we all fell prey to the parson's mousetrap," Grenton said.

"I am in earnest," Stephen stated. "My dog is the only companion that I need."

Hawthorne bobbed his head. "That is good because I do not want you to become enamored with Gemma, giving me a reason to challenge you to a duel."

Stephen pushed back in his chair and took a step back. "Trust me, you do not want to challenge me to a duel, Hawthorne. I am an excellent marksman."

"As am I," Hawthorne asserted.

"Regardless, I can assure you that I will stay away from your cousin," Stephen said. "I would rather chew glass than attempt to court another woman." He tipped his hat at them. "Good day, gentlemen."

As Stephen walked through the main hall of his club, he found it preposterous that Hawthorne would even imply this widow would turn his head. No, he was destined to be alone. His life was not conducive to having a wife and it would be best if he stayed far away from this woman- this Lady Hawkinge.

Gemma, Countess of Hawkinge, was tired. She was tired of pretending that all was well when she had an innate desire to do something more with her life. Her life consisted of sitting around the Dowager House and drinking tea. But she didn't dare complain about her lot in life for fear that it could be taken from her.

Her husband had died over a year and a half ago and he had only left her with a worthless piece of land, leaving her entirely at the whim of her brother-in-law. Henry was not a bad man, but she felt he spent entirely too much of his time trying to manage her. And she didn't need to be managed.

Reaching in the folds of her gown, she removed the letter that her aunt had written to her. Lady Montfort had invited her for the remainder of the Season now that she was out of mourning. She had to admit that she was excited about going. She couldn't wait to see the sights of London and to walk through Hyde Park. It had been far too long since she had last done that.

Gemma felt tears burn in the back of her eyes. Baldwin had confessed his love for her at Hyde Park, and it had been the happiest day of her life. She had naively thought they would have had a life full of love and happiness, but Baldwin had been taken from her much too early.

The main door opened, and she could hear Henry's familiar voice as he conversed with her butler. A moment later, Henry stepped into the room with a smile on his face.

Henry was a handsome man with his dark brown hair,

square jaw, and wide shoulders. Physically, he reminded her so much of her late husband, but Henry did have a temper. It would only flare up on occasion, and she was mindful to avoid him at these times.

"Good morning, Gemma," Henry greeted.

She returned his smile, knowing what was expected of her. "Good morning," she said.

"I came to join you for breakfast this morning. I do hope you haven't eaten yet."

Gemma returned the letter to the folds of her gown. "I have not," she replied. "I was just reading a letter from my aunt."

"I hope all is well."

Rising, Gemma said, "It is." She knew it wasn't the right moment to reveal that her aunt had invited her to Town. Frankly, she wasn't quite sure how Henry would react to her leaving Hawkinge.

Henry approached her and offered his hand. Gemma slipped her gloved hand into his and allowed him to assist her in rising.

As she went to remove her hand, Henry caught hold of it and moved it into the crook of his arm. "You must allow me to escort you into the dining room," he said.

"But, of course," Gemma responded. She wanted to chide him for being too familiar, but she knew he would dismiss it out of hand. She had learned it was better for her if she just accepted the way things were around here.

Henry led her through the entry hall and into the dining room. He dropped his arm, waved off the footman, and went to pull out a chair for her.

"Thank you," Gemma murmured as she sat down.

Henry went to sit at the head of the long rectangular table. "How are you faring this morning?" he asked.

"I am well."

With a watchful eye, he said, "I noticed that you did not go riding this morning."

Gemma leaned to the side as a footman placed a cup of tea in front of her. "I'm afraid I was not feeling up to it," she admitted.

"Should I send for the doctor?"

"That won't be necessary," she rushed to reply. The last thing she wanted was the doctor to suggest bloodletting as a treatment.

A footman placed a plate in front of her with her usual breakfast of a piece of toast and one hard-boiled egg.

Henry looked at her plate with disapproval. "I do not know why you insist on eating so little for breakfast."

"It is sufficient for me."

"That is hardly enough food for a pigeon." Henry snapped his fingers at the footman. "Bring Lady Hawkinge another egg and some chops and liver."

Gemma frowned as she glanced down at her plate. There was no point in arguing with Henry, especially when he got like this.

Henry turned his attention back towards her. "I find that a hearty breakfast prepares me for the day."

Reaching for her piece of toast, she took a bite of it and took her time chewing. It was far more preferable than talking to Henry. If he really knew what she was thinking, he would no doubt punish her for her insolence.

Henry took a sip of his tea and said, "I will be in meetings all day with my solicitor, but I was hoping you would join me for dinner this evening."

Gemma felt dread in the pit of her stomach as she knew the time had come to discuss her plans with him. She had no doubt that this would be a battle of the wills, and she had no desire to back down.

Placing the piece of toast back onto her plate, she gave him a smile and hoped that it would disarm him. "My aunt,

Lady Montfort, has invited me to join them for the remainder of the Season."

Henry just stared at her, his expression giving nothing away. Finally, he asked, "Why would you wish to go to London?"

"I was hoping to go to the opera, tour the menagerie, and visit the shops on Bond Street," Gemma replied.

"London is terribly overcrowded and the smell wafting off the River Thames is horrific this time of year."

"That is true, but I do believe the good outweighs the bad."

Henry shook his head. "It is a terrible idea," he said. "I think it would be best if you remain here."

"Why?" she asked. "Not only am I out of mourning but I am rather bored."

Henry picked up his fork and pointed it at her. "Then we shall acquire new books for your library."

"Books are hardly the issue," she responded.

"Then what is the issue?" Henry asked as he started eating.

Gemma shifted in her seat to face him. "I would like to spend time with my aunt, uncle and cousins," she said. "It would be nice to be around family."

Henry's nostrils flared slightly. "Am I not your family?"

"Yes, you are, and I meant no disrespect," Gemma rushed out. "I just thought a change of scenery might do me good."

"I agree, but it is much too soon for you to return to Society," Henry said.

"I respectfully disagree."

Henry pursed his lips. "Have you forgotten my brother so soon?"

Gemma lowered her gaze and murmured, "There is not a day that goes by that I do not think about Baldwin."

"Yet you are rushing to London like a love-craved debutante."

"I am not going to London to seek another husband," Gemma asserted.

"Good, because I fear that you would be sorely disappointed," Henry remarked. "Baldwin left you hardly anything and you are living off my good graces."

Bringing her gaze back up, Gemma replied, "I am aware, and I am most grateful for your kindness and generosity."

"No respectable man in high Society would offer for a woman that had no dowry or inheritance of her own," Henry pressed. "You may be beautiful, my dear, but you have nothing of value to offer to any man. It is a simple fact."

"I am well aware of my shortcomings, but I still wish to go to London."

"Your dresses are hardly in the height of fashion, and I refuse to pay for a whole new wardrobe for you," Henry said. "You would be a laughingstock the moment you stepped foot into a social event and that would reflect poorly on me."

Gemma took a sip of her tea as she gathered her courage to keep fighting. "My gowns are almost two years old, but I am sure my lady's maid could make some adjustments on them."

"What of the household staff at the Dowager House?" he demanded. "Do you expect me to continue paying their wages while you are cavorting around London?"

"I assure you that I will not be cavorting," she replied. "Furthermore, I do have some money that could go towards their wages. It isn't much, mind you, but I think it will be sufficient."

"I have no doubt that Baldwin would think this was a terrible idea. He cared greatly for the people in the village, and you are just abandoning them."

"I will only be gone for a few months," she argued.

"Who will care for the medicinal herbs in your garden and dispense them, as needed?"

"My housekeeper, Mrs. Wallace, has graciously agreed to take over that responsibility while I am away."

Henry glanced over at the footman before he lowered his voice. "I do hope your desire to go to London is not an attempt to rid yourself of me for a short period of time."

Gemma had to admit that she would enjoy some time away from Henry, especially since he was becoming increasingly familiar with her. But she didn't dare admit that to him.

"Heavens, no," she lied, hoping her words sounded convincing. "That is the farthest thing from the truth. I just need some time away, for my own sanity."

Henry considered her for a long moment before he let out a heavy sigh. "Very well, then," he said. "If you are adamant about going to London, I will go with you, and you can reside at my townhouse."

"I would prefer to stay with my aunt."

"For what purpose?" Henry asked, his voice rising. "Is my townhouse not grand enough for you?"

Gemma knew she needed to proceed cautiously and try to stroke Henry's ego. "No, far from it. Your townhouse is one of the grandest in all of London, but there are far too many painful memories associated with it and Baldwin."

Henry leaned back in his chair. "I know you must think me insensitive, but I promised Baldwin that I would look after you on his deathbed. And I intend to fulfill that promise."

"I can take care of myself," she said, knowing her words lacked conviction.

"You are just a woman, and you cannot possibly understand the depravities of men," Henry said. "Who will protect you from the men that just want to use you and toss you aside?"

Gemma fidgeted with the napkin in her hand. "Not only will I be under my uncle's protection, but I have my cousins, Lord Hawthorne and Lord Hugh, to see after me."

"They won't have time for you since they will be busy

entertaining their new wives," Henry asserted. "You will be forgotten, neglected, and you will be begging to come home."

"I do not think that will be the case, especially since my aunt has sent a coach for me," Gemma revealed. "It should be arriving this afternoon."

Henry narrowed his eyes. "You already agreed to this madness?"

"I did." Gemma lowered her eyes to her lap rather than meet Henry's infuriated gaze. "I did not think you would object so vehemently."

Shoving back his chair, Henry rose and walked over to the window. The silence was deafening as he clasped his hands behind his back. She didn't dare to speak up and risk stoking Henry's ire even more. He would speak when he was ready.

Henry turned towards her and said, "I cannot stop you, but I want you to consider the consequences of your actions." His voice was calm, but stern.

"Which are?" she asked with dread in her voice.

Henry unclasped his arms. "You are still the Countess of Hawkinge, and I will expect you to behave accordingly."

"I know what is expected of me."

He scoffed. "If you did, you wouldn't be wasting your time in London. You would remain here and be content."

Gemma rose from her seat. "I am not doing this to spite you, my lord," she said. "I just want to remember what it is like to laugh again."

"Do I not make you laugh?" Henry asked, the hurt evident on his features.

Coming to stand in front of him, Gemma shook her head. "You have been nothing but kind to me, but I can't keep hiding out here in the Dowager House. I need to do something more with my life."

"And you think you will find it in London?"

"I don't know, but it is worth a try," she admitted softly.

Henry placed a hand on her sleeve. "Go to London, but make sure you come back at the end of the Season."

"I will."

"Promise me that you will not engage in any scandalous behavior," Henry said.

Gemma bobbed her head. "I promise."

Henry dropped his arm from her sleeve. "Very well, then, I would imagine you have much to do before the coach arrives."

"I do."

"I must admit that it will be very lonely here without you," Henry said. "Perhaps I will travel to London as well and call upon you to ensure you are being properly tended to."

"I would like that."

"Would you?" Henry asked as he held her gaze.

Unsure of his meaning and feeling slightly uncomfortable, Gemma took a step back and said, "I should be going."

A flash of disappointment crossed Henry's features. "I do wish you safe travels, my dear," he said before he departed the room.

Gemma watched his retreating figure and knew that she had made the right decision. It would be for the best if they had some time apart.

## Chapter Two

With every rotation of the wheels, Gemma felt more at peace with her decision to travel to London. She knew her experience would be vastly different than what she was accustomed to. She had been the diamond of the first water during her first Season and had caught the eye of many handsome lords. But everything changed when she had been introduced to Baldwin. With his intoxicating blue eyes, she had fallen hard, and he quickly occupied her heart.

When Baldwin died, she had been nearly inconsolable, but time had dulled that pain. She used to frequent his grave every day, hoping to feel close to him, but she always left feeling more alone than she had when she arrived.

Tears came to her eyes, and she wondered if she would ever stop crying when she thought of Baldwin. They had only been married for three years, but he had been her whole world during that time. How could she go on without him?

Her dark-haired lady's maid's voice broke through her musings. "Are you thinking about your husband?" Lydia asked with compassion in her voice.

Gemma reached up and swiped at the tear that was sliding down her cheek. "I am," she admitted.

She was most grateful that she was traveling with Lydia, who had been her lady's maid since before her coming out ball. They had grown close after her husband's death, and she was grateful that she could be so open and honest with her, which was a rarity amongst servants. But Lydia had proven herself to be a trusted confidante over the years.

Lydia gave her an understanding look. "He was a good man."

"That he was. He was the best of men," Gemma agreed. "But I do need to stop crying whenever I think of him."

"There is no shame in that."

"A lady does not cry in public," Gemma said. She could practically hear her mother say those words. Her mother had always taken it upon herself to teach her how to be a proper lady from a young age. When girls were outside playing games, she was with her mother, sipping tea and conversing with the women that had come to call.

Lydia adjusted the sleeves of her maid's uniform. "You must give yourself some allowance since you have only recently ended the mourning period for your husband."

"I do believe I will always mourn for him."

"As well as you should," Lydia said. "You loved him deeply. That kind of love does not just disappear."

"Lord Hawkinge accused me of forgetting my husband by going to Town."

Lydia pressed her lips together. "I would not give Lord Hawkinge's words any credence. They are just that- words."

Gemma glanced out the window and admired the townhouses as they drove by. She did miss the excitement of London and the constant stream of social events.

"Do you intend to see your father while you are in Town?" Lydia asked.

"I do not."

"It has been years since you last saw him."

Gemma frowned. "My father made his choice when he

married that horrible woman," she said. "My mother hadn't been dead a month before they exchanged their vows."

"That was in bad form, but he is still your father."

She brought her gaze back to meet Lydia's. "My father has not attempted to contact me once since his nuptials. He didn't even attend Baldwin's funeral."

"That is true, but—"

Gemma cut her off. "Why are you trying to defend my father's actions?"

"Because there were things I wish I had said to my father before he passed," Lydia replied. "For once they are gone, the opportunity goes away, leaving you wondering what could have been."

"If my father cared a whit for me, he would have been there when I truly needed him." Gemma worked hard to keep the sadness out of her voice. Their estrangement had taken a toll on her, but she refused to acknowledge how much her father had hurt her.

Fortunately, before Lydia could reply, the coach came to a stop in front of a lavish whitewashed townhouse with gold embellishments over the windows.

The footman opened the door and extended his hand to assist her out of the coach. She slipped her gloved hand into his and went to step down onto the pavement.

She had just taken a step towards the main door when it was opened, and the familiar butler greeted her. "Good afternoon, my lady."

Gemma stepped into the entry hall and removed her hat. "It is good to see you looking so well, Balfour."

Balfour's eyes crinkled in the corners as he went to accept her hat. His eyebrows were mostly white, but a few black strands remained. "You are much too kind, but I am slowing down in my old age," he said, placing the hat down onto a table. "Your aunt has been expecting you. If you will follow me, I will announce you."

"That won't be necessary," Gemma insisted. "I know the way."

Balfour tipped his head. "Very good, my lady."

Gemma walked over to the drawing room and promptly recognized her Aunt Edith's voice that was drifting out into the entry hall. She took a moment to smooth down her blue traveling habit, hoping she looked somewhat presentable.

Taking a step into the room, she saw that her aunt was conversing with a blonde-haired young woman.

Her aunt stopped speaking when she saw her, and a smile came to her lips. "Gemma," she said, rising, "you have finally arrived."

"I have," she responded, suddenly feeling very nervous.

Her aunt crossed the room and gave her a warm embrace. As she leaned back, she said, "It is so good to see you, my dear."

Gemma felt herself relax in her aunt's arms. "Thank you."

Dropping her arms, her aunt gestured towards the blonde-haired young woman. "Allow me to introduce you to my daughter-in-law, Dinah, the Countess of Hawthorne."

Gemma dropped into a curtsy. "A pleasure."

Dinah offered her a kind smile. "I have heard so much about you that I feel as if I already know you."

"I am not sure if I should be relieved or frightened," Gemma joked.

Dinah laughed, just as she had intended. "Would you care for some tea?" she asked, waving her hand over the teapot.

"I would love some," Gemma replied.

Her aunt looped arms with her and started leading her towards the settee. "I am so glad that you decided to join us for the rest of the Season."

"I do appreciate the invitation," Gemma said.

"It is the least I could do for my favorite niece."

"I am your only niece."

Aunt Edith slipped Gemma's arms out of hers and returned to her seat. "Regardless, I am excited that you are here, and I know your cousins feel the same."

"Where are Nathaniel and Hugh?" Gemma asked as she sat across from her aunt and Dinah.

Dinah handed her a cup of tea and replied, "Nathaniel is rather busy today and Hugh is spending time with Marielle."

Nathaniel's voice came from the doorway. "I am never too busy to say hello to my favorite cousin."

Gemma placed her cup down onto the table and rose to face him. She was surprised to see that he was wearing a blue jacket that had tattered sleeves and his boots could use a good polish. It was a far cry from what she expected an earl to wear.

As Nathaniel walked further into the room, he asked, "How was your journey to Town?"

"It was uneventful."

"Those are the best kind of trips." Nathaniel went and slipped his arm around his wife's waist before asking, "How are you faring?"

Nathaniel and Dinah exchanged a look of love that caused Gemma to feel a twinge of jealousy. She used to look at Baldwin like that.

"I am well," Dinah replied.

Nathaniel leaned in and pressed his lips against Dinah's. "I will be home for dinner," he said as he leaned back.

"I will be looking forward to it," Dinah responded.

Her aunt spoke up. "Dear heavens, you two must learn to behave when we have company," she chided lightly.

"Gemma isn't company. She is family," Nathaniel pointed out. "Besides, I always am looking for a reason to kiss my wife."

"I think it is admirable," Gemma said. "Baldwin used to do the same thing."

Nathaniel gave her a sad smile. "I do miss Baldwin."

"As do I," Gemma murmured.

Her aunt picked up her teacup and took a sip. Then she said, "You may go, Nathaniel. We have much to discuss with Gemma."

Nathaniel chuckled. "I shall be on my way, but not before I steal another kiss from my wife."

"You can't steal what is freely given, my love," Dinah said.

Gemma went to sit down and reached for her teacup. She was happy for her cousin, but it hurt to see a couple that was so in love. It made her yearn for what she once had.

Once Nathaniel departed from the room, Dinah sat down next to Lady Montfort and said, "I do hope our displays of affection do not upset you."

"Not at all," Gemma lied.

"I wanted to thank you for your most thoughtful gift for our wedding," Dinah said. "You are a very talented painter."

"I will admit that painting helped me through some of the darker days that I had after Baldwin died."

Her aunt's eyes held compassion. "You have had a rough go of it, but you will make it through this most difficult time."

Gemma wanted to believe her aunt, but she didn't think she would ever be happy again. Her heart was shattered and there were too many pieces to pick up.

Dinah picked up a biscuit off the tray and took a bite. "I understand that you enjoy riding."

Gemma perked up. "I do, and I brought my horse with me."

"Wonderful," Dinah said. "We shall have to go riding together."

"I will be looking forward to it."

Aunt Edith perused the length of her. "I hope you do not mind but the dressmaker will be arriving shortly to measure you for some new gowns."

Gemma winced as she was forced to admit, "I'm afraid I do not have the funds to pay for additional gowns."

"I said nothing about you paying for them," her aunt said. "This is my gift to you."

With a shake of her head, she responded, "That is much too generous."

"Nonsense," her aunt asserted. "It is the least I could do for you, considering your father is a dunderhead."

A giggle escaped her lips, which was something that had not happened in a long time. "My father *is* a dunderhead," she agreed.

Her aunt nodded in approval. "I had hoped that he would have come around, but he is still the same hardheaded man that I knew growing up." She shifted her gaze to Dinah. "I am not sure if Nathaniel told you, but Lord Winsley is my brother."

"He did, but I have not had the pleasure of meeting him," Dinah said.

"There is no pleasure, especially if he is with his wife," her aunt responded. "That woman got her claws into him and has refused to release her hold on him."

Gemma took a sip of her drink. "When was the last time you spoke to him?"

"I saw him at Lady Westmoore's soiree a few days ago, but we only exchanged a few words before that woman returned to his side."

"That is most unfortunate," Gemma said. "I'm afraid I haven't spoken to him since he told me that he intended to remarry."

"I can only imagine how hard that conversation must have been for you," her aunt remarked.

Gemma sighed. "I do not understand how my father could have moved on so quickly, as if my mother meant nothing to him."

"I know your parents had an arranged marriage, but they appeared to have genuine affection for one another," her aunt said.

"I thought they did, or at least I hope they did," Gemma said.

Balfour stepped into the room, interrupting their conversation. "A Madame Gallant has arrived with her assistants, and I have set her up in the parlor."

"Wonderful." Her aunt placed the cup of tea down onto the table and rose. "Shall we adjourn to the parlor for your fitting?"

Gemma took a long sip from her teacup before returning it to the tray. As she rose, she said, "I cannot thank you enough for your generosity."

Her aunt dismissed Gemma with a wave of her hand. "It is the least I can do. After all, we can't have you traipsing through London in old gowns, now can we?"

"I suppose not."

***

Stephen grumbled to himself as he sat in his coach. He was annoyed that he had agreed to accept the invitation to dine with Hawthorne and his family. If he wanted to see Marielle, he could have called upon her this afternoon rather than being stuck dining with a plethora of people. Now he had no choice but to pretend that all was well, even though he felt empty inside.

He hadn't always been this miserable. He had loved being a captain in the Royal Navy and overseeing his own ship. But now he was running a shipyard. A very profitable shipyard. His father's man of business had seen to that. Yet, he would give it all up to feel something again.

The coach came to a stop in front of Lord Montfort's townhouse and he opened the door. He knew it was expected of him to wait for the footman, but he was tired of doing what he should. He would much rather do what he *wanted* to do.

He may have been born into this life of privilege, but he had experienced the worst depravities of men when he was in the French prison. It had changed him, and not necessarily for the better. It made him realize that he couldn't keep going on as he had. He felt lost in a world of nothingness; a world of scorn and noise. Something had to give, and he wasn't entirely sure what that was.

After he stepped onto the pavement, he adjusted the black top hat on his head before he approached the main door. He had just reached for the knocker when the door opened.

"Good evening, Mr. Wycomb," Balfour said as he went to stand to the side. "I hope you had a pleasant day."

Stephen resisted the urge to huff. He hadn't had a pleasant day since his ship had been sunk by the French. "It was tolerable," he decided on.

Balfour maintained his stoic expression, showing no reaction to his jaded response. "I was just about to ring the dinner bell," he said. "If you follow me, I will show you to the drawing room."

"That won't be necessary," Stephen said. "I can find my own way."

"If you insist, sir," Balfour responded.

Stephen made his way across the entry hall and stepped in the drawing room. He had been to this townhouse nearly every day since his sister had returned from her wedding tour with Hugh. He wanted to spend as much time with her before the end of the Season. After that, he intended to return home to Brightlingsea- alone. That is what he preferred. Frankly, that is what he deserved.

His eyes roamed the spacious rectangular-shaped room and his eyes landed on the pianoforte. He used to listen to his mother play for hours. He smiled at that memory.

Marielle's voice came from the doorway. "Careful, Brother. If you continue to smile like that, one might think you are actually enjoying yourself," she teased.

He turned to face her. "I was just thinking about how Mother would play the pianoforte for hours as she attempted to memorize the pieces."

"Mother loved nothing more than playing for others," Marielle reflected.

"That she did."

Marielle walked further into the room with a smile on her face. "I am so pleased that you decided to join us for dinner."

"I didn't have much of a choice," Stephen admitted. "I didn't dare refuse Lady Montfort."

"Regardless, I am glad that you are here."

Stephen studied his sister for a moment. Her smile was genuine, and she appeared to radiate happiness. If he didn't love his sister so, he would find it downright irritating.

"You seem happy," he commented.

Marielle's smile grew brighter, if that was even possible. "That is because I am."

"Are you sure?" he asked. "Because if you aren't, I will gladly remove you from this place."

"Hugh would never let that happen."

"I am not afraid of Hugh."

Marielle went to sit down on the settee. "I know you aren't, but he has been the perfect husband."

"There is no such thing."

"True, but he has made me blissfully happy," she responded. "He has even fulfilled his promise not to gamble anymore."

Stephen walked over to a yellow upholstered armchair and placed his hands on the back. "It hasn't been that long since you two were wed. What if he changes his mind?"

"I am not concerned," Marielle said. "He is a man of his word."

He frowned at his sister's response. Could she truly be that naïve? "I just fear that you are blinded by love."

"So what if I am?" Marielle asked. "There is no shame in loving one's husband."

Stephen put his hand up, knowing he was fighting a losing battle. "You are right. Forget I said anything."

Marielle eyed him curiously. "Did you just admit that I was right?"

"I did."

"That was admirable of you, Brother," she said. "You never admit that you are wrong."

"That is because I rarely am."

Marielle laughed as he had intended. "You are incorrigible."

"What will you do when the Season is over?"

"Hugh and I intend to retire to our Brookhaven estate," Marielle shared. "We want to be close to family but still maintain our own residence."

"I think that is wise."

Marielle lifted her brow. "I am surprised that you stayed in Town this long."

"I am here to ensure you are being taken care of." He came around the chair and sat down. "Besides, my man of business is proficient at what he does."

"Father thought so, as well."

The sound of the dinner bell chimed in the distance, beckoning everyone to come.

Stephen turned his head towards the noise. "I do not think I could live as you do."

"It is not so different from the way we were raised," Marielle said. "Our home was filled with servants to tend to our every whim."

"I'm afraid I have become accustomed to caring for myself."

"You will need to get over that," Marielle joked.

Stephen brought his gaze back to meet hers. "Your life is

filled with social events. Do you ever grow tired of the demands that are placed on your time?"

"That is what is expected of me," Marielle said. "I knew what I was getting into when I married a son of a marquess."

"It sounds dreadful."

"To you, perhaps. But I rather enjoy dancing with my husband."

Stephen's lips twitched. "You should know that I danced with Hugh on occasion."

"You did?"

"When our headmaster at Eton brought in the dancing master, we were forced to dance with one another," Stephen shared. "We made it a point to stomp as hard as we could on each other's boots."

"That doesn't surprise me in the least," Marielle said.

Hugh's amused voice came from behind him. "Stephen would never let me lead either."

Stephen shrugged. "One could hardly blame me because you acted more like a girl than a man."

As Hugh went to sit down next to his wife, he said, "I am glad that you decided to join us."

"Liar," Stephen said.

Hugh chuckled. "For some reason, your presence makes my wife happy so I am inclined to tolerate you."

"That is most gracious of you."

With a glance at the door, Hugh said, "My cousin, Lady Hawkinge, arrived this afternoon and she will be down shortly."

"Wonderful," he muttered. Why did that concern him in the least? He wanted nothing to do with Lady Hawkinge.

Hugh lowered his voice. "She is still mourning her husband deeply and it is as if a dark cloud hangs over her."

Marielle spoke up. "I didn't sense that when I met Gemma. She was quite pleasant, and I have enjoyed getting to know her."

"Gemma has always been a force to be reckoned with," Hugh shared. "But now she seems more reserved."

"Perhaps she grew up," Stephen suggested. "I would imagine that marriage has a way of sorting out one's priorities and determining what is truly important."

Hugh glanced at his wife before saying, "Marriage changed me for the better."

"Good, because you were intolerable before," Stephen jested.

Hugh didn't look amused by his joking. "Just promise me that you will behave when you are around Gemma."

Stephen didn't know why it mattered to Hugh how he acted around Lady Hawkinge. He had no intention of showing any attention towards her. Why should he? He had no interest in marriage, not since Evie had rejected his suit.

"I promise," he settled on.

His words seemed to appease Hugh and he reached for his wife's hand. "Did Marielle inform you that we are retiring to our Brookhaven estate after the Season?"

"She did."

"We are pleased with it and—" Hugh's words cut off as he abruptly rose. "Good evening, Cousin."

Rising, Stephen turned towards the doorway and saw a woman with dark brown hair. Her hair was piled high on her head and long curls framed her face. She had pale skin, which contrasted nicely with her deep-set green eyes, high cheekbones, and a pronounced jawline.

Whatever he had been expecting when he thought of Lady Hawkinge, it had not been this. A beautiful young woman stood in front of him, and her eyes spoke volumes before her lips moved. There was a sadness to them, one that he recognized in himself.

Lady Hawkinge smiled weakly at her cousin. "Good evening, Hugh."

Hugh gestured towards Stephen. "Mr. Wycomb, allow me

the privilege of introducing you to my dear cousin, Lady Hawkinge."

Her eyes shifted to him, and the smile left her lips. "It is a pleasure to meet you, Mr. Wycomb." Her words were cordial enough, but he could tell that she was just being polite.

Stephen bowed. "Likewise, Lady Hawkinge."

Lady Hawkinge remained in the doorway and he could see hesitancy on her face. She glanced over her shoulder as if she were debating about fleeing from the room.

Hugh must have sensed this, too, so he encouraged, "Do join us for a moment. The others should be down shortly."

Lady Hawkinge slowly walked further into the room. "I apologize for intruding."

"You did no such thing," Marielle asserted. "We were just discussing our country estate."

Stephen watched as Lady Hawkinge went to sit next to Hugh in an armchair before he claimed his seat. She appeared to relax slightly as she remained close to her cousin.

Keeping hold of his wife's hand, Hugh shifted on the settee to face his cousin. "Did you have a nice rest?"

"I did," Lady Hawkinge said, her voice no louder than a whisper.

Stephen couldn't help but wonder if her shyness was due to his presence, but he felt compelled to speak to the young widow.

"I understand that you are spending the rest of the Season with Lady Montfort," he said.

Lady Hawkinge nodded. "Yes, she was gracious enough to invite me."

"That was kind of her."

"It was," Lady Hawkinge agreed.

Stephen waited for her to expand on the topic, but he was left disappointed. What would it take for her to converse with him?

A silence descended over the group and before it grew

awkward, Marielle revealed, "Gemma and I are going shopping tomorrow with Lady Montfort."

"Wonderful, you are going to spend more of my money," Hugh teased.

"I do believe you said it was 'our money'," Marielle bantered back.

Hugh gave his wife a loving look. "I am just teasing you," he said. "Everything that I have is yours."

Stephen snuck a peek at Lady Hawkinge and saw that she was looking at Hugh and Marielle with a longing look on her face. It was evident that she had been affected by Hugh's words. However, before he could respond, Lady Montfort stepped into the room with Lord and Lady Hawthorne trailing close behind.

Lady Montfort's eyes roamed the room before announcing, "Dinner is ready to be served. Shall we adjourn to the dining room?"

Hugh promptly rose and started leading Marielle towards the door. Rising, Stephen went to offer his hand to Lady Hawkinge to assist her in rising.

Lady Hawkinge tentatively slipped her hand into his and allowed him to assist her. Once she was standing, she withdrew her hand and clasped her hands together.

"May I escort you to the dining room?" he asked as he offered his arm.

With a glance at his arm, he could tell that Lady Hawkinge wished to refuse him, but would she? He would take no offense if she did, but he hoped that she wouldn't. There was something about her that caused him to pause, despite only just meeting her.

Propriety won out and she placed her hand on top of his. "Thank you," she murmured. "You are most kind."

Stephen felt as if he had secured a small victory as he led her into the dining room.

# Chapter Three

Gemma's eyes were downcast as she listened to the lively conversation that was going on around her at the dining table. She wanted to join in, but she found her heart wasn't in it. While she had been in her mourning period, she had spent so much time alone that she had grown accustomed to the silence. It was during this time that she reflected on what she had with Baldwin. He may not have been perfect, but he had been perfect for her.

She felt tears forming in her eyes, but blinked them back. There would be no good that would come from crying in front of her hosts. Furthermore, she had no desire to cry in front of Mr. Wycomb. He may not be as sympathetic as her family would be, not that she cared about what his opinion was of her.

Mr. Wycomb may be a handsome man with his dark hair, broad shoulders and square jaw, but there was a heavy solemnness about him that contrasted with his kind eyes. It made her wonder what battles he was fighting within himself. Not that she was thinking about him.

Her aunt's voice broke through her musings. "Is something wrong with your soup, dear?"

Gemma brought her gaze up and saw that everyone was watching her. "I'm afraid you caught me woolgathering," she admitted with a sheepish smile. It was only then that she noticed that everyone had finished their soup and they had been waiting on her to do the same.

She reached for her spoon and dipped it into the bowl.

As she brought the spoon to her lips, Dinah spoke up. "I understand that there is to be a shopping trip to Bond Street tomorrow."

"There is," Lady Montfort confirmed. "Would you care to join us?"

Dinah bobbed her head. "I would. One never knows what kind of treasures we will find there."

"I'm afraid that Gemma is in desperate need of new hats and accessories," her aunt informed the group.

"My hats are perfectly acceptable," Gemma attempted.

"For the country, perhaps," her aunt pressed, "but everyone is held to an impossible standard in Town."

Gemma placed her spoon down and indicated to the footman that she had finished. She leaned to the side as he collected her bowl.

"I do not wish to be a bother," Gemma remarked.

Her aunt reached for her glass, then said, "You are no such thing. After all, I always look for a reason to go shopping."

"That is true," her uncle declared as he walked into the room. "I do apologize for running late, but I'm afraid it couldn't be helped."

"You are here now," her aunt said with a smile on her face. "That is enough for me."

Her uncle went to sit down at the head of the table and met Gemma's gaze. "It is good to see you looking so well, Gemma."

"I daresay that you are in desperate need of spectacles, then," Gemma joked.

Her uncle chuckled. "And I see that you have not lost that wit that I am so fond of." He turned his attention towards Mr. Wycomb. "I am pleased that you are joining us for dinner again."

Mr. Wycomb tipped his head. "It is my honor, my lord."

While her uncle placed a white linen napkin onto his lap, he shifted his gaze back towards Gemma and said, "I happened upon Lord Hawkinge at the club today. He sends his regards."

Gemma blinked. "Henry is here?"

"You sound surprised," her uncle said. "Weren't you aware that he was in Town?"

"Last we spoke, he mentioned traveling to Town, but I did not expect him so soon," Gemma admitted.

Her uncle eyed her curiously. "Do you take issue with Lord Hawkinge?"

Gemma knew she needed to choose her next words carefully. "Henry has been nothing but kind to me, but at times, I fear that he is too kind."

"Can anyone be too kind to someone?" her uncle asked.

"I suppose not," Gemma said. She knew she was not explaining herself well. She wasn't sure what it was about Henry that caused her to question his behavior, but as of late, she had been on guard around him.

Her aunt interjected, "In your letters, you mentioned that Lord Hawkinge has taken good care of you since Baldwin's death."

"Henry has been very generous to me," Gemma agreed.

"If you have no objections, we shall invite him to dinner so we may properly thank him for caring for you," her aunt said.

Gemma bit her lower lip before saying, "I have no objections." But she did have objections, lots of them. She just didn't want to tell her family that. They would think she was being silly.

"Wonderful," her aunt said.

The footmen brought in the next course and set it onto the table. Gemma reached for her glass and took a long sip. Why was it so hard for her to adequately express what she was thinking? She was one to avoid conflict, at all costs, but sometimes it put her in the most peculiar situations.

Marielle spoke up from across the table and asked, "Where do you hail from?"

Gemma placed her glass back down. "I am from Sussex, but I am residing in Hawkinge at the Dowager House."

"Is the Dowager House sufficient for your needs?" Marielle asked.

"It is," Gemma said. "I thought I would miss the grandeur of the big house, but the Dowager House fits my needs perfectly. I have even taken up gardening."

Her aunt lifted her brow. "But you hate getting your hands dirty."

"It is far more preferable than needlework," Gemma remarked. "It got rather tiresome sitting in the drawing room and embroidering for hours on end. Frankly, it reminded me of how lonely I truly was."

"Then I am even more pleased that you accepted our invitation to reside with us for the remainder of the Season," her aunt said.

Gemma smiled. "I am most grateful for your generosity."

As Nathaniel dished some meat onto her plate, he asked, "Would you care to go riding with us tomorrow?"

"I would enjoy that immensely," Gemma said.

"Very good," Nathaniel remarked. "We ride in the early morning to avoid the crowds at Hyde Park."

"I find I prefer that. I do hate crowds."

"I believe everyone at this table shares your sentiments," Nathaniel said as he returned to his seat.

Gemma picked up her fork and moved the meat around on her plate. She wasn't particularly hungry at the moment.

The thought that Henry was in Town did not settle well with her.

"Gemma," Dinah started, "I'm afraid I do not know much about you, but Nathaniel speaks so highly of you that I know we will be fast friends."

Bringing her gaze up, Gemma said, "I should warn you that Nathaniel is prone to exaggeration."

Nathaniel gave her an amused look. "Nothing I told Dinah was untrue," he stated. "I may have mentioned how you used to tattle on us when we were climbing in trees."

"That is because you and Hugh would climb far too high and I do recall that you got stuck one time," Gemma said.

Hugh interrupted, "One time?" He chuckled. "We would get stuck all the time, but we always found our way down."

"Climbing trees is a good way to break one's neck," Gemma remarked. "That is what my mother always told me."

"It was a good thing that never happened," Hugh teased.

Marielle motioned towards her brother and shared, "Stephen loved climbing trees on our estate, and I thought my mother would grow mad with worry."

"It sounds like you had a good mother," Dinah said.

A reflective look came into Mr. Wycomb's eyes. "We did," he responded. "She was the best of women. She even supported my decision to join the Royal Navy."

Her uncle wiped the sides of his mouth before asking, "Did your father object?"

"He did," Mr. Wycomb replied. "He wanted me to attend Oxford to prepare to take over the day-to-day operations of our shipyard, but I had a desire to serve King and Country."

"That is a noble desire," her uncle said.

Marielle glanced at her brother with pride as she informed everyone, "Stephen was a captain of his own ship."

Gemma watched as Mr. Wycomb visibly stiffened and she wondered why he had such an adverse reaction to his sister's words.

"I'm afraid those days are behind me," Mr. Wycomb said, his voice terse. "I retired my commission once I returned home to England."

"Do you miss the sea?" Gemma inquired. "I only ask because my late uncle served in the Royal Navy, and he spoke frequently about how he missed the freedom that was afforded to him at sea."

Mr. Wycomb grew quiet. "There are many things that I miss, but I saw far too much death for my liking."

A silence descended over the table and Gemma immediately regretted asking her question. The pain in Mr. Wycomb's voice had been undeniable and she felt immense compassion for whatever it was that he had been through.

Hugh cleared his throat. "It might be best if we spoke of something more pleasurable."

"Hear, hear," Nathaniel agreed, bringing his gaze to meet hers. "Do you still play whist?"

"It has been some time, but, yes, I do," Gemma replied.

Nathaniel turned towards Dinah. "Gemma is a sheep in wolf's clothing when it comes to whist. She has managed to best us at the game since we were little."

Gemma shrugged one shoulder. "My mother ensured that I was proficient in all card games."

"You are more than proficient," Hugh stated. "You could easily go to the gambling hells and make a fortune at cards."

"A gambling hell is no place for a lady," her aunt contended.

"Do not worry," Gemma said. "I have no intention of going to a gambling hell. I saw firsthand what gambling can do to one's family."

Her aunt reached out and placed a hand over hers. "I'm sorry that my brother treated his family so distastefully."

Gemma pressed her lips together. "It is in the past. My father can't hurt me now."

"No, he can't," her aunt agreed as she withdrew her hand.

Hugh gave her a sad smile. "It was terribly inconsiderate of me to bring up gambling," he said. "Please forgive me."

"There is nothing to forgive," Gemma responded.

Reaching for his glass, Hugh said, "You are most generous, Cousin."

"My past does not define me or defeat me. It has only strengthened me," Gemma responded. "Or at least that is what I keep telling myself. Perhaps one day it will ring true for me."

Mr. Wycomb met her gaze from across the table. "That is rather poetic," he said. "I wish I had your strength."

"You misunderstood me, sir. I am not strong," Gemma said. "But, rather, I am learning to live with the hand that has been dealt to me."

Mr. Wycomb stared at her, as if he was gauging her sincerity. Then he remarked, "I find that admirable of you. I'm afraid that I cannot say the same."

"You will, in time," Gemma encouraged.

"I daresay you are giving me far too much credit, Lady Hawkinge," Mr. Wycomb said.

Gemma held his gaze for a moment longer than she knew was proper before shifting her gaze towards her aunt. "I would be remiss if I did not ask how your cousin, Mrs. Wadell, is faring."

A bright smile came to her aunt's face. "She is doing well and has just married for the fourth time."

"She is on her fourth husband?" Gemma asked.

"Yes, but she was married, widowed, and married again long before she was your age," her aunt shared. "She is not someone that likes being alone."

"Does anyone like being alone?" Gemma questioned.

As her aunt answered her question, Gemma snuck a glance at Mr. Wycomb. He was sitting rigid in his chair, and he appeared as if he would rather be anywhere else but here. She had surprised herself when she had engaged him in conversation, but she couldn't seem to help herself. He was hurting, just as she was, and she felt a kinship towards him. Which was ridiculous. She hardly knew the man.

So why did she have a nagging feeling to learn more about him?

It was still early in the morning as Gemma exited her bedchamber and headed down the hall in her dark grey riding habit. A door opened and a pale-faced Dinah stepped out into the hall.

A relieved look came to Dinah's face as she said, "I am pleased to catch you in the hall. Unfortunately, Nathaniel had business he had to see to this morning, and I am not feeling well. I'm afraid I won't be able to join you for a ride."

"I am sorry that you are not feeling well," Gemma said. "Should we call for a doctor?"

Dinah shook her head. "I have had bouts of nausea in the morning lately, but it usually subsides if I remain perfectly still in my bed." She paused. "At least until early evening."

Gemma opened her mouth to respond when Dinah's hand flew up to her mouth. A panicked look came to her face as she hurried back into her bedchamber, closing the door behind her.

Her aunt's voice came from behind her. "I have a suspicion as to why Dinah has been so nauseous as of late."

"As do I," Gemma said. "Should we tell her?"

"I think it is best if we let Dinah discover it on her own." Her aunt perused the length of her. "Do you still intend to go riding?"

"I believe I shall."

"Is there any way I can convince you otherwise since it is not prudent for you to be riding alone?"

Gemma smoothed down her riding habit. "You seem to forget that I am a widow. The same rules do not apply to me."

"You can still damage your reputation if you are being too reckless."

"A ride through Hyde Park is hardly being reckless," Gemma contended. "Besides, I doubt that anyone of importance is awake at this hour."

Her aunt looked unsure. "Just promise me that you will take along extra footmen on your ride."

"I promise," Gemma said. "Now, I should be going so I may return for breakfast."

"Very well, then," her aunt responded. "But I shall anxiously wait for your return."

Gemma smiled at her aunt before she proceeded down the hall. She knew her aunt was only looking after her best interests, and she found it endearing. She had no doubt that her mother would have had the same conversation with her had she been alive.

Once she descended the stairs, she saw Balfour was standing in the entry hall. He had his usual stoic look on his face and he was patiently waiting for her to approach him.

Gemma came to a stop in front of him. "I wish to go riding. Will you inform the grooms?"

Balfour's lip twitched. It happened so fast that she feared she imagined it. "Lord Hawthorne instructed me to prepare your horse and to see to two footmen accompanying you."

Taken aback from her cousin's thoughtfulness, she asked, "When did he do this?"

"Not more than an hour ago, my lady," Balfour responded. "I see that he properly assumed you would go riding without him."

"That he did," Gemma said.

Balfour stepped over to the main door and opened it. "Your horse is waiting out front, and the footmen can direct you to Hyde Park."

"That won't be necessary. I could find Hyde Park in my sleep."

As Gemma departed the townhouse, she saw the sun was sitting low in the sky and it was casting orange light and long shadows down the street. She tended to prefer mornings because it reminded her that every dark night eventually ends.

A footman assisted her onto her white gelding and she took a moment to adjust her skirt. Once she was situated, she turned her horse towards Hyde Park and proceeded down the cobblestone street. It wasn't long before she arrived at the east entrance, and she led her horse off the well-worn path. There were many places to explore in Hyde Park and she didn't care a whit about being seen.

She kicked her horse into a run and enjoyed the feeling of the wind on her face. How she missed this. Henry had always chided her on riding too fast. He was worried that she would break her neck and he even went so far as to cut down all of the hedges near the Dowager House to prevent her from jumping them.

The farther she headed into Hyde Park, the more free she felt. In this precise moment, she did not have to dwell on anything other than remaining in the saddle. All of the raw pain that she felt from Baldwin's death slipped away and she found that she was enjoying herself.

Up ahead, she saw the Serpentine River and she slowed her horse's gait. A man was standing on the edge of the river, looking out, and his back was facing her. He was dressed in a blue jacket, buff trousers and a black top hat sat atop his head. A dog was running around him in a playful manner, and she couldn't help but smile at the scene in front of her.

She had no desire to disturb the man so she began to turn her horse around. Unfortunately, her horse whinnied at that precise moment, drawing attention towards her.

The man turned around and she recognized him at once. Mr. Wycomb. As much as she wanted to kick her horse into a run, she knew it would be unfathomably rude to just ignore him. Furthermore, he was Marielle's brother, someone who had shown her nothing but kindness. It would be best if she remained and at least spoke to the man.

Mr. Wycomb bowed at his waist and tipped his top hat. "Lady Hawkinge," he greeted.

She tipped her head. "Mr. Wycomb."

A brown puppy ran up to Mr. Wycomb and tried to bite the stick that was in his hand. In a swift motion, Mr. Wycomb reared his hand back and tossed the stick farther down the bank. The puppy happily chased after it.

Gemma and Mr. Wycomb stared awkwardly at one another. She wasn't quite sure what to say so she settled on, "I see that you have a dog." What a dumb thing to say. Of course, he had a dog. It was obvious to everyone that had eyes. What he must think of her?

Mr. Wycomb nodded. "I acquired the dog a few weeks ago and I have become quite fond of Bandit."

"Bandit?" Gemma repeated back. "What did the dog do to earn such a name?"

"I named my dog after my cabin boy's dog," Mr. Wycomb explained. "He snuck a dog onto our ship and proceeded to hide it from the officers."

"How did you discover the dog?"

Mr. Wycomb looked amused. "A ship is not large enough to keep a dog hidden for long, but we pretended for the boy's sake. At least until it became too obvious to avoid any longer."

"You must have held your cabin boy in high regard then."

A pained look came to Mr. Wycomb's eyes. "I did," he replied. "His name was Johnny and he was like a son to me."

Gemma adjusted the reins in her hands as she asked, "May I ask what happened to him?"

"He died, as did his dog," Mr. Wycomb replied, his voice curt. It was evident that there was a story behind his words, but she didn't dare prod.

"Oh," Gemma murmured. "My condolences for your loss."

Mr. Wycomb shifted his gaze back towards the river and Gemma knew she should go. But something propelled her to stay and dismount her horse.

As she held the reins in her hand, she asked, "Will you tell me about him?" Why had she just asked that? Hadn't she just decided that she wouldn't prod?

Mr. Wycomb turned back to face her. His expression was unreadable. "What do you wish to know?" His words were cordial enough but there was an underlying terseness to them.

"How long was Johnny your cabin boy?"

"Two years," he said. "He was twelve years old when he died."

"Isn't that a little young for a cabin boy?"

"It was, but there were some extenuating circumstances." Mr. Wycomb crouched down and removed the stick from Bandit's mouth before he tossed it again. "Johnny was the son of one of my seamen."

Gemma watched as the puppy rushed over to the stick and picked it up. Then he shook it and returned it to Mr. Wycomb.

Mr. Wycomb reached for the stick, but the puppy backed up, his tail wagging.

"It would appear that Bandit wishes to play," Gemma said.

"That is all that he wants to do," Mr. Wycomb grumbled. "He is nearly impossible to train."

"Bandit is still young."

Mr. Wycomb took a commanding step towards the dog and ordered, "Drop it."

Bandit's ears went up and he stared up at Mr. Wycomb.

"Drop it," Mr. Wycomb repeated.

The puppy dropped the stick on the ground in front of him and took a step back.

Mr. Wycomb looked relieved. "Good job, Bandit," he praised.

As he went to retrieve the stick, Bandit scooped it back up and ran a short distance away.

"Blasted dog," Mr. Wycomb mumbled.

Gemma knew she shouldn't laugh, but she found the situation to be quite amusing. She had never trained a dog before, but she imagined it was rather difficult.

With a sigh, Mr. Wycomb said, "I daresay that it is easier to manage a ship than it is to train Bandit."

"Surely it can't be that bad."

"I'm afraid it is."

Gemma handed the reins off to one of the waiting footmen before she went to approach Bandit. She crouched down and said, "Come here, Bandit."

Bandit dropped the stick and rushed towards her. She started petting the puppy, despite his many attempts to lick her on the mouth.

"I do worry that Bandit will soil your riding habit," Mr. Wycomb said.

"Riding habits can be laundered."

Mr. Wycomb clasped his hands behind his back. "Bandit will enjoy living in Brightlingsea. I have an estate on a cliff overlooking the ocean."

"That sounds wonderful."

"My father purchased the land right after he opened his shipyard and he promised himself that, one day, he would build a magnificent home on that property," Mr. Wycomb shared. "It took many years, but now it stands as a testament to my father's hard work and dedication."

Gemma rubbed her gloved hands off on her riding habit. "What a beautiful legacy that you and your sister have."

"It is," Mr. Wycomb responded. "My father was a good man, and he taught me many valuable lessons that I still carry with me."

She offered him a weak smile. "I wish that I could say the same about my father, but he was too busy gambling and chasing after his mistresses to teach me anything of value."

Mr. Wycomb shifted in his stance. "I'm sorry."

With a dismissive wave of her hand, she said, "It is of little consequence. Frankly, I hardly know the man."

"That is most unfortunate."

"My father made his choice long ago, and because of that, we do not enjoy a close relationship," she said.

Mr. Wycomb eyed her curiously. "Is that what you want?"

Gemma tensed. "It doesn't matter what I want. My father is not one to consider another's feelings."

"May I ask of your mother?" Mr. Wycomb asked.

"I'm afraid my mother passed on many years ago," Gemma revealed. "She loved my father, but he didn't love her in the same regard."

Mr. Wycomb unclasped his hands and brought them to his sides. "The worst kind of agony comes from loving someone you can never have."

Gemma cocked her head. "Pardon me for saying so, but you seem to speak from experience."

"I'm afraid I attempted to court a woman, but my offer of courtship was rejected." Mr. Wycomb turned and stared out over the water. "It is a time that I hope to soon forget."

Her horse neighed behind her, startling her. Gemma knew she had intruded on Mr. Wycomb's time for long enough. "I should be going, but I do thank you for your time."

Gemma wasn't certain but she thought she saw a flash of disappointment on his features.

Mr. Wycomb approached her and held his hand out. "May I assist you onto your horse?" he asked.

"I would greatly appreciate that, sir."

He intertwined his fingers together and bent down. Gemma positioned her foot into his hands before placing her own hands onto his broad shoulders. He gently assisted her onto her horse before he took a step back.

"I do hope that today finds you well, my lady," Mr. Wycomb said.

Gemma accepted the reins from the footman and adjusted them in her hands. "I apologize for intruding on your solitude."

Mr. Wycomb held her gaze as he said, "You could never be an intrusion." The way he spoke his words, she believed him.

Bandit started barking at Mr. Wycomb's heels as he tried to get his master's attention.

Mr. Wycomb glanced down at Bandit and shook his head. "If I can offer you a piece of advice, I would tell you to never acquire a puppy."

"I shall heed your advice," she said. "Good day, Mr. Wycomb."

As she urged her horse away from Mr. Wycomb, she realized that she was smiling.

# Chapter Four

Stephen stared at the brown brick townhouse on the edge of the fashionable part of Town. It was well-maintained but the bricks were showing signs of wear. He had been standing in this same spot for what felt like hours, but he was dreading this upcoming meeting. He was here to offer his condolences to his first lieutenant's family. He had worked closely with Benjamin, and he mourned the man's death deeply.

He let out a sigh. He better get this over with before his courage waned. The only consolation was that he wasn't making a condolence call on a widow this time. Benjamin had left behind his parents and a sister, but, thankfully, no wife.

He crossed the busy street, skirting the carriages, and approached the main door. He picked up the knocker and tapped three times on the door.

The door opened and a middle-aged butler with black hair stared back at him. "May I help you, sir?"

Stephen removed a calling card from his waistcoat pocket. "I was hoping for a moment of Mrs. Heathcote's time."

The butler accepted his card and glanced at it. "Do come in, Mr. Wycomb," he said as he stood to the side to allow him entry. "I will see if Mrs. Heathcote is available for callers."

"Thank you," Stephen acknowledged.

As the butler walked off, his heels clipping on the polished tile, Stephen's eyes roamed the modest entry hall. The papered walls had a floral pattern and it contrasted nicely with the ornate woodwork that ran the length of the hall.

The butler stepped out of a room and informed him, "Mrs. Heathcote will see you now, sir."

Stephen felt like his boots were made of lead as he approached the drawing room. He knew how these meetings usually went but he felt obligated to do it.

Mrs. Heathcote was standing next to a camelback settee and a thin-faced young woman stood next to her. The matron's hair was mostly white, but a few dark strands still resided.

A smile came to Mrs. Heathcote's lips as she greeted him. "Captain Wycomb," she said. "What an honor it is to have you in our home."

He bowed. "The honor is mine, Madam."

Mrs. Heathcote gestured towards the young woman. "Allow me to introduce my daughter, Miss Grace Heathcote."

Stephen turned his attention towards Miss Heathcote. "It is a pleasure to be meeting you."

Miss Heathcote dropped into a curtsy. "Captain Wycomb," she murmured.

A long clock chimed in the corner and Stephen attempted to gather the strength to proceed with this most difficult conversation.

Mrs. Heathcote waved her hand over the tea service. "Would you care for some tea?"

"No, thank you," he said. He didn't want to overstay his welcome. He wanted to say what needed to be said and be done with it.

As he opened his mouth, Mrs. Heathcote spoke first. "I am pleased to be finally meeting you. Benjamin always spoke so highly of you in his letters."

"That is kind of you to say."

Mrs. Heathcote returned to her seat and her daughter did the same. "Please take a seat, Captain."

Stephen walked over to an upholstered armchair and sat down, knowing it would be rude to refuse her invitation.

Mrs. Heathcote leaned forward and poured a cup of tea. She placed the teapot down and picked up the cup. Then she extended him the cup.

"You look like you could use a cup of tea," Mrs. Heathcote said.

Stephen accepted the cup. "Thank you, kindly." He took a sip of the lukewarm tea before he lowered it to his lap. "I was Benjamin's captain for two years on the *HMS Intrepid*."

Mrs. Heathcote nodded. "Yes, and he cherished that time with you."

"As my first lieutenant, we worked closely together, and I grew to depend on him and his expertise," Stephen said.

Mrs. Heathcote retrieved her teacup and took a sip. "Did you know that Benjamin snuck off and joined the Royal Navy?"

"I did not."

She nodded. "My son wanted to see what the world had to offer. He was never content with what he had," she shared. "We discovered what he had done by way of a letter."

"That must have been difficult."

"At first, yes, but we came to respect his decision," Mrs. Heathcote said. "We had hoped he would have followed in his father's steps and become a barrister."

"For what it is worth, Benjamin was an accomplished officer, and he saved many people's lives through his quick thinking and determination."

Mrs. Heathcote pressed her lips together. "And look at what it has done for him."

Stephen leaned forward and placed his teacup onto the table. "I wanted to offer my condolences for your loss, and to assure you that your son's sacrifice was not in vain. He was fighting for something much bigger than him."

A gasp escaped Mrs. Heathcote's lips. "Benjamin is dead?"

Stephen gave her an odd look. "Did the War Office not inform you of his death?"

"Yes, but I thought it was a mistake."

With a steady voice, Stephen said, "I regret to inform you that Benjamin died when the *HMS Intrepid* went down."

"You are mistaken," Mrs. Heathcote asserted. "Benjamin retired from the Royal Navy when he returned nearly seven months ago."

It was his turn to act surprised. "I beg your pardon?"

It was Mrs. Heathcote's turn to give him an odd look. "Did you not know he retired from the Royal Navy?"

"No, but more importantly, I didn't know he was alive," he said. "He was on the list of casualties that died that day."

"I'm afraid your list was wrong."

Stephen lowered his gaze as he tried to take in what he had just been told. How was Benjamin alive? All the survivors of the *HMS Intrepid* were taken captive by the French and sent off to that wretched prison.

Bringing his gaze back up, Stephen asked, "May I speak to Benjamin?"

"Unfortunately, I do not know where my son is," Mrs. Heathcote replied. "He walked out of the door one day and has yet to return."

"How long has that been?"

"About six weeks."

Stephen had been back in London for about six weeks. Surely that was just a coincidence.

Mrs. Heathcote lowered her teacup to her lap. "I had been hoping that you would know where my son is."

"I'm afraid not."

"That is a shame," Mrs. Heathcote said. "He left behind his responsibilities, and I would like to ensure he is all right."

"Do you have any idea of where he might be?" Stephen questioned, attempting to keep the eagerness out of his voice.

Miss Heathcote spoke up. "Benjamin was known to frequent the Scarlet Lady gambling hell."

Shifting in her seat, Mrs. Heathcote asked, "How would you know such a thing?"

"On occasion, he would come home drunk and start shouting about how the Scarlet Lady had stolen his money," Miss Heathcote shared.

"I do not recall this," Mrs. Heathcote said.

"That is because you take your medicine and retire to your bedchamber shortly after supper," Miss Heathcote informed her.

"Regardless, Benjamin would not be foolish enough to gamble," Mrs. Heathcote pressed.

"But, Mother—"

Mrs. Heathcote cut her off. "You must have imagined it." She turned her attention towards him. "You will have to excuse my daughter. She has the most vivid imagination."

"Of course, consider it forgotten," Stephen readily responded.

Rising, Mrs. Heathcote said, "If you will excuse me, I'm afraid I need to lie down."

Stephen rose. "I do thank you for your time," he acknowledged before he walked over to the door.

"If you see my Benjamin, please inform him that he has responsibilities at home that he must see to," Mrs. Heathcote said.

Turning around, he tipped his head. "Yes, Ma'am."

As he exited the townhouse, Stephen couldn't seem to wrap his head around the fact that Benjamin was still alive. How did he escape capture by the French? He had so many questions to ask Benjamin and he thought it would be prudent to go to the Scarlet Lady. Perhaps someone would know Benjamin or at least where he had gone to.

He held his hand up to secure a hackney. It didn't take long before a black coach came to a stop in front of him.

"Where to, Mister?" the driver shouted down at him.

"The Scarlet Lady," Stephen replied.

The driver shook his head. "You don't want to go there," he said. "That gambling hell is close to the rookeries and has a reputation for cheating."

"I will pay you three pounds to take me."

"Get in, then," the driver said.

Stephen opened the door and stepped inside of the foul-smelling hackney. His boots stuck to the floor, and he saw the fabric on the bench had pulled apart at the seams. It was a far cry from what he was accustomed to.

The coach jerked into traffic and Stephen went to open the window. Unfortunately, it was broken and only a sliver of air came through. He wished that he had brought his pistol with him, considering he was going to be in close proximity to the rookeries.

A short time later, the coach came to a stop in front of a red brick building. Three rough-looking men were loitering outside, and they were heckling people that walked by.

He opened the door and stepped out. After he paid the driver, he approached the main door but one of the men moved to block his path.

"What do you think ye are doing?" the man asked.

Stephen didn't cower in front of the man. "I think it is fairly obvious," he replied. "I wish to go inside."

The man held his hand out. "Ye have to pay us each a few coins if ye want to do that."

"And why is that?" Stephen asked.

The man smiled, revealing a row of rotten teeth. "If ye don't, ye ain't going anywhere."

Stephen watched as the other men came to stand behind their friend. He had no intention of paying the men to step aside so he knew he would have to fight through them.

"I'm not going to pay you a farthing," Stephen said. "I suggest you let me pass before you make me angry."

The man's smile dimmed. "What's it to ye?" he asked. "Ye look like ye have plenty of money to spare."

"That is beside the point."

One of the men in the back spoke up. "Come on, bloke. We don't want to have to rough you up. Just give us the money."

Stephen stood his ground. "You don't want to fight me."

The man with rotting teeth stepped closer until he stood toe to toe with Stephen. "This is yer last warning. Just give us some coins and ye can be on yer way."

Ignoring the man's bad breath, Stephen said, "I can assure you this is not a fair fight."

"Ye got that right," the last man shouted.

As they stood there staring at one another, he heard a familiar voice next to him. "What in the blazes are you doing here?"

Stephen turned his head and saw Lord Hawthorne standing there with a bewildered look on his face.

"I had an errand I needed to see to," Stephen replied.

"Did that errand involve fighting with ruffians?" Hawthorne asked.

The man with rotten teeth turned towards Hawthorne. "Who are ye calling ruffians?" he demanded.

Hawthorne chuckled. "You did well, David." He reached into his waistcoat pocket and pulled out a few coins. "Now leave this man be."

David collected the coins and clutched them in his hand. "It is a pleasure to do business with ye," he said with a flamboyant bow.

As the three men walked off, Stephen turned towards Hawthorne. "I had that under control. There was no need to pay them to let me pass."

"I didn't," Hawthorne said. "They handled a job for me a few days ago."

"What kind of job?"

Hawthorne brushed his question to the side and asked one of his own. "What are you doing here, Stephen?"

---

Stephen delayed his response as he studied Hawthorne's tattered clothing. His jacket was ill-fitting, threadbare, and his boots were scuffed. What was an earl doing wearing such clothing? Although, he did not look out of place in this section of town. Most of the men wore clothing that needed to be mended and a good washing. But for what purpose was Hawthorne trying to blend in?

Hawthorne crossed his arms over his chest. "I hadn't taken you for a gambler," he said in an accusing tone.

"I'm not," Stephen responded.

"Then what are you doing here?"

Stephen tugged down on the lapels of his jacket. "I am looking for someone."

"Here?" Hawthorne glanced up at the building. "The Scarlet Lady is a notorious gambling hell and spits out more people than it can chew."

"I was not aware of its reputation but that means little to me."

"Go home, Stephen," Hawthorne encouraged. "This is not a place for someone like you."

"But it is for you?"

Hawthorne shrugged. "I have been in worse places."

That didn't answer Stephen's question, but he knew it would be best to bring Hawthorne into his confidences so they could get off the street. "I am looking for my first lieutenant,

Benjamin Heathcote, and his sister said that he was known to frequent the Scarlet Lady."

"I have never heard of Benjamin Heathcote."

"That is because he is entirely below your notice," Stephen said. "I am hoping that someone in the Scarlet Lady knows where he is."

"How long has he been missing?"

"About six weeks."

Hawthorne looked unsure. "Why is it important that you find this man?"

"Benjamin was my first lieutenant aboard my ship, and he was presumed dead after the French defeated us," Stephen explained. "But, somehow, he made it out alive and evaded capture. I just want to know what happened."

Hawthorne looked reluctant but, eventually, he sighed. "I will help you. But if you value your life, you will never return to the Scarlet Lady," he said.

"Surely you exaggerate."

"I'm afraid not." Hawthorne uncrossed his arms and walked over to the door. "Come along, then."

As Hawthorne opened the door, the sound of riotous laughter could be heard from within. He disappeared inside and Stephen hurried to follow him. He didn't quite know what to expect, but he reminded himself that he had been in worse situations than this- most notably, a French prison. Surely a gambling hell couldn't be as heinous as Hawthorne described.

Stephen stepped in the gambling hell and his steps faltered. The place was filled with round tables that were surrounded by men and the smoke from the cigars wafted low in the room. Women, wearing scantily made clothing, walked around with trays in their hands, providing drinks to the men. A few of the women were sitting in the men's laps as they played cards.

Hawthorne came to stand next to him. "Do you see him?"

Stephen's eyes scanned over the room before replying, "I do not."

"Have you ever been in a gambling hell before?"

"I have not," he admitted. "My father always told me that gambling was a vice that could bring down the mightiest of men."

"Your father sounds like a wise man." Hawthorne's eyes scanned the room. "This place has earned the distinction of a 'gambling hell' because impropriety is flaunted here."

"I can see that."

A young woman with blonde hair walked up to him in a gown that had a provocative neckline. "Would you care for something to drink, handsome?"

"No, thank you," Stephen replied, hoping she would leave him be.

She stepped closer to him and asked, "Do you want me to help you join a game?"

"That won't be necessary."

The young woman frowned. "Pardon me for asking, but why are you here?"

"I am looking for some information."

"That is going to cost you."

Stephen removed a coin from his waistcoat pocket and extended it to her. The young woman looked down and said, "You will have to do better than that."

Hawthorne spoke up from next to him. "We will gladly pay more, once you have answered my friend's questions."

The young woman shifted her gaze back to him. "What is it that you are wanting to know?"

Stephen leaned closer so she could hear him over the noise. "Have you heard of a Benjamin Heathcote?"

"Sure, we all have," the young woman replied. "He was a regular here. Although, he lost more than he won."

"Do you know where I can find him?"

The young woman shook her head. "I'm afraid I haven't seen him in days, but he usually sits at table six."

"Where is table six?"

"It is the table in the center of the room," the young woman responded as she gestured towards the table. "He would sit there for hours upon hours."

Stephen's eyes shifted towards table six and saw that there were two seats open. He retrieved a few coins and handed them to the young woman. "That will be all."

The young woman smiled as she accepted the coins. "It was a pleasure doing business with you, handsome."

Stephen turned to Hawthorne. "I'm going to join the game at table six and see if I can garner any more information."

"I will join you."

"That won't be necessary."

Hawthorne put his hand up. "Trust me, it is wholly necessary."

Stephen tipped his head before he started walking over to table six. As he reached for one of the empty chairs, a balding man that sat at the table spoke up. "That seat is taken."

"By whom?" Stephen asked.

"By anyone other than you," the man said as he glanced down at the cards in his hands.

Hawthorne pulled out a chair and sat down, not bothering to ask for permission. "My friend and I want to join the game."

"Do you have money?" the man asked.

"We do," Hawthorne replied.

"Loads of it?" the man pressed.

Hawthorne huffed. "I will once I take it from you."

The man let out a bark of laughter. "I like you." He glanced up at Stephen and scowled. "But you, not so much."

Stephen went to sit down and said, "I'm looking for someone."

The man glared at him. "We are not snitches here."

"He isn't in trouble or at least I don't believe he is, but…"

Hawthorne spoke over him. "What my friend is trying to say is that we will play."

Placing a card into the center, the man said, "You will have to wait until this game is over."

Stephen counted four men at the table, and they all seemed to have the same hollowed out looks in their eyes. He wondered how long they had been gambling.

A man with a rounded face met his gaze and asked, "Do you even know how to play Loo?"

"I do," Stephen replied.

The man gave him a disbelieving look. "You don't belong here, Mister," he said. "Go home and stop wasting our time."

"We will go, but we need some information first," Hawthorne said, leaning forward. "And we are not leaving until we get it."

The balding man tossed his cards into the center. "That will cost you."

Hawthorne retrieved two gold coins and slid them towards the man. "Where can we find Benjamin Heathcote?"

The man's eyes remained fixed on the gold coins. "What did he do?"

"Nothing, we are just looking for him," Hawthorne replied.

"Why?"

"Does it matter?" Hawthorne asked.

The round-faced man interjected, "I know where Benjamin Heathcote is."

"Where?" Hawthorne asked.

"He is staying at a boarding house a few blocks over," the round-faced man revealed.

"What boarding house?" Stephen inquired.

The man rubbed his chin. "The Canterbury."

Hawthorne picked up the coins and handed them to the

round-faced man. "Thank you," he said. "You have been most helpful."

Stephen pushed back his chair and rose. "Thank you, gentlemen."

The balding man scoffed. "There are no gentlemen here."

A burly man approached Stephen and grabbed his arm tightly. "It is time for you to leave," he declared.

"Why?"

"We don't take kindly to people asking too many questions," the burly man replied as he started leading him away from the table.

Stephen jerked his arm away from the man. "I don't need your assistance."

The burly man went to open the door and ordered, "Get out, and don't come back. Your kind is not welcome here."

"I have no intention of coming back," Stephen said.

After he stepped out, the door was slammed shut. Where was Hawthorne? The thought of Hawthorne being in the gambling hell without him did not sit well with him.

He opened the door and saw the burly man was still standing guard.

The guard narrowed his eyes. "I told you to stay away."

"I am looking for someone."

Taking a commanding step towards him, the guard said, "You are starting to make me angry, bloke."

Hawthorne appeared behind the guard and placed a hand on his shoulder. "Stand down, Ronald," he ordered. "I will ensure my friend will never return."

"Your friend?" the guard asked. "You might want to pick better friends."

Hawthorne grinned. "I was thinking the same thing," he said before he proceeded to walk out the door.

The guard gave Stephen a menacing look before he slammed the door shut again.

With a look of disbelief, Stephen asked, "How is it that you are acquainted with the guard?"

"I make it my business to know everyone." Hawthorne started walking down the pavement. "It would be best if you went home straightaway since it is getting late."

"I want to go to the Canterbury," Stephen said.

"Not today," Hawthorne asserted. "It isn't safe for you to be in this part of town at night."

"But not for you?"

Hawthorne glanced over at him and replied, "My business is my own." His tone brokered no argument.

Stephen was a wise enough man not to argue with Hawthorne, especially since he had helped discover Benjamin's whereabouts. "Fair enough, but I intend to visit the Canterbury first thing tomorrow."

"I am unable to go tomorrow morning so it will have to wait until the afternoon."

Stephen stepped over a dog carcass in the street. "I will go alone."

"You won't get past the front door without me," Hawthorne said. "Trust me, you don't want to go traipsing through this part of town without me."

"I don't traipse," Stephen muttered.

Hawthorne stopped on the pavement and put his hand up. "I will help you find Benjamin, but it will be on my terms."

"What does that mean?"

"You will see." Hawthorne lowered his hand as a hackney came to a stop in front of him. "Take the hackney home and I will send word about tomorrow."

Stephen glanced around and saw men loitering outside of buildings. They were all watching them with particular interest that caused him to be concerned for Hawthorne. "Are you sure you will be all right?"

"Yes. You do not need to concern yourself about me."

Knowing he was fighting a losing battle, Stephen shouted

up his address to the driver before he opened the door. "I wish you luck."

Hawthorne took a step back. "I don't have time for luck."

As the hackney pulled away from the pavement, Stephen watched as Hawthorne stepped into the alley, disappearing into the shadows.

## Chapter Five

Gemma was happy that she'd made the decision to come to London. She had enjoyed the time immensely with her family and she found that she was in no rush to return to Hawkinge. There was something liberating about being away from Henry. He was kind to her and ensured she was taken care of, but she had grown tired of his constant presence in her life.

As she descended the stairs, she heard the sound of infectious laughter coming from the drawing room. She wondered what was so amusing.

She saw Balfour at the base of the stairs and she approached him. "May I ask who is in the drawing room?"

"Lady Hawthorne's sister, the Marchioness of Haddington, called upon her nearly an hour ago," Balfour replied.

Another bout of laughter came from the direction of the drawing room and Gemma decided it would be rude of her to interrupt their lively conversation.

A knock came at the door and Balfour went to open it. He stood to the side as Mr. Wycomb stepped into the townhouse.

When Mr. Wycomb saw her, he stopped, removed his black top hat and bowed. "Good morning, Lady Hawkinge."

She dropped into a curtsy. "Mr. Wycomb," she greeted. "How are you this fine morning?"

"I am well." He turned towards Balfour and extended his hat. "Is Lady Hugh available for callers?"

Balfour accepted the hat and replied, "I shall find out at once, sir."

Once Balfour started to walk away, Gemma gave Mr. Wycomb a nervous smile. "I would invite you into the drawing room for a cup of tea, but I'm afraid it is occupied at the moment."

"You do not need to concern yourself over me." Mr. Wycomb patted his stomach. "Besides, I do not think I could stomach another cup of tea this morning."

"That is not very British of you to say," she teased.

"I'm afraid I did not drink much tea on my ship," Mr. Wycomb shared. "It was a commodity that was hard to acquire when at sea."

Gemma clasped her hands in front of her. "Do you miss the sea?"

A myriad of emotions crossed Mr. Wycomb's face and his next words seemed very contrived. "There is a time and a place for everything and I'm afraid my time serving in the Royal Navy was up."

"I do thank you for what you have done for King and Country."

"I didn't sign up for the Royal Navy to be thanked," Mr. Wycomb said. "I did it because I wanted to command a ship."

"And you succeeded in your efforts."

Mr. Wycomb clenched his jaw. "Had I known what I know now, I would never have left English soil."

"Surely you don't mean that?"

"I saw far too much death in my many years in the Royal Navy," Mr. Wycomb said. "Deaths that I could have prevented."

Gemma felt compassion towards Mr. Wycomb and

attempted to convey that by asking, "Is death not a part of war?"

"Try telling that to the families that lost their sons," Mr. Wycomb replied, his voice curt.

Marielle's voice came from behind her. "Stephen," she said sternly. "I do hope you are behaving yourself around Lady Hawkinge."

Gemma turned towards Marielle. "We were just having a lively debate."

Marielle eyed her curiously but, thankfully, she let the matter drop. "We should all adjourn to the drawing room."

"Lady Hawthorne is visiting with her sister," Gemma informed them.

Stephen stiffened. "Lady Haddington is here?" he asked as he glanced over at the drawing room. "Perhaps I should go."

Marielle came to a stop in front of him. "It is only a matter of time before you must face her," she said. "It might as well be in the privacy of the drawing room."

Stephen nodded slowly. "You might be right."

"Of course I am right." Marielle flashed him a bright smile. "I usually am."

"And you are very humble about it," Stephen joked.

Marielle looped arms with her brother. "You may as well get this over with," she said as she started leading him towards the drawing room.

Gemma followed behind and she was curious as to why Mr. Wycomb had such apprehension towards Lady Haddington.

Once she stepped into the drawing room, she saw a thin, brown-haired young woman sitting next to Dinah. They had stopped speaking and were watching Marielle and her brother.

Mr. Wycomb cleared his throat. "You are looking well, Lady Haddington."

Lady Haddington tipped her head. "As are you, Mr. Wycomb."

A small silence descended over the group before Marielle gestured towards Gemma. "Lady Haddington, allow me to introduce you to Lady Hawkinge."

Lady Haddington smiled. "It is a pleasure, but I must insist you call me Evie," she said.

"Then you must call me Gemma."

Evie nodded approvingly. "Dinah has informed me that you intend to stay in London for the remainder of the Season."

"That is true, assuming that they do not tire of me."

Dinah spoke up. "Never," she said. "Gemma has been a delight and I have found her to be an excellent shopping companion."

Evie made a face. "I detest shopping with my sister. I have never seen someone that analyzes every part of a hat."

"I must ensure the hat is up to my standards," Dinah defended.

"You go into the shop, buy a hat, and you leave. It is a simple process," Evie said. "Yet, my sister has found a way to complicate it."

Dinah leaned forward and retrieved her teacup. "You will have to excuse my sister. She seems to think that shopping is akin to torture."

"Only when I shop with you, dear sister," Evie teased.

Marielle walked over to sit down next to Evie. "Have you been to the orphanage as of late?" she asked.

"I went this morning, but I'm afraid Georgie wouldn't let the girls practice climbing walls," Evie shared.

"Pardon?" Gemma asked, fearing she'd misheard Evie. "Why would girls wish to climb walls?"

"It is a simple but practical thing to do," Evie explained. "Besides, it has come in handy on occasion."

Gemma gave her a questioning look. "Why would anyone need to climb a wall?"

"What if the doors are locked?" Evie asked.

"Then you wait for them to be unlocked," Gemma replied.

Evie gave her an amused look. "I'm afraid it is not quite that simple." She turned her attention towards Mr. Wycomb. "What say you, sir?"

"I may have climbed a wall in my youth but that was so I could torment Hugh," Mr. Wycomb said.

Marielle shook her head. "You two were terrible to one another."

"I won't disagree with you there," Mr. Wycomb remarked.

"I am of the mindset that you and Hugh are more alike than you realize," Marielle said.

Mr. Wycomb reared back slightly. "I am nothing like Hugh and I resent the implication."

"Stop being so sensitive, Brother," Marielle responded. "Besides, you two get along now."

"Only because of you," Mr. Wycomb asserted.

Gemma sat down next to Dinah and reached for the teapot. She glanced up at Mr. Wycomb and asked, "Would you care for a cup of tea?"

"No, thank you," Mr. Wycomb said. "My position has not changed on it."

Gemma smiled. "Does your sister know about your aversion to tea?"

Marielle lifted her brow. "When did you stop liking tea?"

"I tolerate tea," Mr. Wycomb said. "Although, I would prefer to drink anything else."

Dinah put a hand to her stomach and winced. "You must excuse me, but I think it is time I go rest."

"Are you feeling unwell?" Evie asked.

"Nothing that a good rest won't cure," Dinah said as she rose and walked out of the room.

Evie's eyes trailed after her sister. "I do hope she feels well soon enough."

Marielle exchanged a pointed look with Gemma, then said, "She should, in about seven or eight months."

With wide eyes, Evie asked, "You think she is increasing?"

"I do, but I am not a doctor," Marielle said. "I have encouraged her to seek out a doctor, but she is under the impression they are all quacks."

Evie gave her an understanding look. "When my sister was younger, she used to get terrible headaches and the doctors treated it by bloodletting."

"Did it help?" Gemma asked.

"No, they only got worse, and she grew weaker every time they put those leeches on her," Evie replied. "It wasn't until the doctors stopped bloodletting that she started to feel better."

"How terrible," Marielle murmured.

"Ever since then, she has avoided doctors," Evie said.

Gemma poured herself a cup of tea and remarked, "I can see why."

Rising, Evie said, "I should be going as well. I'm afraid I have some things I need to see to before supper."

Mr. Wycomb bowed. "It was good to see you again, Lady Haddington."

Evie gave him a kind smile. "Do take care of yourself," she said before she walked over to the door.

Marielle shifted in her seat and said, "That went well."

Mr. Wycomb lifted his eyes heavenward. "You had to press the issue."

"Aren't you glad that I did?" Marielle asked. "As you can see, there is no animosity between you two."

"There never was," Mr. Wycomb said.

Marielle met Gemma's gaze and explained, "Stephen attempted to court Evie, but her heart was already with Lord Haddington."

"Thank you for recapping that," Mr. Wycomb grumbled.

"It was purely for Gemma's sake," Marielle said. "There is no shame in admitting what happened to you."

Mr. Wycomb frowned. "Will you not drop it?"

"I will," Marielle replied with a smile.

Gemma took a sip of her tea as Mr. Wycomb walked over to the window and stared out. His face was solemn, but there was a sadness to his eyes that made her heart lurch. She suspected that Evie's rejection of his suit had hurt him more than he would ever admit.

Marielle's voice broke up the silence. "Do you intend to go to Lady Croft's ball tonight?" she asked her brother.

"No."

"But you must," Marielle insisted. "You haven't been to a social gathering in weeks."

"I am well aware," Mr. Wycomb said.

A pout came to Marielle's lips. "You promised, Stephen."

Mr. Wycomb heaved a sigh. "Fine. I will be in attendance, but I shall leave before the supper dance."

Marielle's lips turned into a smile. "Wonderful," she said as she clasped her hands together. "Hugh will be thrilled to spend time with you."

"I somehow doubt that to be true," Mr. Wycomb stated.

"You two will become best friends before you know it," Marielle quipped.

Mr. Wycomb walked over to his sister and kissed her cheek. "I shall see you tonight." He turned towards Gemma. "Will I be seeing you this evening, as well?"

"You shall," Gemma replied.

"Would it be too presumptuous to ask for you to save me a dance?"

"It would not."

"Then I shall collect it this evening," Mr. Wycomb said before he offered a bow and departed.

A thrill of excitement coursed through her at the thought

of dancing with Mr. Wycomb. What was the matter with her? Had she forgotten about Baldwin so soon? Mr. Wycomb may be handsome, but her head would not be so easily turned.

---

Stephen sat in his study as he reviewed the documents that his man of business had requested he sign. It was becoming increasingly difficult to efficiently oversee his shipyard when he was so far away from Brightlingsea. He needed to return home, but something was stopping him.

As much as he hated to admit it, his sister was happy with Hugh, and they complemented one another. He was beginning to realize he didn't need to worry about his sister's welfare because Hugh would ensure she was taken care of. Which both grated on his nerves and pleased him.

What was truly keeping him in Town? An image of Lady Hawkinge came to his mind but he quickly banished it from his thoughts. Where had that thought even come from? He had no intention of courting Lady Hawkinge. And even if he did, she was still mourning the loss of her husband deeply. He refused to pay court to a woman who had already given her heart away. Hadn't he already learned his lesson before with Lady Haddington? Besides, he didn't need a wife at this time.

When he had laid in his bed on the ship, he dreamed of getting married and having children. He wanted what his parents had, but it was becoming nearly impossible to obtain. What if he spent the rest of his life chasing after the promise of love?

Bandit let out a whimper in his sleep as he laid next to the hearth. Stephen leaned back in his seat and reflected on how Lady Hawkinge reacted to Bandit. Her face had lit up at the sight of Bandit and she didn't flinch at his dirty paws on her riding habit. She was truly a remarkable woman. Furthermore, the way she spoke her words, he knew they were genuine and from the heart.

Stephen stifled a groan. Hadn't he decided that Lady Hawkinge was not the one for him? There was no denying that she was beautiful, but he couldn't risk getting hurt again. When it was time for him to settle down, he would be more practical on who he wished to court. He still yearned for a love match, but love could be cultivated over time. He would just need to find someone that he could fall in love with.

With a shake of his head, he turned his attention back towards the documents that were in front of him. He reached for the quill and signed each one.

His aged butler shuffled into the room. "Excuse me, but a Lord Hawthorne is here to see you, sir," Pratt said.

"Send him in," he ordered.

"I shall see to it." Pratt slowly turned on his heel and departed from the room.

Stephen was fearful that Pratt might collapse at any time, but he didn't dare insult him by insinuating that he couldn't handle his job.

A long moment later, Hawthorne stepped into the room with a quizzical look on his face. "Your choice in a butler is an interesting one," he said as he walked closer to the desk.

"The household staff came with the townhouse," Stephen explained.

"Ah," Hawthorne said. "That makes sense."

Stephen rose. "Shall we depart for the Canterbury?" he asked eagerly.

"Are you sure you want to do this?"

"I do," he replied. "Why do you ask?"

Hawthorne held his gaze and said, "Because sometimes it is best to not go prying into other people's lives. You never know what you will find."

Stephen came around his desk. "I need to know what happened with Benjamin. I can't just let this go."

"All right, but do try and remember that I warned you against this."

"Duly noted." Stephen gestured towards the door. "Shall we?"

As they headed out of the small study, Hawthorne asked, "How well do you know Benjamin?"

"I thought I knew him quite well."

"But not now?"

Stephen shook his head. "The Benjamin that I knew would never have shirked his responsibilities to spend time at a gambling hell."

"War can change people," Hawthorne remarked.

"You don't need to remind me of that," Stephen said. "There is not a day that goes by that I do not relive the moment the French boarded our ship and took us captive. It was my greatest failure."

Stephen stepped into the entry hall and saw Pratt was holding the door open. Although he was leaning into the door for support. That poor man, he thought to himself.

He stepped outside and saw a hackney was positioned in front of his townhouse. Hawthorne brushed past him and went to step into the hackney.

Once they were both situated, Hawthorne gave him a pointed look and said, "You mustn't torture yourself with the past. It is over, and you managed to survive it."

"I wish I didn't."

"Surely you don't mean that."

"I do, wholeheartedly," Stephen replied. "The only reason I survived was because I was wounded and fell into a state of unconsciousness. If it hadn't been for that, I would have fought until my last dying breath."

"What good would that have done?" Hawthorne asked.

"I was the captain of my ship. It was a failure on my part to be taken alive," Stephen expressed. "The main deck was covered with dead bodies and I should not have escaped the onslaught."

Hawthorne opened the window, allowing fresh air to circulate in the coach. "I must assume that you did all that you could to help your crew."

"I did, but it wasn't enough." He paused. "I wasn't enough."

Hawthorne didn't speak for a moment. Then he said, "The past cannot be changed, but it can be accepted."

"I cannot accept what I did."

"Then it will consume you, leaving you a shell of the man that you once were."

Stephen huffed. "Pardon me for saying so, but I doubt you understand what I have been through."

"You are right," Hawthorne said. "I was never in the Royal Navy. However, I know a thing or two about regrets."

"What kind of regrets does an earl have?"

"Too many."

Stephen eyed Hawthorne curiously. "How is that possible?"

"It matters not, but you are not alone in suffering for things that you wish could have been different," Hawthorne replied. "Life has a funny way of keeping you humble."

"That it does," Stephen agreed.

The coach came to a stop in front of a brown brick building and Stephen asked, "Where is the Canterbury?"

Hawthorne reached for the handle. "I informed the driver to drop us off a block away."

"For what purpose?"

"A hackney already draws too much attention in this section of town," Hawthorne explained. "If we want to remain inconspicuous, we need to go the rest of the way on foot."

Stephen followed Hawthorne out of the coach and came

to stand next to him on the pavement. Hawthorne paid the driver before stepping back.

A drunken man sat a short distance away, leaning his back against the building, and he was loudly singing.

Hawthorne approached the dark-haired man and dropped a coin into a cup that sat in front of him. The man stopped singing and smiled up at him. "Thank you," the man said with a slur. "You are indeed kind."

"Perhaps you should keep the singing down," Hawthorne suggested.

"And deny everyone the privilege of hearing my singing?" the man asked. "Never."

Hawthorne chuckled. "I suppose this is better than attempting to sell stray cats."

"That was ingenious on our part," the man defended. "You may move along. I am trying to collect enough coins for a hearty meal today."

Stephen couldn't help but notice that the slur in the man's voice had disappeared the longer he spoke to Hawthorne. That was odd. Although, it was more odd that Hawthorne appeared to know this man.

Hawthorne continued down the street and Stephen matched his stride. "Do you know that man?" he asked.

"I do."

When Stephen realized that Hawthorne had no intention of revealing anything more, he pressed, "May I ask how?"

"That man has done some work for me."

"What kind of work?"

Hawthorne glanced over at him and replied, "You are being rather nosy today."

"I am just trying to make sense of it all."

"I thought we agreed that there would be no questions," Hawthorne remarked.

Stephen knew he wasn't going to get any further information out of Hawthorne so he decided it would be best if he dropped it.

Up ahead, Stephen saw the Canterbury. It was a two-level brick building that was positioned between two other structures. A worn plaque by the door identified the boarding house.

Hawthorne came to a stop in front of the door and said, "Let me do the talking."

"Why is that?"

"Because I know how to deal with these people."

Stephen went to open the door. "After you, then."

After he followed Hawthorne inside the dimly lit entry hall, a man brushed past him and muttered an apology under his breath.

Hawthorne reached out and grabbed the man's arm. "I do not take kindly to having my friend robbed."

"I ain't robbed anyone," the man declared.

Hawthorne kept hold of the man's arm. "I saw you take his coin purse from his left pocket." He leaned in. "If you don't give it back nicely, then I will have no choice but to make you."

Indecision crossed the man's face before saying, "You can't blame a man for trying." He extended a small leather purse to Hawthorne. "You should tell your friend to be more careful in these parts."

Hawthorne accepted the purse before he dropped the man's arm. "Go on, then."

Stephen stared at Hawthorne in disbelief. "How did you know he robbed me of my coin purse?"

Hawthorne extended it towards him. "Just try not to stand out so much."

Depositing the coin purse back into his left pocket, Stephen asked, "How can I do that?"

"I daresay that it might be impossible."

A woman with silver-streaked hair and a pointed nose approached them. "How may I help you, gentlemen?"

Hawthorne stepped forward. "We are looking for someone."

"Then you can just turn around and go out that door," the woman said. "I am no snitch."

"I didn't imply that you were." Hawthorne removed some coins from his waistcoat pocket. "I was just hoping you would point us towards the direction of Benjamin Heathcote's room."

The woman eyed the coins with interest. "There is no one here by that name."

"Are you sure?" Hawthorne pressed.

With a frown, the woman said, "I know each of my tenants."

Stephen spoke up. "The man that we are looking for is tall, dark-haired and he has a scar along his chin."

"That would be Colin Staley," the woman said. "His room is on the second floor; room twenty-two."

Hawthorne handed the money towards the woman. "Thank you for your time."

The woman deposited the coins into her pocket. "I don't want trouble. This is a respectable establishment."

"We just want to speak to him," Hawthorne assured her.

"Then make it quick," the woman said with a jerk of her head.

They headed towards the stairs and ascended them in silence. Stephen wasn't quite sure what to expect when he saw Benjamin, but he was intent on asking him a few questions.

Hawthorne stopped by the door that read "Twenty-two". He lifted his fist up and pounded on the door.

Stephen saw a shadow moving from under the door. He pointed towards it and Hawthorne nodded his understanding.

Reaching behind him, Hawthorne retrieved a pistol and

moved it to his side. He pounded on the door again and said, "We know you are in there."

A moment later, the handle slowly turned and the door opened partially, revealing a redheaded, petite young woman.

"Can I help you?" she asked softly.

Stephen stared back at the woman in surprise. "We were told this was Colin Staley's room."

"It is," she replied. "I am his wife- Lavinia Staley."

# Chapter Six

*His wife?*

Mrs. Heathcote mentioned nothing about Benjamin having a wife. Then again, he doubted that Benjamin's mother knew anything about her son using a fake name or living at the Canterbury.

Hawthorne smiled at the young woman, no doubt in an attempt to disarm her. "Is your husband home?" he asked as he tucked the pistol into the waistband of his trousers.

Mrs. Staley shook her head. "I'm afraid not."

"Do you know where he is?" Hawthorne asked.

"No."

"Will he be returning home shortly?"

"I'm not entirely sure," she replied. "He tends to come and go as he pleases."

Mrs. Staley's body blocked most of the view of her room, but Stephen was able to see that a map hung on the back wall. Unfortunately, he couldn't see what it was a map to.

She followed his gaze before she stepped back and closed the door even more. "May I get your names and I will inform Colin that you came to see him?"

"My name is Step…"

Hawthorne cut him off. "Our names aren't important," he said. "We will return at a later date to speak to Mr. Staley."

Mrs. Staley gave them a weak smile before she closed the door, ending their conversation.

Hawthorne gestured that Stephen should follow him as he walked towards the stairs. They didn't speak as they exited the boarding house.

Once they were on the pavement, Stephen glanced up at the second level and saw Mrs. Staley watching them from behind a curtain. Her eyes went wide when their eyes met, and she closed the curtain.

Hawthorne's voice drew his attention. "That was odd."

"It was," Stephen agreed. "Do you think Mrs. Staley knew her husband is using a fake name?"

"I'm unsure since she introduced herself as Mrs. Staley." Hawthorne's expression grew solemn. "What do you think your friend might be involved in?"

"I don't rightly know, but it can't be good."

"No, it can't," Hawthorne said. "I will make some inquiries and I will see what I can learn about Benjamin Heathcote, or, should I say, Colin Staley."

"Who are you making inquiries to?"

Hawthorne shrugged. "Just some people that I have become acquainted with."

"Like the people at the Scarlet Lady?"

"It is beneficial for someone like me to be well acquainted with people from all walks of life," Hawthorne replied.

"Someone like you?" Stephen repeated back. "Need I remind you that you are an earl."

Hawthorne smirked. "I am well aware."

Stephen furrowed his brow. "You are a man of many secrets."

"I have no more than most men."

"I don't believe that to be true."

Hawthorne's gaze left his and roamed over the buildings. "We have tarried long enough," he advised. "It would be best if we got you into a hackney."

"What about you?"

"I have some business I need to see to," Hawthorne said.

Stephen wasn't quite sure what to make of Hawthorne. He was unlike any earl that he had ever met before. He had an air of secrecy about him that made him seem dangerous.

They had just started walking down the pavement when he saw Lord Haddington, dressed in a bold purple jacket, approaching them from the opposite direction.

Blazes. Haddington was the last person he wanted to see. Ever since he had attempted to pursue Evie before she had become Haddington's wife, they held thinly veiled hostility for one another. But he didn't regret his actions. Evie was a woman that was worth fighting for, but, in the end, she had followed her heart.

Haddington came to a stop in front of Hawthorne and asked, "What brings you to this section of Town?"

"Stephen wanted to look up an old friend and I offered to go with him," Hawthorne replied.

"Did you find him?" Haddington asked.

Stephen spoke up. "We did not," he replied.

Haddington shifted his gaze to meet Stephen's. "That is most unfortunate."

"I am beginning to believe this friend does not wish to be found," Stephen admitted.

"Is that going to stop you?" Haddington asked.

Stephen shook his head. "Not in the least."

Haddington's eyes left his and watched the patrons that were passing them on the pavement. "I'm glad that you had the sense to bring Hawthorne along with you," he said. "You are no match for the ruffians here."

"I could have managed."

Haddington huffed. "You would have been attacked and left for dead."

"I daresay you do not give me enough credit," Stephen said. "You seem to forget that I was a captain in the Royal Navy."

"But you aren't any longer," Haddington stated.

"I can still fight my way through a few ruffians," Stephen asserted.

Haddington didn't look convinced by his assurances. "I sincerely doubt that, and there is no shame in that."

Stephen took a step closer to Haddington. "I am not some hoity-toity dandy that needs protection."

Haddington's eyes narrowed slightly. "I contend that you are."

As he opened his mouth to respond, Hawthorne cleared his throat. "Are you two done with-whatever it is that you are attempting to do?"

Stephen reluctantly took a step back, but he wished that they had been anywhere else so they could have settled this with a bout of fisticuffs. He had longed to hit Haddington. Frankly, nothing else would give him such great satisfaction.

Haddington turned his gaze towards Hawthorne. "It is most fortunate that I ran into you because I need to speak to you."

Hawthorne acknowledged his words with a tip of his head. He turned towards Stephen. "Do you think you can find your way home?"

"Again, I am not some simpering miss," Stephen grumbled. "Will you stop treating me as such?"

Haddington opened his mouth to no doubt disagree with him, but Hawthorne spoke first. "Then we shall leave you to it."

Stephen watched as Hawthorne and Haddington walked further into the rookeries, neither showing a glimpse of hesitation.

Finding himself alone, he started walking back from whence they had come. His alert eyes watched the men loitering in the doorways, appearing far too interested in him. He was smart enough to bring an overcoat pistol this time, but there was only one shot in it. He would have to make it count, assuming it came to that.

He passed the drunken man and continued down the pavement. Once he saw a hackney, he put his hand up to signal it when he saw a man walking towards him. He would recognize the man's gait anywhere. It was his old first lieutenant.

Surprise, then panic, came to Benjamin's face as their gazes met. In the next moment, Benjamin darted across the street, skirting the carriages, and disappeared into an alleyway.

Stephen rushed after him but was forced to stop when a carriage passed in front of him. Once the coach was past him, he hurried over to the alleyway and saw that it was empty. He ran towards the other side but he didn't see any sign of Benjamin.

Botheration. He slammed his fist into the sides of a brick building. Why was Benjamin avoiding him and using an alias? This didn't make any sense.

Stephen retraced his steps and was fortunate enough to see a hackney coming down the street. He put his hand up and the hackney came to a stop in front of him.

"Where to, Mister?" the driver shouted down to him.

Stephen informed him of the address before he stepped inside. He leaned his back against the bench as he attempted to decipher why Benjamin had acted in such a fashion when he'd seen him. He had considered Benjamin his comrade and he had mourned his death.

He turned his head towards the window and watched as the buildings passed by. It wasn't long before he realized that they were on Bond Street. He watched all the ladies walking down the pavement with their servants trailing behind, holding their packages. How droll was this life in Town.

This is not the life that he wanted. He wanted to be far away from London and live an idyllic life in Brightlingsea. He wanted to give his kids the same opportunities that he was afforded as a child.

He was about to turn from the window when he saw Lady Hawkinge. She was standing next to Lady Montfort and she was pointing towards a hat in a window's storefront.

Not entirely sure what he was about, he tapped the side of the hackney and it came to a rolling stop. He exited and extended a few coins to the driver.

Stephen turned back towards where he had last seen Lady Hawkinge but she was nowhere to be found. He walked towards the window and looked inside. He saw Lady Hawkinge was holding the hat that she had been admiring in her hand and she was speaking to Lady Montfort.

A man brushed up against him, causing him to stagger back. "My apologies," the man muttered before he continued down the pavement.

When his eyes strayed back towards the window, he saw that Lady Montfort was watching him with a curious expression. He had been caught staring. He knew he should just tip his hat and walk away, but something propelled him to open the door.

As he entered the milliner's shop, he watched as all the women turned to face him. He ignored their blatant looks and approached Lady Hawkinge and Lady Montfort.

He bowed. "Lady Hawkinge," he greeted. "Lady Montfort."

Lady Hawkinge smiled politely, still holding the hat in her hands. "What a pleasant surprise to see you in here."

"Yes, it certainly is," Lady Montfort said.

Stephen pointed towards the hat in Lady Hawkinge's hands. "That is a lovely hat."

Lady Hawkinge held it up. "I was thinking the same thing," she replied. "Do you often visit millinery shops?" There was a teasing tilt in her voice.

He felt like a fool. What had he been thinking coming into the shop? This was a shop for ladies, not gentlemen.

A shopkeeper walked over to him and asked, "Are you interested in purchasing a hat, sir?"

"I… um…" He paused to collect his thoughts. "I think I would like to purchase a hat for my sister." There. That was an excellent reason to be in a milliner's shop.

The shopkeeper nodded. "Very good. What kind of hat are you looking for?"

"One with flowers," Stephen replied.

"Do you know what her favorite flower is?" the shopkeeper pressed.

Stephen blanched. "I do not." How would he know what his sister's favorite flower was?

With a wave of her hand, the shopkeeper said, "We have over a hundred hats that have flowers on them. Would you care to select one that fits her tastes?"

Stephen's eyes roamed the collection of hats until he saw a simple one with pink flowers on it. "That one will do," he said.

"Very good, sir," the shopkeeper responded. "You have exquisite taste. I shall prepare it for you."

Stephen met Lady Hawkinge's gaze and he could see amusement in her eyes.

"Marielle is fortunate to have a brother that is most attentive to her," Lady Hawkinge remarked. "I have no doubt that she will treasure your gift to her."

"You are too kind, my lady," Stephen acknowledged.

Lady Montfort removed the hat from Lady Hawkinge's hand. "I will go see this boxed up," she said. "I will be back in a moment."

"Thank you," Lady Hawkinge murmured.

Stephen stood there, feeling immensely awkward. "I should be going."

"Not before you get your hat," Lady Hawkinge encouraged.

He let out a nervous chuckle. "Yes, there is that." Why was he acting like such a buffoon around Lady Hawkinge?

Lady Hawkinge seemed to take pity on him and said, "If you would like, I would be willing to give Marielle the hat."

"That would be most helpful." He started backing up. "She might even wear it this evening."

Lady Montfort handed Lady Hawkinge a box and informed him, "Ladies do not wear hats to balls, Mr. Wycomb."

"Of course not," Stephen said. "Silly me." His back bumped against the back of the door and he let out a sigh of relief. "Good day, ladies."

He quickly departed from the shop, wondering what in the blazes had he been thinking going in there in the first place.

***

Gemma resisted the urge to smile as she watched Mr. Wycomb depart or should she say "flee" from the milliner's shop? He had appeared uncomfortable in the shop, but she had enjoyed conversing with him, even if it was for only a few moments. Frankly, she was beginning to look forward to these unexpected meetings. He always managed to brighten her spirits.

Her aunt gave her a knowing look. "It would appear that Mr. Wycomb fancies you."

Gemma shook her head. "No, you are mistaken."

"Then why would he come in a milliner's shop to speak to you?"

Gemma bit her lower lip. Could Mr. Wycomb hold her in

high regard? That thought both thrilled and terrified her. Knowing Lady Montfort was still waiting for her response, she replied, "I do believe he came in for a hat for Marielle."

Thankfully, before her aunt could respond, the shopkeeper walked up with a hat box and said, "The gentlemen left without his hat."

"I shall take it and put it on my account," her aunt responded.

"Yes, my lady," the shopkeeper said as she extended her the box.

Her aunt accepted it and turned towards her. "Shall we go home now?"

"Yes, please," Gemma replied.

After they exited the shop, they handed their packages to their servants and approached the coach. A footman opened the door and assisted them inside.

Gemma went to sit across from her aunt. "I cannot thank you enough for your generosity."

"It is the least I can do," her aunt responded as the coach jerked forward. "Besides, I have enjoyed spoiling you."

As she played with the strings of her reticule that hung around her wrist, she said, "I must admit that I hate that Baldwin left me in this position."

"What position is that, dear?"

"Forcing me to live off the good graces of others," Gemma admitted. "I wish that Baldwin had left me a jointure rather than some piece of land."

"Perhaps he thought the land was worth something?"

Gemma sighed softly. "Sadly, it is not," she replied. "Although Henry has offered to buy it from me at a generous price."

"That was kind of him."

"It was, but I have turned him down," Gemma said. "I might just be sentimental, but Baldwin did want me to have it."

Her aunt's eyes held compassion. "Then you must not part with it."

"I might one day have to," Gemma said. "I can't keep living off Henry's generosity forever."

"You are still the Countess of Hawkinge, and it is Lord Hawkinge's duty to care for you," she said. "You will always be his brother's wife."

Gemma's gaze grew downcast. "I know I am being foolish, but I just want my life to go back to the way it was before Baldwin died."

"There is nothing foolish about that."

"I want to be happy again," she admitted softly.

Her aunt didn't speak for a moment. Then she said, "The happiest people are the ones that know how fleeting happiness can truly be."

"I'm afraid I don't understand."

Her aunt's face softened as she asked, "Do you want to be happy?"

"I do."

"Then you must work at it," her aunt said. "It is not something that is just given to you. You must put forth some effort to obtain it. Happiness is not a guarantee to anyone."

Gemma met her aunt's gaze. "What if I never experience happiness again?"

"That is poppycock," her aunt replied. "I have seen the way your eyes light up when you look at Mr. Wycomb."

Gemma tensed. "No, absolutely not! I love my husband."

Her aunt gave her a kind smile. "There is no disputing that, but Baldwin is not here anymore. You are allowed to live your life."

"By forgetting Baldwin?" she huffed. "I think not."

"No, you are honoring Baldwin by choosing to be happy."

Gemma pressed her lips together. "How can I be happy without Baldwin?"

Her aunt gave her a knowing look. "Do you think Baldwin would want you to wallow in sadness?"

She shook her head.

"Baldwin loved you more than anything else in this world and he would want you to seek out happiness."

"And you think Mr. Wycomb could bring me happiness?"

Her aunt shrugged. "I don't rightly know. That is for you to decide."

"Mr. Wycomb is…" Her voice trailed off as she tried to collect her thoughts. What was he, exactly? He was a solemn man, but his voice seemed to calm her raging soul.

Gemma felt herself go rigid. How could she even consider Mr. Wycomb as a suitor? She loved Baldwin, and she would not allow her fickle heart to change that.

In a steady voice, Gemma said, "I am not ready to entertain suitors."

"In time, you will."

"I do not see myself ever remarrying."

Her aunt looked as if she had more that she wanted to say but the coach came to a stop in front of their townhouse, effectively ending their conversation.

After they exited the coach, they approached the main door and Balfour stood to the side to allow them entry.

Balfour closed the door and addressed her aunt. "Lord Montfort was hoping you would join him in his study."

"I believe I shall." Her aunt turned towards her and reached for her hand. "We will continue our conversation later."

Gemma bobbed her head in agreement, but she secretly hoped that her aunt would forget their discussion. She had made her decision. She had no intention of allowing Mr. Wycomb to court her, assuming he even asked.

As her aunt walked away, she could hear music drifting out of the music room and she felt drawn towards the noise. She came to a stop outside of the door and saw Marielle was sitting at the pianoforte. Her fingers were moving over the keys at a brisk pace. Her eyes were closed, and she was swaying to the music.

The music came to a stop and Marielle lowered her hands to her lap. Feeling foolish for intruding, Gemma went to leave but Marielle's voice stopped her.

"Do you play?" Marielle asked, shifting to face her.

"I used to," Gemma admitted.

Marielle eyed her curiously. "May I ask why you stopped?"

Gemma stepped into the music room and replied, "When Baldwin was dying, he asked for me to play the pianoforte, over and over. It was the only thing that seemed to comfort him towards the end."

Tears came to her eyes as she continued. "Our bedchamber was right above the music room so we opened the windows to allow him to hear the music," she shared. "I would play for hours and he never seemed to tire of it."

"Did he have a favorite piece?"

"He preferred Handel," Gemma replied. "The Messiah's 'Hallelujah' chorus was what he requested most of all."

Marielle patted the seat next to her. "I am familiar with that piece. I would be happy to accompany you."

Gemma put her hand up. "I wouldn't dare," she said. "It would bring back too many painful memories."

"Are all of them bad?"

Gemma paused. "Not all of them," she admitted. "But I am not ready yet."

Marielle gave her an understanding smile. "My mother taught me how to play the pianoforte, and after she died, I didn't feel like playing it either."

"What changed?"

"Now, whenever I touch the keys, I remember my mother," Marielle said. "I remember her smile, her eyes, and, most importantly, I remember how she made me feel."

Gemma walked closer to the pianoforte. "Do you not get sad?"

"I do, all the time, but it is the only time that I feel as if my mother is watching over me." Marielle waved her hand in front of her. "I know I must sound silly."

"Not to me," Gemma rushed out.

Marielle retrieved the sheets of music that sat on the pianoforte and shuffled them. "I am sorry that I missed the opportunity to go shopping this afternoon, but Hugh wanted to take a stroll through the gardens."

"You should know that we ran into your brother in the most unusual place."

Rising, Marielle asked, "Which was?"

"The milliner's shop," Gemma replied.

Marielle furrowed her brows. "Why was Stephen at the milliner's shop?"

"Apparently, he wanted to purchase you a hat," Gemma responded.

"He bought me a hat?"

Gemma smiled. "Yes, it has the most beautiful pink flowers."

Marielle made a face. "But I hate pink."

"I do not think your brother was aware of that," Gemma responded. "I think it was sweet that he was thinking about you."

Walking over to a table, Marielle put the music down and said, "Stephen has never bought me a hat before. I do wonder what he was about."

Gemma walked over to the window and looked out into the gardens. "You might be overthinking this."

"I don't think I am," Marielle said. "I suspect it wasn't as much of what was in the shop but 'who' was in the shop."

Not liking the direction of the conversation, Gemma asked, "Are you close with your brother?"

"Stephen is many years older than me, but he has always

been my protector," Marielle replied. "It was extremely hard on me when his ship went down, and he was presumed dead."

"I can only imagine what you must have endured during that time."

Marielle smiled. "If Hugh hadn't won me in a card game, I don't know where I would have ended up since my inheritance was tied up in probate court."

"My cousin won you in a card game?" Gemma asked.

"My guardian wagered me and lost," Marielle explained. "Hugh was my guardian until Stephen arrived at his doorstep."

"I remember you saying that there was some animosity between them so how did Mr. Wycomb respond to Hugh being your guardian?"

With a laugh, Marielle replied, "He was furious, at least until he realized how well Hugh and the rest of his family had cared for me."

Gemma moved from her place at the window and sat down on a camelback settee. "I'm having a hard time imagining my cousin being a guardian."

"Hugh was a perfect gentleman."

"I have no doubt," Gemma said. "My cousin may be many things, but he has always treated women with the utmost respect."

Marielle looked through some sheet music before she selected one. "Before I met Hugh, I was determined to run my father's shipyard and I had no intention of marrying."

"What changed your mind?"

A reflective look came to Marielle's eyes. "I fell in love with a man that values me above all else."

"Then you made the right choice."

Marielle took the sheet music over to the pianoforte. "Every day I wake up with Hugh by my side. I know that nothing but our love matters." She sat down on the bench. "It is a wonderful feeling to be in love."

"Yes, it is," Gemma readily agreed.

Moving her hands to rest above the keys, Marielle said, "I have learned that love is always worth the risk."

Gemma sat back as Marielle started playing the pianoforte and she decided to stop overthinking everything. She didn't know what her future held, but she shouldn't be trying to run from it.

# Chapter Seven

Stephen stood in the back of the stuffy ballroom and adjusted his white cravat. He vaguely heard the patrons being announced as he attempted to determine why the blazes he had agreed to come to this ball. But he already knew the answer. Lady Hawkinge. He was drawn to her and it was unlike anything that he had ever experienced before.

He had been interested in Evie, cared for her even, but he had never been so beguiled as he was by Lady Hawkinge. Which was proving to be a problem for him, considering he had repeatedly decided that he would not show her any favor. Yet, he couldn't seem to help himself.

He needed to regain his senses before he made a fool of himself again. Even if Lady Hawkinge wasn't mourning her late husband, he was still far beneath her. He owned a ship-yard and wasn't a member of the peerage. He didn't belong amongst the *ton*, but his sister kept ensuring he received invitations to social events. It was maddening, but he knew his sister had good intentions.

"Botheration," he muttered under his breath. He didn't want to be here, but he couldn't very well leave now. He had asked Lady Hawkinge to save him a dance. What if she was anticipating the dance as much as he was? Although, he sincerely doubted that. She would have a line of suitors if she were so inclined.

His sister was announced, and he turned his attention towards the door. Hugh was leading Marielle into the ballroom, but they appeared to only have eyes for one another. If he waited for them to find him, he would be waiting all night.

"Excuse me," Stephen said as he brushed past a couple that were standing in front of him. He crossed the room and came to a stop in front of Marielle.

Marielle smiled up at him. "You came."

"I did." Stephen shifted uncomfortably in his stance. "It is deucedly warm in here."

Hugh chuckled. "It always is, but you will get used to it."

"I doubt it." Stephen perused his sister's ballgown. "You look lovely. I see that you acquired a new gown."

"I did, but apparently you purchased a new hat for me, as well," Marielle said, her eyes sparkling with amusement.

Stephen winced. "I did."

"You do realize that I do not favor pink," Marielle remarked.

"I hadn't realized that when I selected the hat."

Marielle lifted her brow. "Pray tell, why did you purchase me a hat?"

"Doesn't a woman always need more hats?" he attempted.

"They do, but I am perfectly capable of selecting my own hats," Marielle replied. "Which poses the question- why did you select the same milliner's shop that Gemma was frequenting?"

"Oh, yes..." Stephen cleared his throat. "I just happened upon the hat shop and Lady Hawkinge was already inside."

Marielle placed a hand on her hip. "Do try again, Brother."

Stephen turned towards Hugh and said, "I do hope she doesn't interrogate you like this."

"She has never had a need," Hugh remarked, "but it would be much better for you if you just tell her the truth."

Stephen didn't want to confess that he held Lady Hawkinge in some regard, at least, not yet. But he needed to say something that would appease his sister's curiosity. While he was thinking of something to say, Lady Hawkinge was announced, along with Lord and Lady Hawthorne.

He shifted his gaze towards the door and saw Lady Hawkinge walk further into the room. She was dressed in a gold-colored ballgown with puffy sleeves. Her hair was piled high atop her head and small curls framed her face. She looked exquisite, but he could see that he was not alone in his opinion. All eyes seemed to be on her as she approached Marielle and Hugh.

Lady Hawkinge came to a stop next to Marielle and he managed to catch her eye. She smiled, and he was lost all over again.

Marielle nudged him with her elbow and murmured, "You are staring."

Stephen blinked. "My apologies," he rushed out, embarrassed that he had been caught staring. "I'm afraid I was caught woolgathering."

"There is no shame in that," Lady Hawkinge graciously replied.

He wasted no time in bowing. "You are looking lovely this evening, my lady," he said.

Lady Hawkinge glanced down at her gown. "My aunt just had this ballgown commissioned for me."

"It suits you nicely." Stephen stifled the groan on his lips. Why had he said that?

"You are too kind," Lady Hawkinge said, lowering her gaze.

Lord Hawthorne stepped up with his wife and greeted him. "I hadn't expected to see you here this evening."

"I promised Marielle that I would attend," Stephen

shared.

Marielle patted his arm with her hand. "If Stephen hadn't come, I have no doubt he would have been sitting in that ramshackle townhouse of his and be drinking away his woes."

"You sound as if you disapprove," Stephen joked.

"I do wish you would come live with us until the end of the Season. There is plenty of room and it is much more pleasant than where you are living now," Marielle said.

Stephen shuddered. "I can't imagine the torture of living under the same roof as two sets of newlyweds."

Hawthorne looked amused. "I do not fault you for that."

The orchestra began warming up and the next set was announced. Before he had a chance to ask Lady Hawkinge to dance, another gentleman did just that.

As Lady Hawkinge was escorted towards the dance floor, Marielle leaned in and said, "You shouldn't have waited so long."

Hugh held his hand out and asked, "Would you care to dance, my love?"

"I would love to," she replied.

Stephen gave Hawthorne a questioning look. "Are you not dancing with your wife?"

Dinah spoke up. "I do not feel like dancing this evening."

"Then may I ask, why did you come?" Stephen asked.

"We already accepted the invitation and my mother-in-law said it would be inconceivable for us to miss this ball," Dinah replied.

"Are Lord and Lady Montfort in attendance this evening?" Stephen asked, his eyes roaming over the room.

"They always are fashionably late," Hawthorne said. "My mother rather enjoys making a grand entrance."

"I see," Stephen said, even though he didn't see.

Stephen wished that he could speak freely to Hawthorne but they were surrounded by people, including his wife. But Hawthorne didn't have any such qualms about it.

"I spoke to my contacts, and no one knows anything about Benjamin Heathcote, or Colin Staley, for that matter," Hawthorne said, keeping his voice low.

"I did see Benjamin when I was trying to secure a hackney and he ran from me," Stephen shared.

"Why would he run from you?" Hawthorne asked.

"I don't know, but by the time I arrived at the alley, he was gone."

Hawthorne grew pensive. "What is Benjamin about?" he asked. "People only run when they have something to hide."

Lady Hawthorne placed her hand on her husband's sleeve and commented, "It is rather warm in here. Would you mind terribly if we step outside for a moment?"

With a loving smile at his wife, Hawthorne placed her hand into the crook of his arm. "Not in the least bit," he said.

Lady Hawthorne offered Stephen an apologetic smile. "You are welcome to join us."

"Thank you, but I do believe I will remain here," Stephen said.

It hadn't been a moment after Lord and Lady Hawthorne had walked off when a blonde-haired woman approached him. The neckline on her gown was far too revealing and she had a look of determination on her face.

She kept her gaze focused on the large crowd as she asked, "Is your income truly twenty thousand pounds a year on your shipyard?"

"I beg your pardon?"

The woman turned to face him with an unimpressed look on her face. "It really is a simple question. I do not think I need to simplify it even more."

"I do apologize, but we have not been properly introduced." He bowed. "If you will excuse me, I—"

She cut him off. "I hadn't taken you for a stickler of propriety, but if you insist." She took a breath. "I am Lady Susanna, daughter of Lord Audubon." The way she said her words made him believe that she expected him to be impressed. But he wasn't.

Stephen took a step back. "I'm afraid I am needed elsewhere. Excuse me."

Before he could take a step, Lady Susanna said, "I am in need of a husband, and I suppose you will do. I am willing to overlook your lack of connections and low social status in favor of your generous income."

Stephen was stunned by Lady Susanna's brazenness and she mistakenly mistook it for acceptance.

Lady Susanna smiled coyly. "I see that you are considering my offer."

"You are mistaken," Stephen said. "You may be in need of a husband, but I do not have need of a wife."

Lady Susanna's smile disappeared. "Surely you are not in earnest. Just think of the doors that will be opened for you if we are married."

He bowed. "I wish you luck on your search for a husband, but I am not interested."

"You are an arrogant man," Lady Susanna said, her voice rising. "If you even took a moment to consider—"

Her words came to a stop when Lady Hawkinge appeared at his side. "I do apologize for interrupting," she paused, "whatever this is, but I need to speak to Mr. Wycomb," she said, placing her hand on his arm. "Please excuse us."

As Stephen led Lady Hawkinge away, he said, "Thank you."

Lady Hawkinge patted his arm. "When I saw Lady Susanna speaking to you, I assumed you needed to be rescued."

"You were correct in your assumption, but why was that?"

"Lady Susanna is my husband's cousin," Lady Hawkinge explained. "She is in her ninth Season, and I have heard that she is getting desperate."

Stephen glanced over his shoulder and saw that Lady

Susanna was watching them with narrowed eyes. "She offered for me."

Lady Hawkinge's mouth dropped but she quickly recovered. "She offered for you?" she repeated. "My, that was bold."

"I thought so, as well." Stephen stepped out onto the veranda and welcomed the cool night air on his skin.

Lady Hawkinge removed her hand and created more distance between them. "I would not concern yourself with Susanna."

"I do not intend to." Stephen tipped his head at a couple sitting on a bench. "Lady Susanna was willing to overlook my lack of connections in favor of my income."

"How generous of her," Lady Hawkinge teased.

Stephen came to a stop next to an iron railing that ran the length of the veranda. "I don't belong here," he sighed.

Lady Hawkinge looked up at the night sky as she said, "You are right. You don't belong with these people."

Stephen knew she spoke the truth, but it still stung, nonetheless.

She brought her gaze to meet his. "You are a good, honest man, and members of high Society do not care for anyone that is genuine."

Feeling bold, he asked, "Do you belong here, then?"

A puff of air escaped her lips. "I am a countess, and these are my peers," she said as she gestured towards the French doors. "But, no, I do not belong here either. I'm afraid it took me being away from all of this to discover that."

"May I be so bold to ask where you belong?"

Lady Hawkinge grew quiet. "I haven't figured that out yet."

The next set was announced, and Stephen didn't want to miss his chance to dance with Lady Hawkinge again. He held his hand out. "Would you care to dance?"

"But this is the waltz."

"Is that an issue?" he asked, not withdrawing his hand.

Lady Hawkinge tentatively placed her hand into his. "I suppose not."

———

Gemma knew she was being silly, but the last time she had danced the waltz was with her husband. It was such an intimate dance, and she wasn't sure if her heart could take being in another's arms.

She allowed Mr. Wycomb to escort her to the dance floor, despite feeling an overwhelming need to flee from the ballroom.

Mr. Wycomb dropped his arm and turned to face her. He must have sensed her apprehension because he leaned in and lowered his voice. "We don't have to dance, if you don't want."

Gemma decided that she should just be honest with what she was feeling. "The last time I danced the waltz was with Baldwin."

Understanding crossed his features. "What would you like to do?"

That was the one question that she couldn't answer. What kind of feelings would surface if she started dancing the waltz with Mr. Wycomb?

Mr. Wycomb met her gaze, and she could see compassion stirring deep within his eyes. "I can see that you are not ready," he said, offering his arm. "It is all right. We shall dance another time."

As she held his gaze, she admired his hazel-colored eyes that could never decide whether they wanted to be green or brown. His eyes held her captive, holding her there, just with his gaze, memorizing her.

Mr. Wycomb's voice broke through her musings. "My

lady," he said. "The music is about to begin. We should leave the dance floor."

Finding strength deep inside of her, she said, "I think I would like to dance with you, Mr. Wycomb."

"As you wish." Mr. Wycomb took a small step towards her, and slowly, as if she might scare at any moment, slipped his arm around her waist. Then, ever so gently, he took her gloved hand into his and brought it up.

Gemma's heart was pounding so hard in her chest that she feared Mr. Wycomb could hear it over the music. She hesitantly placed a hand on his shoulder and allowed him to start leading her across the dance floor.

It was after a few trips around the room that she found herself relaxing in Mr. Wycomb's arms. He smelled of sandalwood and a hint of orange. That was a stark contrast to what her husband smelled like. Baldwin always smelled like leather because he spent so much time in the saddle.

"You dance superbly," Mr. Wycomb said.

"Only because you haven't let me fall yet," she teased.

She had meant her words lightly, but Mr. Wycomb's expression grew solemn. "I would never let you fall," he said.

"I believe you." And she did. She felt safe in his arms. It was a feeling she hadn't felt in a long time; a feeling that she had missed.

Mr. Wycomb tightened his hold on her waist. "Are you enjoying yourself?"

"I believe I am."

His lips twitched. "That is a high endorsement."

"I know you must think me foolish…"

"Never, and you don't need to explain yourself to me," Mr. Wycomb said, speaking over her. "I can hear in your voice how much you loved your husband."

"I did, with my whole heart."

Mr. Wycomb clenched his jaw for a moment before it relaxed. "How did you meet your husband?"

"At a ball," she replied. "The moment I saw him, I knew he was the one."

"Was it love at first sight for him, as well?"

She smiled at that memory. "Not at all. He later told me that he found my beauty to be off-putting."

"He wasn't wrong."

"You are sweet, but it has been many years since I have been a diamond of the first water," Gemma responded.

Mr. Wycomb brought her closer and she didn't resist him. "You are still the most beautiful woman in this room, and everyone knows it," he said.

Gemma felt a blush forming on her cheeks and she brought her gaze down to the lapels of his jacket. "You shouldn't say such things to me, sir."

"I am only speaking the truth."

She pressed her lips together, then said, "I'm afraid I am not ready for the truth yet."

Mr. Wycomb bobbed his head. "Then I shall strive to be patient."

"I might not ever be ready… for the truth."

"The truth can be scary, but I do believe the truth could set you free," he said. "You just have to be strong enough to embrace the truth."

Gemma brought her gaze up. "I wish it was that simple."

"It can be as simple as you want it to be."

"Not for me," Gemma said. "I tend to overthink things. It used to drive Baldwin mad."

Mr. Wycomb smiled. "You never did tell me how your husband won your heart."

"He tripped me."

Rearing back, Mr. Wycomb asked, "He tripped you?"

"Yes," Gemma replied. "It wasn't on purpose, mind you, but we were dancing, and I have never met someone that danced so poorly. He stuck his foot out and I tripped over it."

"Are you sure he didn't mean to trap you into marriage?"

"Heavens, no!" she said. "Baldwin was mortified but my father demanded that we be wed at once. He even went and secured us a special license."

"It sounds like a rough way to start a marriage."

"It does, but we were in love before we stood in front of the vicar," Gemma said. "Baldwin said he fell in love the moment I landed in a heap on the dance floor and laughed."

"You two were most fortunate to have found one another."

"That we were." Gemma grew quiet. "We were only married for a few years before he grew sick. One minute he was there, and the next… he was gone." Her voice was soft.

Mr. Wycomb winced. "I am sorry. I do not mean to dredge up bad memories."

"That's just it, however. Every memory with Baldwin in it is a good one," Gemma said. "The memories without him are what makes me sad."

The music came to an end and Mr. Wycomb dropped his arms. He took a step back and bowed slightly at the hips. "Thank you for dancing with me, my lady."

"You are most kindly welcome."

Mr. Wycomb offered his arm. "Allow me to escort you back to your cousins."

Gemma placed her hand on his and they departed the dance floor. They walked through the crowd of people until she saw Hugh and Marielle standing next to a column. She was just about to point them out when Mr. Wycomb shifted his direction towards them.

Once they arrived, Mr. Wycomb didn't drop his arm and she saw no need to do so either. She found she enjoyed being this close to him.

Her aunt's voice came from behind her, startling her. "I saw you dancing the waltz, my dear," she said. "You were flawless in your movements."

Gemma removed her hand from Mr. Wycomb's and

turned to face her aunt. "That is because of my partner, Mr. Wycomb."

Mr. Wycomb bowed. "Lady Montfort," he greeted. "It is a pleasure to see you again."

She tipped her head to acknowledge him before she turned back to Gemma. "If you will come with me, I have a few people that I would like to introduce you to."

"Yes, Aunt Edith," Gemma said.

As they walked away, her aunt leaned closer to her and said, "A word of advice- you cannot dance with a gentleman like you did with Mr. Wycomb and not expect people to talk."

"How exactly did I dance with Mr. Wycomb?"

"You appeared beguiled by the man."

Gemma pursed her lips. "I am not beguiled by Mr. Wycomb."

"Just be cautious," her aunt advised. "You may be a widow, but you are not untouchable. Gossips will still talk."

"Why should I care?"

Her aunt came to an abrupt stop and turned to face her. "You are a part of this family, and a shameful scandal could ruin our good name," she replied.

"I understand."

Placing her hands on Gemma's shoulders, Aunt Edith said, "Keep your chin up. Just remember that everything you do is on display for others to see."

"How wonderful," she muttered.

"You have been in the country for far too long. The *ton* delights in watching people's failures." Her aunt perused the length of her. "I see that your ballgown turned out splendidly."

"Yes, it did."

Her aunt dropped her arms to her sides. "I know that it has been some time, but it is imperative that you do not dance with Mr. Wycomb again this evening."

"I remember," Gemma muttered. "To do so would imply

that we have an understanding between us."

Her aunt frowned as she glanced over her shoulder. "I hadn't realized that your father would be in attendance this evening."

"My father is here?" Gemma followed her aunt's gaze and saw her father and stepmother approaching them.

"Try not to create a scene," her aunt counseled as she brought a smile to her face. "Andrew, what a delight it is to see you here."

Her stone-faced father came to a stop next to them and tipped his head at his sister. "Edith." He turned his attention towards her, and his expression did not soften a bit. Not that she expected it to. He was like a stranger to her. "Gemma."

Knowing what was expected of her, she dropped into a curtsy. "Father."

Her stepmother was tall, with dark brown hair, and wore clothing that left little to the imagination. She looped her hand through her husband's arm and greeted her politely. "You are looking well, Gemma."

Gemma had little to say to her stepmother, so she remained quiet.

Her father either didn't care about her insolence or didn't notice because he demanded, "Do you want to explain to me why you were dancing with someone so far below your station?"

"If you must know, Mr. Wycomb's sister is married to Lord Hugh."

"Yes, his sister may be an upstart, but he doesn't belong in high Society," her father pressed. "He owns a shipyard."

"I am well aware of his occupation," Gemma said.

Her father narrowed his eyes. "I didn't have you marry an earl only to watch you throw your life away for some shipbuilder."

Gemma attempted to stay calm even though she felt her temper rising. "Mr. Wycomb and I are just friends."

"Friends?" he huffed. "Friends do not dance the waltz in a sensual way."

"Nothing about our dance was sensual," she stated.

With a shake of his head, her father asked, "Do you even think of Baldwin anymore?"

Gemma pursed her lips together. "That isn't fair of you to say."

Her father wasn't done with her, and he took a step forward, towering over her. "How do you think Baldwin would react to your shameful behavior on the dance floor?"

"I don't know because he is dead, Father," Gemma spat out.

Her aunt gasped. "Gemma."

Gemma turned towards her aunt. "I'm sorry, but I can't do this," she said before she started to walk away. She had to put as much distance between her and her father as she could. How did her father always manage to grate on her nerves? He was impossible, and she would never understand why he was so cruel to her.

She barely acknowledged her cousins and wives as she passed by them and headed out the French doors. She saw their concerned looks, but she didn't want to stop and explain herself. She just wanted to be alone.

How dare her father ask her if she thought about Baldwin! What audacity he had. He had no idea of how much she missed him; how much it hurt to think about him.

Gemma hurried down the path of the gardens until she found a bench that was set back under the trees. She went to sit down and blinked back the tears that were threatening to fall from her eyes. For a brief moment, she had a respite from her grief when she danced with Mr. Wycomb, and her father found a way to ruin it.

As she swiped at her eyes, she didn't think her father would let her have an ounce of happiness. He never did before, so why should he start now?

# Chapter Eight

Stephen had watched as Lady Hawkinge had walked across the ballroom with a determined stride and a hardened look on her face, but he couldn't help but notice the slightest quiver of her chin.

"It would appear that Uncle Andrew managed to upset Gemma... again," Hugh remarked with a frustrated sigh. "I should go speak with her."

"Allow me," Stephen said.

Hugh opened his mouth to no doubt object but Marielle spoke first. "I think that is a grand idea."

"You do?" Hugh asked, looking skeptical.

Marielle nodded. "I do," she said.

It took a long moment, but Hugh finally relented. "Very well," he encouraged. "But do not put my cousin in a compromising position."

"I have no intention of doing so," Stephen said.

Hawthorne spoke up. "Dinah and I will step onto the veranda to ensure you and Gemma are properly chaperoned."

Before Stephen even took his first step, Marielle leaned in and said, "Be sure to listen to what she isn't saying."

"What does that even mean?"

"Women don't always say what they are truly feeling," Marielle explained. "They are afraid to reveal too much of themselves."

"Then how can one solve their problems?"

"Sometimes women just want to be heard. They don't want their problems solved."

"That is illogical."

Marielle grinned. "Women aren't known to be the most rational creatures, especially when we are upset."

Hugh interjected, "It is true."

Stephen was growing tired of this conversation. He wanted to go find Lady Hawkinge and ensure that she was all right. Nothing else seemed as important as that at this very moment.

"If you will excuse me," Stephen said before he started to walk off. He didn't want to give his sister a chance to give him anymore of her "so-called" advice, especially since he knew how to speak to a woman.

He stepped out onto the veranda and his eyes roamed over the gardens, but he saw no sign of Lady Hawkinge. He started down the path, tipping his head at the couples that he was passing by, and kept his alert eyes open. He had seen her leave the ballroom, so he knew she had to be somewhere in these gardens.

As he reached the back gate, he was about to head back towards the townhouse when he heard a woman sniffling. He turned towards the noise and saw a bench was set back under a large tree. But, more importantly, he saw Lady Hawkinge sitting in the center of it, her eyes downcast.

He stepped off the path and walked the short distance towards the bench. Lady Hawkinge brought her gaze up and there was enough light from the moon to see that she had been crying.

Stephen reached into his jacket pocket and removed a

white handkerchief. He extended it to her without saying a word.

"Thank you," she murmured as she wiped her eyes.

Now that he was here with Lady Hawkinge, he was at a loss for words. What could he say to bring back the light that was so prevalent in her eyes?

The only noise was an owl hooting in the distance and the sound of the wind rustling through the tree leaves.

Stephen decided that the silence had gone on long enough so he thought it would be best to start with something safe.

"It is a lovely evening," Stephen said, glancing up at the stars.

When she didn't respond, he decided to try again. "The gardens are exquisite," he attempted.

This time, Lady Hawkinge responded with a slight bob of her head. "That they are," she murmured, keeping her gaze fixed on her lap.

Botheration. They were going to get nowhere if he kept to polite conversational topics. He would need to press her a little and hope that she didn't resent him for doing so.

In a steady voice, he said, "I understand that your father was in attendance this evening."

"That he was."

"Did you speak to him?"

"I did."

Stephen took a step closer to her, being mindful to maintain a proper distance. "Did he say something that upset you?"

Lady Hawkinge brought her gaze up. "My father is the most aggravating of men, and he can't help but upset me."

"Do I need to challenge him to a duel?" Stephen asked in an attempt at humor.

"No, that would solve nothing." Lady Hawkinge clenched his handkerchief in her hand. "Besides, I do believe my father is too surly to die."

Stephen took another step towards the bench, the leaves

crinkling under the weight of his boots. "May I be so bold as to ask what he said to upset you?"

"It matters not. He will always find a way to criticize me."

"But it matters to me."

Lady Hawkinge bit her lower lip. "My father took issue with my dancing the waltz," she hesitated, "with you."

"I see." He cocked his head. "Do you regret dancing with me?"

Her eyes widened. "Heavens, no," she rushed out. "I wouldn't change a thing about dancing with you, but my father…" Her words trailed off.

Stephen decided to take his sister's advice and boldly asked, "What aren't you saying?"

She sighed. "My father does not approve of you," she revealed. "He thinks working for a living is degrading."

Stephen paused. "Do you want me to seek your father's approval?"

"No, I do not," she replied. "For it is something that is unobtainable, even for me."

"I can't imagine that to be true."

Lady Hawkinge rose from her seat on the bench. "I'm afraid the moment I was born, I was a grand disappointment to him," she said. "My father hardly came around the nursery, but when he did, he would make it a point to chastise me for the tiniest infraction."

Not sure what to say, he settled on, "I'm sorry."

With a shrug, she continued. "It has been this way for my entire life. I know no other way."

"That doesn't make it right."

"And what am I to do about it?" she asked, her voice rising. "My father didn't even attend Baldwin's funeral. What kind of father does that?"

Stephen could hear the pain in her voice and was smart enough not to interrupt.

Lady Hawkinge scoffed. "We hadn't spoken since he

married his mistress, but I had hoped he would have traveled the short distance to be there for me."

"He should have been," Stephen said.

A tear ran down her cheek and Lady Hawkinge reached up to wipe it away. "He was too busy entertaining his wife, a woman he married a month after my mother died." Her voice grew shaky. "One month. That is all my mother meant to him."

Stephen took a step closer to her and she had to tilt her head to look up at him. "I would be irate if my father had done something so despicable."

"My father didn't see it that way. He was upset that I missed their nuptials," Lady Hawkinge said. "He sent me a scathing letter after he returned home from their wedding tour."

"That must have been hard to read."

"It was," Lady Hawkinge murmured. "But nothing beat his audacity until this evening when he accused me of forgetting about Baldwin since I danced the waltz with you."

Stephen noticed that her eyes had grown moist with tears and felt a surge of protectiveness wash over him. "You did nothing wrong. It was just a dance."

Her eyes met his, and for a moment, her face was open and vulnerable in the moonlight. "It was more than just a dance for me," she said softly.

He felt elated by her words. It meant that he was making more progress with her than he realized. Maybe, just maybe, she could begin to start caring for him, as he did for her.

Stephen reached for her hand and brought her gloved hand up to his lips. "It was more than a dance for me, too."

Gemma smiled shyly at him. "I'm glad."

As he held her gaze, he said, "Whatever happens between us, I do not want you to shy away from speaking to me about Baldwin."

"No?"

"Baldwin is a part of you, and I want to know the true you," Stephen said. "I don't want you to hide a part of yourself away."

Stephen almost breathed a sigh of relief when he saw the light return to Lady Hawkinge's eyes. For they were brighter than any star in the night sky.

"I feel the same way," she murmured.

While he held her hand close to his mouth, he realized that he had no intention of letting her go. He would do whatever it took to fight to win her affections.

"Gemma." He breathed her name with all the reverence it deserved. "I apologize if I am being too familiar."

"I will allow it."

"I do hope that means you will call me Stephen."

"I would like that," she said as her eyes briefly dropped to his lips.

It took everything that Stephen possessed not to pull her into his arms and kiss her senseless. He desperately wanted to kiss her, but not here, not now.

A clearing of a throat came from next to them.

Stephen dropped her hand and stepped back to create more distance between them. He turned his head and saw Lord and Lady Hawthorne were watching them with guarded expressions.

Hawthorne met his gaze and said in a firm voice, "I do believe you have taken enough of my cousin's attention for the evening." He offered his other arm to Gemma. "I will escort you back into the ballroom."

Gemma lifted her eyebrow. "Thank you, but I do believe I can find my own way back."

Hawthorne looked displeased by her response. "I'm afraid I must insist since it isn't proper for you to be alone in the gardens."

"Very well, but you must first allow me to say my goodbyes to Mr. Wycomb," Gemma said.

Hawthorne gave a reluctant nod. "Make it quick, then."

Gemma smiled up at Stephen. "Thank you for cheering me up this evening."

"You are welcome," he said, returning her smile. "Would you care to join me for a trip to the museum tomorrow?"

"I would very much like to do so."

"Wonderful," Stephen said. "I shall call upon you tomorrow."

Gemma held up his handkerchief. "I shall have this laundered and returned to you at once."

"I would prefer if you kept it."

Stephen swore that her smile faded a little, growing softer, more intimate. He watched as she moved to stand next to Hawthorne, accepting his proffered arm.

As Hawthorne led his wife and Gemma back into the ballroom, Stephen found that his smile had not dimmed in the least. He was making progress with Gemma, and he couldn't wait until he could see her tomorrow.

He walked over to the back gate and exited the gardens. There was no reason for him to return to the ballroom. He had done what he had set out to do.

---

Gemma woke up to the sun streaming into her bedchamber. She sat up in bed and stretched her arms. For the first time in ages, she felt rested, and she couldn't wait to see what the day would bring forth.

The door opened and Lydia slipped into the room, holding a tray. "Good morning, my lady," she greeted. "I see that you are finally awake."

"Did I oversleep?"

Lydia placed the tray down on the dressing table. "Breakfast was served nearly an hour ago and Lady Montfort has been inquiring after you."

"I hadn't meant to sleep so long."

"I would imagine your body needed the rest." Lydia walked over to the wardrobe and opened it. "What would you like to wear today?"

"I would prefer my green gown," Gemma replied as she put her legs over the side of the bed.

Lydia retrieved the gown and went to drape it over the back of her settee. "Would you care to eat first or shall we style your hair?"

"I can eat while you style my hair." Gemma rose and sat down at the dressing table. She picked up a piece of toast from the plate and took a bite.

Lydia removed the cap from her head and started brushing her hair. "It was late when you returned home from the ball and we didn't have a chance to talk," she said. "How was the ball?"

Gemma brought her hand up to her mouth as she chewed. "It was..." Her words trailed off as she tried to think of a way to describe it. Finally, she settled on, "It was blissfully eventful."

"What does that mean?"

After she swallowed the bite in her mouth, Gemma replied, "I danced the waltz with Mr. Wycomb."

"You did?"

Gemma bobbed her head. "At first I was hesitant, but I am glad that I danced with him."

"Is it because he is incredibly handsome?"

"Is he?" Gemma asked innocently. "I'm afraid I haven't noticed."

Lydia laughed. "You are a terrible liar, my lady."

"All right, I may have noticed that he is exceptionally handsome," Gemma said. "But that was not the reason why I accepted his invitation to dance."

"Then why did you?"

Gemma wiped the crumbs off her hands as she confessed, "I think I have developed feelings for Mr. Wycomb."

"And?"

Gemma turned in her seat to meet Lydia's gaze. "Are you not the least bit surprised?"

"Not in the least," Lydia replied as she made a motion with her hand, indicating that she should turn back around. "I have heard the way you speak about him, and I only assumed you had feelings for him."

"Mr. Wycomb is the first man that has shown me favor since Baldwin died."

Lydia shook her head. "No, Mr. Wycomb is the first man that you have noticed showing you favor," she said. "You just have never wanted to look before."

Gemma reached for her cup of chocolate and took a sip. "My father was there last night," she revealed.

"Did he make a scene?"

"Thankfully not, but he did chastise me for embarrassing myself with Mr. Wycomb," Gemma responded.

"How exactly did you embarrass yourself?"

"I danced with a man that was well below my station, and there is nothing worse in the eyes of my father." Leaning forward, Gemma placed her cup back onto the tray. "That is one advantage of being a widow. I am no longer under his thumb."

"Was your stepmother there?"

Gemma made a face. "Yes, and her gown was entirely too revealing. I should have shoved a grapefruit in her cleavage, and I daresay she wouldn't have noticed."

Lydia giggled. "That is terrible of you."

A knock came at the door, interrupting their conversation.

"Enter," Gemma ordered.

The door opened and a young maid stepped into the room. "Lord Hawkinge has come to call," she revealed.

Gemma resisted the urge to groan. She didn't feel like entertaining Henry, but she had no choice but to do so. She didn't dare insult him by turning him away.

"Will you inform him that I shall be down shortly?"

The young maid dropped into a curtsy. "Yes, my lady."

Once the door was closed, Lydia placed her hair into a tight chignon. "It is simple, but it will do for now," she said. "We must hurry and dress you so Lord Hawkinge will not chide you for making him wait long."

Gemma walked over to the wardrobe and pulled out a simple pale blue gown. "I would prefer to wear this when I receive Lord Hawkinge."

"Is there a particular reason why?"

"I do not feel like dressing up for Lord Hawkinge," Gemma replied.

Lydia accepted the gown and placed it next to the green gown. She stepped back towards Gemma and asked, "Shall we?"

A short while later, Gemma descended the stairs of the townhouse and headed for the drawing room. She stepped inside and saw Henry was staring out the tall window, an annoyed look on his face.

"Henry," she greeted, dropping into a curtsy. "How pleased I am that you have come to call on me."

Henry's eyes perused the length of her and she saw approval inside of them. "You look lovely, my dear."

"You always flatter me." Gemma gestured towards the settees. "Would you care to have a seat?"

"I would like that very much."

Gemma went to sit down in the middle of the yellow settee in anticipation of Henry sitting across from her. However, he claimed the seat next to her and she quickly moved over, creating more distance between them.

Henry removed his pocket watch and glanced at it. "I would be remiss if I did not mention that my time is precious and I do not have time to wait in a drawing room, for anyone."

"I apologize, but I'm afraid it couldn't be helped," Gemma said. "I woke up much later than I intended and—"

He cut her off. "I abhor excuses. Just promise me that it won't happen again and we can move past this."

Gemma brought a smile to her lips. "I promise."

"Very good," Henry said. "I was hoping to take you on a carriage ride around Hyde Park today during the fashionable hour."

"As fun as that sounds, I'm afraid my afternoon is already spoken for," Gemma said. "I intend to visit the museum."

"May I ask with whom?"

Gemma clasped her hands in her lap. "Mr. Wycomb. He is the brother of Lady Hugh."

Henry looked unimpressed. "If you would like to see the museum, I would gladly accompany you," he said. "You don't need to waste your time or energy with a man like Mr. Wycomb."

"What exactly does that mean?"

"Mr. Wycomb is common, and you are a countess. My countess," Henry said.

"That is only until you marry, and then I become the dowager countess."

Henry moved closer to her on the settee. "Yes, and your actions affect me. Imagine what the gossips would say if the Countess of Hawkinge was mingling with commoners."

"Mr. Wycomb and I are friends," Gemma said.

"You must be careful who you make friends with because they could reflect poorly on you," Henry advised.

Gemma tried to create more distance by moving to the side of the settee, but that did little to deter Henry. It wasn't long before she was pressed up against the side of the settee.

A serving maid stepped into the room with a tea service and placed it down on a table in front of them.

In a soft voice, the maid inquired, "Would you like me to pour?"

"No, but would you inform my aunt that we have company?" Gemma asked.

The maid dropped into a curtsy. "Yes, my lady."

As the maid departed from the room, Gemma leaned forward in her seat and asked, "Would you like some tea?"

"Yes, I think that would be nice."

Gemma poured him a cup of tea and extended it towards him.

Henry accepted it and took a sip of his tea. He pressed his lips together as he went to put the cup and saucer onto the tray. "I am surprised that Lady Montfort would serve this tea."

"What is wrong with it?"

"It is much too bitter for my tastes."

Gemma poured herself a cup and took a sip. "I do not think it is bitter," she said as she lowered the teacup to her lap.

Henry gave her a haughty look. "I'm afraid my palate is much more refined than yours, my dear," he said. "Now, what were we speaking about before we were interrupted?"

"I think you were chastising me on the friends that I was keeping."

"Not chastising, but I was advising you," he corrected. "You are naive to the ways of the world and need to be protected."

"I do thank you for your concern, but I do believe it is unfounded."

Henry leaned closer to her. "It is my duty to watch over you, and I do not shirk my responsibilities."

"That is kind of you, but I am residing with my aunt and uncle for the remainder of the Season."

Henry huffed. "And they are doing a poor job of watching over you."

"I disagree."

With a glance at the neckline of her gown, Henry said,

"Come reside at my townhouse and I shall care for you properly."

"There is no need since I enjoy it here."

Henry leaned closer and tucked a piece of hair behind her ear, his fingers lingering on her skin. Gemma resisted the urge to shudder but knew she had to do something drastic to remove herself from this situation.

She spilled the tea onto her lap and jumped up, feigning outrage. "Drats," she said. "I can't believe I am so clumsy."

Henry rose. "It is just a spot. It will wash out."

"I need to have my lady's maid treat this gown at once so the stain won't set," Gemma said as she placed the teacup onto the tray. "I am sorry to cut our meeting short."

Henry reached for her hand and brought it to his lips. "I have enjoyed our time together immensely."

"As have I," Gemma replied, choking on the words.

He continued to hold her hand, making her feel even more uncomfortable than she already was. Fortunately, her aunt's voice came from the doorway.

"Lord Hawkinge," her aunt said. "What a pleasant surprise."

Henry dropped her hand and moved to create more distance between them. He bowed. "Lady Montfort."

Her aunt glanced down at the stain on her gown and gave her a disapproving look. "Tea is exceptionally difficult to remove from clothing," she tsked. "You should go at once and I will keep Lord Hawkinge company."

Henry held his hand up. "Thank you, but I have work that I need to see to," he informed her. "Perhaps another time, my lady."

"How disappointing," her aunt said. "But I do understand."

With a parting look at Gemma, Henry departed from the drawing room, and she didn't breathe a sigh of relief until she heard the main door close.

Her aunt gave her a knowing look. "Did you truly spill your tea to avoid Lord Hawkinge?"

"I did," she replied, seeing no reason to deny it.

"May I ask why?"

Gemma walked over to the window and watched as Henry stepped into his black coach. "Henry has always flirted with me, but he has grown bolder with each passing day."

"He couldn't possibly intend to marry you since it is illegal to marry a brother's widow in England."

"I do not believe that is the arrangement he has in mind for me," Gemma admitted.

Her aunt's eyes grew wide. "That audacious man!" she exclaimed. "What nerve of him to try to take you as a mistress."

Gemma turned back towards her aunt. "What am I to do? I rely upon his good graces to live," she said. "Without him, where would I go?"

"You would live here, with us," her aunt declared.

"I couldn't possibly intrude."

Her aunt had a determined look on her face. "I couldn't live with myself if I sent you back to Hawkinge with that man, knowing what I know now," she said.

Gemma hoped her words properly expressed the gratitude that she felt in her heart. "Thank you."

"Now, go and take care of that stain before it sets," her aunt advised. "We wouldn't want you to ruin a gown over Lord Hawkinge, now would we?"

"No, we would not," Gemma replied, pleased that she had the foresight to set her green gown aside for her outing with Mr. Wycomb.

# Chapter Nine

Stephen found himself whistling as he stepped out of his carriage. He was in a rather fine mood this afternoon. He found himself anxious to see Gemma again. He didn't think he would ever tire of being in her presence. There was something about her that seemed to brighten everything around her. And when she smiled, he couldn't help but smile back.

He approached the main door of Lord Montfort's townhouse and knocked. It was promptly opened by the butler, and he greeted Stephen in a cordial tone.

"Mr. Wycomb, do come in," the butler said as he stood to the side to allow him entry.

Stephen stepped into the entry hall and waited as the door was closed behind him.

"Lady Hawkinge is expecting you," the butler informed him. "If you will follow me, I will announce you."

The butler turned on his heel and walked the short distance to the drawing room. He stepped inside and announced, "Mr. Wycomb has arrived, my lady."

Stephen followed the butler into the room and saw Gemma was standing in front of the settee. She was dressed in an alluring green gown that flattered her features immensely.

She curtsied when their eyes met. "Mr. Wycomb," she murmured.

He bowed. "My lady."

Gemma gestured towards an upholstered armchair near her. "Would you care to sit down for a moment?"

"I would," he said.

As he approached the proffered chair, a maid stepped into the room, and she walked over to a chair in the corner.

Gemma gracefully lowered herself onto the settee. "I would offer you some tea, but I know you do not care for it." Her words were spoken lightly.

"You speak as if I am the only person that has an aversion for tea."

"I have yet to meet another."

"Perhaps you are not looking hard enough," he joked.

Gemma reached for her teacup on the table and took a sip. As she lowered the cup and saucer to her lap, she said, "I must admit that I am looking forward to the museum today."

"As am I."

"Baldwin and I would visit the museum every time we were in London," she shared. "He was particularly fond of the coins that were on display, but I preferred the antiquities."

"I am afraid that I have never been to the museum before."

"Then you are in for a treat," Gemma said.

His sister stepped into the room with a hat in her hand. "Hugh should be down in a moment and we can depart."

Stephen had risen when his sister had entered the room. "We?" he asked, glancing between Gemma and Marielle.

Marielle approached him and kissed him on the cheek. "When we discovered that we both had plans to attend the museum this afternoon, we decided it would be fun to go together."

"What a pleasant surprise," Stephen said, hoping his words sounded somewhat convincing.

Marielle went to sit down next to Gemma and reached for a biscuit off the tray. "I can't wait to see what books they have on display. Last time, they had a first edition Gutenberg Bible."

As his sister rambled on about the significance of the Gutenberg Bible, he found himself slightly disappointed that he would have to compete for Gemma's attention on this outing.

The long clock chimed in the corner and Marielle jumped up. "I should see what is taking Hugh so long. Please excuse me."

Stephen rose and waited until his sister departed from the room. Then he returned to his seat and hoped that the disappointment didn't show on his face.

Gemma leaned forward and placed her teacup down onto the tray. "I know you must be terribly disappointed, but my aunt thought it would be best if Marielle and Hugh accompanied us for propriety's sake."

"I am not disappointed," he lied, wondering how Gemma had known precisely what he had been thinking.

Gemma gave him a look that implied she didn't believe him. "Regardless, it will be fun to spend time with Marielle and Hugh."

"Are you close with your cousin?"

"I am," she replied. "My mother thought it was important that I knew my cousins, so we visited them frequently in my youth."

"But not your father?"

Gemma huffed. "My father was hardly around," she said. "He was much too busy with his mistresses or gambling."

"That is most unfortunate."

"My father acquired a hefty gambling debt and should have been thrown into debtor's prison," she said. "It was no less than he deserved."

"Why wasn't he?"

"Baldwin paid off his debts as a wedding gift to me," Gemma revealed. "He didn't want the scandal associated with my name."

"That was most thoughtful of him."

"It was, but my father didn't stop gambling. He kept approaching Baldwin for more funds until it became too much," Gemma said. "Baldwin cut my father off and that incited my father's anger. He threatened to drag my name through the mud if Baldwin didn't continue to fund his lavish lifestyle."

Stephen lifted his brow. "Your own father tried to blackmail you?"

"He did, but it didn't work. The *ton* was well acquainted with my father's disreputable behavior, and they didn't give his words any heed," Gemma explained. "Sadly, the person that suffered the most was my mother. She refused to leave my father and come live with me and Baldwin."

"Did she state why that was?"

"My mother said she loved my father, but I don't know how that was possible. He mistreated her terribly and she still stood by his side," Gemma said. "He wasn't even by my mother's side when she died because he was too busy entertaining his mistress."

Stephen winced. "That is awful."

Gemma clenched her hands in her lap. "I do not think I can ever forgive my father for his ill-treatment of my mother," she admitted. "What he did to her was cruel."

"I agree, wholeheartedly." He moved to sit on the edge of his seat and placed his hand over her clenched hands. "Blood means you are related, but it doesn't mean they are your family. Your father lost his right to claim you as his daughter when he treated you so distastefully."

Glancing down at their hands, she asked, "You don't think I should forgive him then?"

"Forgiveness is a tricky thing," he replied. "You can forgive someone without accepting their behavior or even trusting them. But you can forgive them for *you* so you can let go and move on with your life."

"I don't think I can," she admitted.

"I am not saying it is easy or even the right path for you," Stephen said. "Only you can decide what is best for you."

Gemma brought her gaze up to meet his. "I don't know what I want to do."

"Then that is your answer… for now." Stephen removed his hand and leaned back. "But you, and only you, have that right to make the decision."

"Baldwin said something similar," Gemma said.

Stephen smirked. "Great men think alike," he quipped.

Gemma laughed as he had intended. "I think you would have really liked Baldwin," she said.

"Will you tell me about him?"

Her face grew solemn and she didn't speak for a moment. Then, she shared, "Baldwin was loyal, charming, and preferred nothing more than the solitude of our country estate. He would help his tenants when needed and I don't believe I ever heard him complain about it."

Stephen remained quiet, hoping Gemma would continue to confide in him.

Gemma continued. "He was really talented at woodworking, and he would whittle animals out of wood as gifts for the children of his tenants. I suppose he was always looking for a reason to brighten someone's day."

"He sounds like a good man."

"He was; the best of men, in my opinion." Gemma gave him a weak smile. "I do apologize. I'm afraid I could go on and on about Baldwin."

"As well as you should," he said. "I meant what I said before. I want to know the whole you and Baldwin helped to make you the way you are now."

"Yes, but speaking about one's deceased husband is hardly romantic."

Holding her gaze, he asked, "Who gets to decide what is romantic?"

Gemma was about to respond when Marielle and Hugh walked into the drawing room. Stephen promptly rose and turned towards his sister.

"I apologize for the delay, but Hugh was meeting with his solicitor," Marielle explained.

Hugh gave them a wry smile. "I'm afraid I was not properly notified about our trip to the museum."

Marielle gave him an amused look. "I did tell you, but you weren't listening."

"I always listen to you, my love," Hugh said.

"Apparently not," Marielle teased.

Hugh slipped his arm around his wife's waist. "Well, I am here now, and I am pleased to spend the afternoon with my wife and cousin."

"And Stephen," Marielle prompted.

"And Stephen," Hugh repeated, albeit reluctantly. "I have seen to our carriage being brought out front."

"That wasn't necessary since I brought a carriage," Stephen attempted.

Hugh furrowed his brow. "Surely you can't be serious," he said. "My family has some of the finest carriages in all of London."

"I think my carriage is adequate."

"Yes, but I do not want to parade my wife and cousin around in a carriage that is merely 'adequate', do you?" Hugh asked.

As much as Stephen wanted to argue with Hugh, he knew that it would just waste his time with Gemma. "Very well," he said. "We shall take your carriage."

Hugh clasped his hands together. "Wonderful," he declared. "I knew you would be sensible about this."

Stephen offered his hand to Gemma. "Allow me to escort you to the carriage."

"Thank you, sir," Gemma said as she placed her hand in his.

Once Gemma was standing, he took her hand and placed it into the crook of his arm. "Did I mention how lovely you look today?"

"You did not."

"Then you must allow me to correct that grievous error right now," he said as he led her towards the entry hall. "Your beauty outshines even the brightest star."

Gemma scrunched her nose. "That was terrible."

Marielle interjected, "I must agree with Gemma. You are no Lord Byron."

Stephen shook his head. "I wasn't trying to be like Lord Byron."

"Good, because the ladies swoon for him, and you do not have a 'swoonable' persona about you," Hugh said.

Marielle swatted at her husband's sleeve. "Be nice to Stephen," she encouraged. "He is trying his best."

"Do you want me to lie to him?" Hugh asked as he led Marielle outside.

Stephen gave Gemma an apologetic smile. "I must admit my attempt to compliment you was awful," he said. "I shall have to work on my compliments."

"Don't try too hard because I thought it was sweet," Gemma responded with a smile.

---

Gemma's eyes roamed over Sir William Hamilton's drawings as she stood in the gallery of the museum. She had always been a fan of his work, and Baldwin had even commissioned Sir William to paint a portrait of him as a gift to her.

Sadly, that painting hung at Henry's country estate because he insisted it remain behind when she moved into the Dowager House. She didn't see it as often as she liked because she dreaded going to the main house. That is where Henry was and she attempted to avoid him at all costs.

"Do you have a favorite painting by Sir William Hamilton?" Stephen asked, breaking the silence.

"I do," Gemma said. "His painting of Marie Antoinette being led to her execution is my favorite."

Stephen eyed her curiously. "Why is that?"

Gemma continued to admire the drawings on the wall as she explained, "I can't imagine how scared she must have been, knowing that her death was imminent, but she kept her head held high for all to see. To me, she was brave."

"That she was," Stephen agreed. "I remember my father was aghast when he read the newssheets announcing her death. He couldn't believe the French had the audacity to behead their queen."

"Some people always need someone to blame for their woes, and Marie Antoinette was an easy target. They even convicted her of treason."

"She was only thirty-seven at the time," Stephen said. "She should have had a long life ahead of her."

"I agree." Gemma glanced over at him. "Do you have a favorite Sir William Hamilton portrait?"

"I'm afraid that I do not have one," Stephen replied. "I do, however, enjoy all of his paintings that depicted episodes from the plays of Shakespeare."

"I take it that you enjoy Shakespeare."

"I do," Stephen said. "My love of Shakespeare came from my father. He was constantly quoting him to entertain my mother."

Gemma moved to the next painting and Stephen followed suit. "Did your parents have a love match?" she asked.

"They did," he replied. "I do not believe I have ever seen two people that were so in love."

"How wonderful," Gemma murmured.

Stephen clasped his hands behind his back. "Sadly, my father never was quite the same after my mother died. I don't believe I ever saw him smile after that," he admitted. "Although, I did not come around often due to my time in the Royal Navy."

"Did you enjoy serving in the Royal Navy?" Gemma asked.

Stephen visibly tensed. "I did my duty to King and Country, nothing more." His tone was curt, leading her to believe that he did not wish to discuss his time in the Royal Navy.

Gemma knew she should change subjects, but she wanted to keep prying in hopes that he would confide in her. "I understand that you were a captain of your own ship."

Stephen kept his gaze straight ahead. "I was."

"I imagine that would be quite the honor."

A pained look came to his eyes. "It was an honor that I did not deserve."

"Surely you don't mean that," Gemma pressed.

Stephen unclasped his hands and said, "Please excuse me for a moment."

As he walked away, Marielle approached her with a curious look and asked, "Where is Stephen going?"

"He said he needed a moment alone," Gemma replied, her eyes remaining on his retreating figure.

"From you?"

Gemma gave her a weak smile. "I do believe I asked one too many questions about his time in the Royal Navy."

An understanding look came to Marielle's eyes. "Stephen can be rather tight-lipped about his time aboard his ship."

"I shouldn't have pried," Gemma said.

Marielle shook her head. "You did nothing wrong.

Stephen is fighting a battle deep within himself, and only he can determine the outcome."

"I wish I could help him."

"A person can only be helped if they are willing to put forth an effort to change, and Stephen just needs more time to come to terms with what happened to him."

Gemma turned towards Marielle and asked, "What did happen to him?"

"Terrible things, I'm afraid," Marielle replied. "But it is not my story to share."

"Do you think Stephen will ever confide in me?"

Marielle nodded. "I do."

Hugh stepped next to his wife and said, "I think we have explored Sir William Hamilton's paintings for long enough. Shall we move onto the Egyptian antiquities?"

"I think that is a fine idea," Marielle responded.

Gemma glanced at the doorway that Stephen had disappeared through. Where had he gone? Perhaps she should go after him to ensure he was all right.

"He will come back," Marielle assured her.

"I know, but I am just worried about him," Gemma said.

Hugh offered his arm to his wife. "Stephen is a grown man," he insisted. "He has managed perfectly well on his own, and he doesn't need you chasing after him like a nursemaid."

Gemma sighed. "You are right."

"Of course I am," Hugh responded before he started leading Marielle towards the next exhibit.

Gemma reluctantly followed them and listened to Hugh as he started to identify a few of the Egyptian antiquities.

Her eyes strayed to a golden scarab amulet that was on display and she leaned closer to examine it. She had learned that these amulets were believed to have different powers and the wearer could access these magical powers.

Stephen's voice came from behind her. "It is beautiful."

"It is," Gemma agreed as she turned around to face him.

"Amulets were very popular with the Egyptians, and they would wear them even into death."

"That is fascinating."

"Did you know that amulet meant protector in the dynastic period?" Gemma asked. Why was she rambling on about useless facts about amulets?

Stephen looked amused. "I did not realize that."

"I read that in a book," Gemma said as she pressed her lips together. Good heavens, why couldn't she stop herself from talking? What did Stephen think about her?

With a smile, Stephen responded, "I'm afraid I have yet to read that book."

Gemma's eyes darted to his lips before saying, "I want to apologize…"

He put his hand up, stilling her words. "It is I that should apologize," he said. "I had no right to abandon you."

"You hardly abandoned me."

"Regardless, it was poorly done on my part, and I am sorry."

Gemma tipped her head. "You are forgiven."

"That is generous of you, my lady," he acknowledged. "How is it that you are so quick to forgive?"

"Denying forgiveness would only hurt me, not you."

Stephen stepped closer and offered his arm. "Allow me the privilege of showing you around the rest of the exhibit."

"I would like that very much," she said, accepting his arm.

Stephen pointed at a dagger and shared, "That is the dagger that killed Ramses the Third."

"Truly?"

With a slight shrug of his shoulders, Stephen replied, "It is possible, but, quite frankly, I don't even know how Ramses the Third died. Do you?"

Gemma giggled and brought a hand up to her lips. "You are a terrible guide."

"You offend me," Stephen said, placing a hand over his heart.

"I doubt you offend so easily."

Stephen lowered his hand to his side. "Thou art as wise as thou art beautiful," he said, quoting Shakespeare.

Gemma was pleased that Stephen was acting more like himself, but she knew she couldn't ignore the other part of him that he was trying to hide from her. She would find a way to get him to confide in her.

As they started walking towards the next glass case, a rough-looking man, dressed in a plain brown jacket and matching trousers, approached Stephen and reared his fist back, hitting him squarely in the jaw.

Gemma gasped as Stephen staggered back, but he didn't fall to the ground. He brought his hand up to his reddened jaw and demanded, "What is the meaning of this?"

The man narrowed his eyes and pointed his finger angrily at him. "This is your only warning- Stay away from Lady Hawkinge."

"Or what?" Stephen demanded as he moved to stand directly in front of the man.

"You don't want to know, bloke," the man replied. "But it ain't pretty. My boss isn't a patient man."

A guard ran up to the ruffian and grabbed his arm. "You need to leave, now!" he ordered.

The man jerked his arm back. "I was just leaving."

"Good," Hugh said as he moved to stand next to Stephen. "Your kind is not welcome here."

"My kind?" the man repeated back in disdain.

"The kind of man that would sneak up on someone and hit them without provocation. You have no honor," Hugh said.

The man chortled. "This is coming from a man that frequents gambling hells."

"I put that life behind me when I wed," Hugh said.

"We shall see," the man spat out. "You men are all the same. You just take and take, not caring for anyone but yourselves."

Another guard approached and commanded, "It is time for you to go meet with the constable."

The man glared at Stephen. "Heed my warning, Mr. Wycomb."

Both guards grabbed the man's arms and started dragging him towards the door.

Gemma remained rooted where she was but Marielle ran towards her brother, throwing her arms around him.

"Are you all right?" she asked as she leaned back. "I was so scared for you."

Stephen gave her a reassuring smile. "I'm fine," he replied. "I have been hit much harder before. It was nothing that I couldn't handle."

Marielle touched his jaw and Stephen winced. "Perhaps we should call the doctor."

"There is no need," Stephen said as he lowered her hand. "You do not need to fuss over me."

Hugh's eyes remained fixed on the door. "How did that man know I frequented gambling hells?"

"He must have read about it in the Society pages," Marielle replied.

Not looking convinced, Hugh said, "He didn't seem like the person that would read the Society pages."

Marielle went to stand next to her husband. "It wasn't exactly a secret that you visited gambling hells."

"True, but I have never seen that man before so how did he know who I was?" Hugh asked.

"Perhaps you beat him in a hand of cards?" Stephen asked.

Hugh shrugged. "I beat a lot of people and sometimes the details grew fuzzy the more the night went on."

Stephen shifted his gaze to Gemma. "Are you all right?"

Gemma let out a shaky laugh. "You are asking me if I am all right?" she asked. "I should be asking you that question."

He closed the distance between them. "You do not need to fear for me."

"How can I not?" she asked. "Someone just ran up to you and struck you in the face because of me."

"Do you know of anyone who would have sent someone to threaten me to stay away from you?" Stephen asked.

"No," she replied.

"Think, Gemma," Stephen pressed.

Gemma brought a hand to her forehead. "I suppose my father or Henry, but they wouldn't have done such a thing."

"Who is Henry?"

"He is my brother-in-law," Gemma revealed as she lowered her hand. "He can be possessive of me at times, but he is not a violent man."

Stephen placed his hand on her sleeve and in a calm voice said, "We need to get you out of here before we garner any more attention."

Gemma turned her head and saw that a small crowd had begun to gather around them. She didn't fight Stephen as he led her towards the door, down the hall and out the main door. He assisted her into the carriage, and she felt great relief once the vehicle started down the street.

None of this made any sense. Why would someone attack Stephen and threaten him to stay away from her?

## Chapter Ten

Stephen sat at a corner table in White's as he sipped his drink. He saw people glance his way, but they were smart enough not to approach him. He wasn't in the mood to talk to anyone. He had engaged in fisticuffs before, but he had never been threatened before. Not that it would change his mind about spending time with Gemma. He intended to continue to show her favor, with the hopes she would agree to a courtship.

He placed his drink down and rubbed his sore jaw. How had he not seen the man approach him? Well, he already knew that answer. He had been so distracted by Gemma that he hadn't even seen the threat coming.

Gemma was the most beautiful distraction, and he needed her desperately in his life. Just by being around her, it lifted his spirits, making him forget about the atrocities that he had experienced at the hands of the French. He had scars. They were marks on his skin that proved the battles he had won, and the one that he had lost. But these weren't the only scars he had; some went below the skin.

As Stephen reached for his drink, he saw Haddington, dressed in an emerald green jacket, approach his table and he stifled the groan that was on his lips. What now?

Without bothering to ask for permission, Haddington pulled out a chair and sat down. "You look awful," he said.

Stephen huffed. "Is there a purpose to this visit or do you intend to just insult me?"

"I was merely stating a fact."

"Then do try to keep those facts to yourself."

Haddington caught the eye of a passing servant and indicated that he wanted something to drink.

Botheration. It was evident that Haddington intended to invade his solace, at least long enough to finish his drink.

Haddington shifted his gaze to meet Stephen's. "I heard what happened at the museum and I took the liberty of speaking to the constable on your behalf."

"You didn't have to trouble yourself."

"It was no trouble at all," Haddington said. "The man that assaulted you was charged and is in Newgate."

"That is good news."

"Although he was not forthcoming on who his boss is."

Stephen took a sip of his drink, then said, "Lady Hawkinge seems to believe it could be her father or her brother-in-law, Lord Hawkinge."

"I am not acquainted with Lord Hawkinge, but I have heard rumors of Lord Winsley's disreputable behavior."

"Lord Winsley has already expressed his displeasure to his daughter about my lowly status amongst Society," Stephen shared.

A server placed a drink in front of Haddington and asked, "Will there be anything else, my lord?"

"Not at this time," Haddington said as he reached for his drink.

The server tipped his head before moving on to another table.

"How is your jaw?" Haddington asked.

Stephen didn't want to admit that it still ached, at least not to a man as infuriating as Haddington. "It is of little consequence."

Haddington sipped his drink. "You were wise to show restraint on your attacker since ladies were present."

"Was that a compliment?"

"No, it was merely a comment."

Hawthorne approached the table and sat down next to Haddington. "I am glad that you are here, Stephen," he said. "It saves me a trip to the hovel that you call home."

"It is hardly a hovel," Stephen muttered.

"Furthermore, your butler appeared on death's door the last time I came to call," Hawthorne remarked.

"It is rather difficult to find a townhouse to rent after the Season has already started," Stephen pointed out.

"I can only imagine, but that is not what I wish to speak to you about," Hawthorne said. "I went back to the boarding house where Benjamin rented a room to speak to his wife, and I was informed that Mrs. Staley had left in the middle of the night, leaving no forwarding address."

"That is awful news. How will we ever find Benjamin now?" Stephen asked.

Hawthorne smirked. "You didn't let me finish." He paused. "I found his wife."

Now Hawthorne had his full attention. "Where?"

"She works near the docks, and she has agreed to speak to us, for the right price," Hawthorne replied.

"Benjamin's wife works near the docks?" Stephen asked.

"About that, she isn't his wife," Hawthorne shared. "She was only posing as his wife since the boarding house doesn't rent to single people."

Stephen furrowed his brow. "How did you discover that?"

"I told you that I have informants around town," Hawthorne said. "It is only a matter of time before we track down Benjamin and you can speak to him."

"Thank you," Stephen said.

"Would you care to speak to her tomorrow?"

"I would, very much so."

Hawthorne eyed him curiously. "Hugh told me about what happened at the museum. Are you all right?"

"This isn't the first time I have been hit before," Stephen grumbled.

Haddington grinned. "That is true, considering I had the pleasure of hitting you before."

Stephen pushed his empty glass away from him. "I would have gladly engaged in a bout of fisticuffs if it wasn't for Lady Haddington."

At the mention of his wife's name, Haddington's face softened. "I may have overreacted."

"May have?" Stephen asked.

"Well, you were trying to offer for my wife," Haddington said.

"She wasn't your wife at the time."

Haddington conceded. "Fair point, but it was only a matter of time before she fell for my charms."

Hawthorne interjected, "What charms?"

With a chuckle, Haddington replied, "I may have had to do some groveling to convince her to be my wife. But it was well worth it."

Stephen watched as Hugh crossed the hall, skirting the tables, and came to a stop next to his brother.

As Hugh pulled out a chair, he met Stephen's gaze and said, "Marielle wanted me to ask how you are faring after the museum."

Stephen groaned. "Will everyone please stop asking about how I am faring?" he asked. "My jaw is sore, but I have been hit much harder before."

Haddington puffed out his chest. "I do believe he means by me."

"No," Stephen said with a shake of his head. "You hit like a girl. It was akin to a feather hitting me across the face."

"I doubt that," Haddington muttered.

Stephen held his glass up to a server to indicate he wished for another. He needed something strong to drink to get through this conversation.

Lord Graylocke arrived at the table and sat down. "I can't believe that everyone started drinking without me."

"Does your wife let you drink anymore?" Haddington asked with amusement in his tone.

Graylocke looked heavenward. "She takes no issue with me drinking as long as I do not take it to excess."

Haddington shifted his gaze to Stephen and shared, "Graylocke showed up drunk to his own wedding and Beatrice was smart enough to send him on his way."

"Why on earth would you show up drunk to your wedding?" Stephen asked in disbelief.

Graylocke frowned. "It was an arranged marriage, and I didn't have the foresight to call upon Beatrice before our wedding," he replied. "If I had, I wouldn't have done something so foolish."

Hawthorne gave Graylocke a pointed look. "I do believe I suggested you do so."

Putting his hand up, Graylocke said," I admit that I was wrong, and it took a lot of groveling for me to convince Beatrice to be my wife."

"Groveling is acceptable when you are speaking from the heart," Haddington remarked, holding his glass up.

"Regardless, I have never been so happy as I have been with my wife," Graylocke said. "I wouldn't change anything because the path I took allowed me to win Beatrice's heart."

A server walked over and placed glasses onto the table before he collected the empty ones.

Graylocke reached for a glass and took a sip. Then he met Stephen's gaze. "I heard you were accosted in the museum."

"Good heavens, do the gossips have nothing else to talk about?" Stephen griped. "I can assure you that I am perfectly fine. Can we please drop it and move on to something else?"

"I hadn't realized you were so touchy about it," Graylocke said.

Stephen sighed. "I apologize. I just want to pretend it never happened."

Hawthorne leaned back in his chair and said, "We could discuss your growing attachment to my cousin."

"Please, no," Stephen muttered as he shifted uncomfortably in his seat. "Surely there is something else we could discuss."

"We could, but it is much more interesting to see you squirm," Hugh said.

"I am not squirming," Stephen contended. "I just do not want to discuss Gemma with you."

Hugh's brow shot up. "Gemma?" he repeated. "You are calling each other by given names now?"

"She gave me leave to," Stephen responded. "But I can assure you that I am not being too familiar."

"I hope not," Hawthorne asserted. "She is family, and we protect our family."

"I mean her no harm," Stephen rushed to assure him.

Hawthorne considered him for a moment before asking, "What are your intentions towards her?"

"I… uh…" Stephen stammered out. He wasn't ready to announce his intentions towards Gemma, especially not to her cousins. What if they told her and it scared her off? It was a chance that he didn't want to risk.

"Surely you don't consider my cousin a dalliance?" Hawthorne pressed.

"Of course not!" Stephen exclaimed. "I have the greatest respect for Gemma, and I would never treat her so distastefully."

Hugh tossed back his drink before saying, "Just don't give us a reason to challenge you to a duel."

"I have no intention to."

"Good," Hugh responded. "Because I would ask Lady Haddington to be my second."

"Not me?" Haddington asked.

Hugh shook his head. "Your wife is a much better shot than you."

"He isn't wrong," Hawthorne remarked, giving Haddington a pointed look.

Lord Grenton approached the table and announced, "I just heard the news about Stephen getting attacked at the museum."

Stephen shoved back his chair. "I have had enough. Good night, gentlemen." He didn't bother to wait for their replies before he headed towards the main door. He could only take so much of his newfound friends, and he had just reached his limit.

---

With the morning sun streaming into the tall windows, Gemma sat at the dining table as she ate her breakfast of an egg and a piece of toast. She hoped that Stephen would call upon her today. Her thoughts of him had increased as of late and she found herself smiling more times than not.

Dear heavens, she was acting like a love-craved debutante again. She loved Baldwin, and she always would, but she felt that it was time to start living her life again. Perhaps that meant she was to spend it with Stephen, but she didn't want to get ahead of herself. He may hold her in high regard, but that was a far cry from courting her.

She wanted to proceed cautiously so as not to make a mistake. Her heart was still tender, and she didn't want to risk having it broken all over again.

Nathaniel stepped into the room with Dinah on his arm.

"Good morning, Cousin," he greeted as he went to assist his wife onto her chair.

"Good morning," she said.

Dinah gave her a weak smile as she glanced down at her cup of chocolate. "Would you mind terribly moving that?"

"The chocolate?"

"Yes, it has rather a strong smell to it," Dinah said as she scrunched her nose.

Gemma picked up the cup and held it up for a footman to take. "Do you take issue with tea?" she asked.

"No, I do not," Dinah said. "At least at this time."

A footman accepted the cup and Gemma ordered, "Will you bring me a cup of tea?"

As the footman went to do her bidding, Nathaniel placed a plate of food in front of Dinah and said, "You should eat."

Dinah pushed back her plate. "I'm not hungry."

Nathaniel moved the plate back in front of her. "You have to try to eat something."

"I will eat the toast," Dinah responded, picking it up off her plate.

With a nod of approval, Nathaniel went to sit at the head of the table and picked up his fork. He met Gemma's gaze and said, "I have been meaning to ask you about something."

Gemma leaned to the side as the footman placed the teacup and saucer in front of her.

"Hugh overheard you telling Stephen that you believe it is possible your father or Lord Hawkinge sent that man to attack him in the museum," Nathaniel stated.

"That is somewhat true," Gemma said. "However, I do not believe either my father or Henry would be capable of such a thing."

"I know your father does not approve of Stephen, but what of Lord Hawkinge?"

"Henry doesn't know Stephen, nor would he ever attempt to get to know him since he is beneath him," Gemma replied.

Nathaniel took a bite of his eggs and chewed them thoughtfully. Then he said, "My mother mentioned that Lord Hawkinge has an unnatural fascination towards you."

"That is true," Gemma admitted. "Henry flirts with me at every opportunity."

"Does he ever make you uncomfortable?"

"All the time."

Nathaniel looked displeased. "If that is the case, I am pleased you will be residing with us for the foreseeable future."

"I do hope that won't be a burden on your family."

Dinah smiled warmly at her. "You are family, and you are more than welcome here."

"That is kind of you," Gemma said. "I do wonder how Henry will take the news."

"You answer to no one since you are a widow," Dinah remarked.

Gemma reached for her teacup and held it in her hand. "Henry has been graciously taking care of me since Baldwin died."

With a knowing look, Nathaniel commented, "It almost sounds like he had another motive for caring for you."

"Perhaps, but I would never have agreed to be his mistress," Gemma said firmly.

"I believe you, but it does give Lord Hawkinge a reason to threaten Stephen to stay away from you," Nathaniel pointed out.

"Henry is not a violent man. He may be misguided, but he knows I do not belong to him," Gemma stated.

"Does he?" Nathaniel pressed.

"Yes," Gemma replied. "Henry has always been fond of the ladies, and it was a great source of contention between Baldwin and him."

Dinah pushed the plate away from her, earning a displeased look from Nathaniel, and asked, "Why is that?"

"Henry was always chasing after one woman or another

and he never seemed to have a desire to settle down with anyone," Gemma explained. "Whereas Baldwin greatly enjoyed being married and grew tired of his brother's philandering ways."

"Sadly, Lord Hawkinge's behavior isn't uncommon for gentlemen of the *ton*, and I daresay, encouraged by many," Dinah said.

Nathaniel placed his hand over his wife's. "There are still good men that are devoted to their wives."

"That is only because you are afraid of Evie," Dinah teased.

Nathaniel chuckled. "She has threatened me, multiple times, about what happens if I ever betray you."

"Evie is very protective of me," Dinah said.

"You need not fear, because I would die before I ever betrayed you." Nathaniel brought Dinah's hand up to his lips. "I love you too much."

Dinah offered her husband a private smile. "I feel the same way." Her face grew pale, and she snatched her hand back. "I will be right back."

Gemma watched as Dinah ran out of the room with her hand over her mouth.

"I'm worried about Dinah," Nathaniel said, his eyes remaining on the door that Dinah just ran through. "I think it is time I call for the doctor."

Gemma nodded. "I agree."

Nathaniel turned towards the footman and ordered, "Send for Doctor Branch at once." He brought his gaze back to meet hers. "Dinah won't be pleased with my decision, but it is for the best."

Balfour stepped into the room and met her gaze. "A Lady Winsley has requested a moment of your time."

Gemma blinked. Her stepmother was here, to see her? For what purpose? She had married her father years ago, and she had never called upon her once.

Nathaniel's voice broke through her musings. "You should see what she wants."

"Why?" Gemma asked. "I have no loyalty towards this woman."

"She is still your stepmother."

"In name only."

Nathaniel's eyes held compassion. "Would you like me to accompany you to the drawing room?"

"I haven't agreed to see her yet."

"But you will."

Gemma cocked her head. "Why do you say that?"

"Because you are just as curious as to why she is here as I am."

She had to admit that her cousin did have a point. Why did her stepmother travel here without her father?

Gemma pushed back her chair and rose. "I will speak to her, but I cannot promise that I will be cordial." She turned towards Balfour. "Is my stepmother in the drawing room?"

"She is, my lady," Balfour confirmed.

With a sigh, Gemma said, "I best get this over with."

"That is the spirit," Nathaniel joked.

Gemma departed from the dining room and crossed the entry hall. She stopped outside of the drawing room and peered in. She saw her stepmother was sitting on the settee, her back rigid. The yellow gown she was wearing was much more conservative than the one she had worn at the ball, but her decolletage was still far too low for an afternoon gown.

As Gemma stepped into the room, her stepmother perked up and smiled. "Gemma," she greeted. "You are looking well."

Gemma came to stop in the middle of the room and clasped her hands in front of her. She decided to forgo the pleasantries and asked, "What is it that you want?"

Her stepmother's smile dimmed. "I heard about Mr. Wycomb's attack in the Society page and I came to see how you were faring since it mentioned you were present at the museum."

"I am well."

"Your father is also very worried——"

Gemma cut her off. "Please do not insult me by sitting there and lying to me. We both know my father does not care a whit about me."

"That isn't true," her stepmother asserted. "Your father does care for you, but he shows it in his own way."

"By ignoring me?" she asked. "Or does he show that he cares for me by insulting me?"

Rising, her stepmother said, "I know there is some bad blood between you two, but I am here to try to bridge the gap, so to speak."

"I am grateful for the bridge," Gemma stated. "There is no reason to attempt to fix something that is broken beyond repair."

"Surely you do not mean that?"

"I do, wholeheartedly."

Her stepmother started fidgeting with her hands. "Your father has recently come into some money, and he is in a position to help you," she said. "He hopes that you will return home and live with us."

"No, thank you," she promptly replied. "I am happy where I am."

Her stepmother glanced around the room. "Your father's townhouse isn't as impressive as this one, but it is a stately home."

"If my father wanted me to come home, why didn't he come himself?" Gemma demanded.

A sheepish look came to her stepmother's face. "I'm afraid he doesn't know I am here."

Gemma let out a dry laugh. "If that is the case, then why would I take anything you say seriously?"

"I know the toll your estrangement has caused him but he is too proud to admit it," her stepmother said.

"I don't know what my father has told you about me, but we have never been close, far from it, in fact," Gemma shared. "I do not have any fond memories of my father."

Her stepmother took a step towards her. "I want to change that," she said. "After your mother died—"

"Do not speak of my mother," Gemma declared, speaking over her. "You don't know the first thing about her."

"I know that your father cared for her."

Gemma arched an eyebrow. "Is that why he wasn't at her side when she died?"

Her stepmother winced. "I would admit that was poor judgment on his part, but he told me that he cared for her."

"Then I shall take your word for it, and not his actions," Gemma said dryly.

"Gemma…" Her words stopped. "I know you have no reason to trust me, but I do want what's best for you."

"I do not trust you," Gemma admitted. "You married my father one month after my mother died."

"Your father was lonely and I was—"

"What?" Gemma demanded. "What could have possibly justified your actions?"

Her stepmother lowered her gaze as she admitted, "I was with child."

"That is your excuse?" she asked in disbelief. "You admit to sleeping with my father when my mother was still alive."

After a long moment, her stepmother shared, "I lost the baby right before your husband died. That is why we couldn't attend his funeral."

"I do not care what your reasonings were," Gemma said. "I want nothing to do with you or my father."

Her stepmother had a crestfallen look on her face. "I know you are angry, but I am not here to fight with you. I am here to make amends."

"I'm sorry, but it is too late for that." Gemma gestured towards the door. "I believe it is time for you to go."

Her stepmother slowly nodded. "I agree, but I do hope you will reconsider."

"Why should I?" Gemma asked.

"I know, deep down, that your father wants you in his life."

Gemma shook her head. "No, my father always wanted a boy. I was just the consolation prize."

Her stepmother walked over to the door and stopped. "I don't have any children of my own, but I had hoped that we could have had a relationship."

"You thought wrong," she said without a hint of remorse. "By your own admission, you admitted to being my father's mistress while my mother was still alive. What kind of woman would be with a man when his wife was dying?"

Lowering her gaze, her stepmother responded, "I realize now that my actions could be called into question—"

Gemma cut her off. "Just to be clear, I do not want anything to do with you or my father. He doesn't want a relationship with me. He just wants to control me. And I refuse to give him that power."

"Gemma, please be reasonable..." her stepmother attempted.

"Good day," Gemma said before she turned her back to her stepmother. She didn't want to hear one more thing that woman had to say. She had spoken her piece and now it was time for her to leave. With any luck, she would never have to see or speak to her stepmother, or father, for that matter, ever again.

## Chapter Eleven

Stephen was not one to eavesdrop, but he couldn't help overhearing some of Gemma's conversation as he stood in the entry hall. He could hear the pain and anger in her voice as she spoke, causing his heart to ache for her. He wanted to help her, but he knew it wasn't his place to do so.

Hawthorne came up behind him and said, "I see that Gemma is still speaking to her stepmother."

"I take it that she is not close with her stepmother."

"I'm afraid not." Hawthorne grew solemn. "Considering what Gemma has been through, she deserves a lifetime of happiness."

Stephen went to respond but stopped himself when Lady Winsley stepped out of the drawing room. Her eyes were full of tears, and she ducked her head as she moved towards the main door. The butler opened the door and she hurried out of the townhouse.

Hawthorne gave him an encouraging nod. "Good luck with Gemma."

"I don't need luck." He paused. "Do I?"

With a chuckle, Hawthorne replied, "You obviously have

never dealt with an emotional woman before. They tend to not think clearly."

"You seem to forget that I have a sister," Stephen said. "Marielle can be quite unreasonable when she is emotional."

Hawthorne placed a hand on his shoulder. "I will inform my aunt that you have come to call, which should give you a small period of time alone with Gemma. Use your time wisely, and don't make me regret this."

Stephen didn't want to waste a moment of his time with Gemma so he proceeded into the drawing room and saw that her back was to him. Her shoulders were slightly slumped, and he could see her wiping at her eyes.

"Gemma," he said softly.

Gemma brought her head up but she didn't turn around. "I'm afraid I need just a moment." Her voice was shaky.

Stephen removed a handkerchief from his jacket pocket and approached her. He held it out and she accepted it.

"Thank you," she murmured.

He walked over to the window and stared out as he waited for Gemma to compose herself. He didn't want to rush her. He wanted her to confide in him, in her own due time.

After a long moment, Gemma turned to face him with a smile on her lips. "I am sorry for keeping you waiting."

Her words were courteous enough, but he wasn't fooled by her sudden transformation, especially since her eyes were still red and puffy.

"Are you all right?" he asked.

"I am," she said.

He took a step closer to her. "I wasn't trying to eavesdrop, but I did happen to overhear some of your conversation."

"That is to be expected since we were not striving to be quiet." Gemma walked over to the table and gestured towards the tray. "Would you care for some biscuits?"

"You seemed upset when you were speaking to your stepmother."

Gemma picked up a plate. "I daresay that the cook here makes the best biscuits. They are simply divine."

Stephen walked over to Gemma and took the plate from her hand. As he set it down onto the tray, he said, "I do not want any biscuits, Gemma."

"Then what would you like?" she asked as she avoided his gaze. "The cook can make anything that you desire."

He placed his hands on her shoulders and waited for her to look at him. "It is evident that you are upset, and I am here if you want to talk about it."

"I'm not upset," Gemma said. "To be upset implies that I care about my stepmother, which I most assuredly do not."

"I think you care more than you are letting on."

Gemma's chest rose and fell with each breath. "I do not wish to discuss my stepmother. She is not worthy of my time or notice."

"Gemma…" he started.

"I will not have my stepmother ruin our time together, Stephen," Gemma said, her chin shaking slightly.

Before he could think about the consequences of his actions, he pulled her into an embrace and held her tightly against him. Gemma didn't hesitate to go into his arms, and she laid her head onto his chest. He marveled how perfectly she fit there, as if she had always belonged.

"You don't have to say anything, but it pains me to see you this upset," Stephen said. "I want to know how I can help you."

"You can't help me, no one can."

"I can try." He leaned back until he looked deep into her red-lined eyes. "But you must let me in."

Gemma's eyes held vulnerability as she whispered, "I want to, but I am scared, Stephen."

"What could you possibly be scared of?" he asked.

Gemma hesitated before saying, "I am a coward."

"Not from where I am standing."

Tears came to Gemma's eyes. "I have always run from my problems and just pretended that all is well until the storm passes."

"There is no shame in that."

Gemma wiped away a tear that was rolling down her cheek. "Do you want to know why my stepmother came today?" she asked.

"I do."

"She wants me to make amends with my father and come live with him," Gemma shared. "Can you imagine the audacity of her?"

"Why didn't your father come himself?"

Gemma bobbed her head. "That is precisely what I said, and she started saying that our estrangement has taken a toll on him," she replied. "It was utter nonsense. My father has never, and will never, care about anyone but himself."

Stephen reached up and tucked an errant piece of hair behind her ear. "What if she is telling the truth?"

Gemma huffed. "My father does not love me. He never has so why the sudden change of heart?" she asked.

"I can't answer that."

"If my father wanted me to come home, then he should have the decency to come here himself so I could turn him down."

Stephen could hear the anguish in her voice, and he knew that she was hurt more deeply than she was letting on.

Gemma laid her head back onto his chest and said, "I don't want anything to do with my father. He has managed to disappoint me, time and time again, until that is all I have come to expect from him."

"I'm sorry," he murmured, not knowing what else he could say.

"What is worse is that my stepmother had the nerve to say she wanted a relationship with me," Gemma shared.

"Would that be so wrong?"

Gemma stiffened in his arms. "My stepmother is awful," she said. "She admitted to having an affair with my father while my mother was still alive."

"That is terrible, but she sounded genuine in her affections when she was speaking to you."

"Most likely out of guilt," Gemma declared. "I assure you that there would be no good that would come from associating with that woman."

"What do you truly know about your stepmother?"

Gemma stepped out of his arms and gave him a look of disbelief. "Whose side are you on?"

"Why do there have to be sides?"

"Even after everything I have told you about my stepmother, you still believe I should let her into my life?" Gemma demanded.

"I just want to do right by you."

"Then know this, my stepmother is a conniving woman that will do anything to achieve her purposes," Gemma said. "She is not to be trusted."

"I believe you, but I am well acquainted with the effects of letting hatred occupy a place in your heart. It will consume you, body and soul, until you are only left with despair."

Gemma's expression grew unreadable as she said, "I don't hate my stepmother. Quite frankly, I don't know her well enough to do so." She paused. "May I ask why you are so acquainted with hatred?"

Stephen realized his misstep. He should never have shared his experience with Gemma. If she knew how much hate and resentment he had chosen to hold on to, she would never look at him the same way again.

He reached down and picked up the plate of biscuits. "Would you care for a biscuit?" he asked, hoping to distract her.

Gemma removed the plate from his hand and replied, "I would prefer if you answered my question."

"I assure you that it is not a question that you want an answer to."

"Let me be the judge of that," Gemma said.

Stephen grew quiet. He was trying to think of something to say that would appease Gemma but wouldn't reveal too much about himself.

Gemma placed the plate down onto the tray and stepped closer to him, causing her to tilt her head to look at him. "You can trust me, Stephen."

"I do trust you."

"Then tell me what troubles you."

"I don't even know where to begin."

"It generally helps if you start from the beginning."

Stephen sighed as he ran a hand through his hair. "You don't know what you are asking of me."

Gemma went to place a hand on his sleeve. "Just as you want to know the real me, I want to know the real you."

"But I assure you that I am not very interesting."

"I disagree."

Stephen reached for her hand on his sleeve and held it tightly. "You are good and kindhearted, and I am not. I am deeply flawed- far more than you even realize."

"I have a fairly good idea of who you are."

Gemma stared at him with nothing but trust in those big, green eyes, and he wanted to warn her to stay away from him. But he couldn't seem to find the words to do so.

Lady Montfort's voice came from behind them. "It is a beautiful day we are having, is it not?"

Stephen dropped his hand and took a step back from Gemma.

Gemma seemed to recover first because she picked up the plate of biscuits and addressed her aunt. "Would you care for a biscuit?"

Lady Montfort did not look amused. "I shall pass." She

shifted her gaze towards him. "Mr. Wycomb, it is a pleasure to see you again."

He bowed. "Lady Montfort."

An uncomfortable silence descended over the group and Stephen knew it was time for him to remove himself.

Turning towards Gemma, he asked, "Would it be permissible if I called upon you tomorrow for a carriage ride through Hyde Park?"

Gemma nodded. "I will be looking forward to it."

"Wonderful." He tipped his head at Lady Montfort and said, "My lady."

As he walked out of the drawing room, he knew he was in trouble. He had no doubt that he could easily fall in love with Gemma because he was already halfway there.

---

Judging by the way that her aunt was looking at her, Gemma knew she was in for a lecture. Not that she didn't deserve it. She had been too familiar with Stephen and she even had wayward thoughts on what his lips would feel like pressed against hers. She closed her eyes as she tried to imagine it. His lips would be warm and soft as they met hers.

"Dear child, are you even listening to me?" her aunt asked in an exasperated voice.

Gemma gave her a sheepish smile. "I'm afraid you caught me woolgathering."

"One does not need to be a mind reader to know what, or should I say 'whom', you are thinking about." Her aunt shook her head. "You may be a widow, but you must still follow the rules of polite Society."

"I am trying to."

"You were alone with a man," her aunt pointed out. "Why

did you not ask Balfour to send in a maid to act as a chaperone?"

"I was rather distracted."

"With what?"

Gemma frowned. "My stepmother made an unexpected call this morning," she shared. "Apparently, my father has come into some money and wants me to move back home."

Her aunt slowly lowered herself onto the settee. "What did you say?"

"I told her that I had no intention of ever moving back in with my father and I asked why he hadn't come himself."

"What did she say to that?"

Gemma waved a hand in front of her. "Supposedly, our estrangement has taken a toll on my father and my stepmother is worried about him."

"How thoughtful of her," her aunt muttered.

"I took no issue with sending her on her way, especially after she admitted to being my father's mistress when my mother was alive."

"That is no surprise there since he married her one month after your mother died."

Gemma walked over to the settee and gracelessly dropped down next to her aunt. "When I was younger, I always used to hope that my father would take notice of something good that I had done, but he never did. Not once," she shared. "My father no more wanted me in his life than he wanted a thorn in his boot."

"That is not true," her aunt attempted.

"Please do not insult me by saying that he loved me in his own way," Gemma said. "That is what my stepmother tried to do."

Her aunt reached for her gloved hand. "You have had a rough go of it, but you don't need to rely on your father or Lord Hawkinge anymore. This is your home now."

Gemma smiled. "Thank you."

"But your uncle and I do expect you to behave appropriately for a woman of your station," her aunt said. "No more clandestine meetings with Mr. Wycomb."

"It was hardly a secret since we were in your drawing room."

With a knowing look, her aunt asked, "Can you imagine the scandal if one of my friends had come to call and witnessed how familiar you and Mr. Wycomb were with one another?"

"That is a fair point."

Her aunt released her hand and reached for a biscuit. "Although a wedding wouldn't be the worst thing, considering you are enamored by the charming Mr. Wycomb."

"I most certainly am not," Gemma lied.

"You are a terrible liar, my dear," her aunt teased. "You can deny it all you want, but your eyes light up when you look at him."

Gemma bit her lower lip. "Am I a terrible person?"

Her aunt's expression grew bemused. "Why would you ask such a thing?"

"Baldwin has only been dead for a little over a year and a half and I am already becoming too familiar with another man."

"You did not die alongside Baldwin," her aunt asserted. "You are free to experience life, and that means pursue another chance at love."

"I just love Baldwin so much."

"No one is disputing that, but you are in danger of living a life so comfortable and soft that you will die without ever experiencing true joy again."

Gemma grew quiet. "I do care for Mr. Wycomb, but we are such different people," she murmured.

"Differences in a marriage can make your relationship stronger, but only if you let them."

"I said nothing about marriage."

Her aunt leaned closer and patted her cheek. "You didn't have to."

Balfour stepped into the room and announced, "Lord Hawkinge has come to call on Lady Hawkinge."

As much as she wanted to send Henry on his way, she knew that would be intolerably rude of her to do so. "Please send him in," she ordered as she rose.

A moment later, Henry stepped into the room and his possessive eyes landed on her. "You are looking as enchanting as ever, my lady." He bowed before turning his attention towards her Aunt Edith. "Lady Montfort," he acknowledged.

Her aunt tipped her head. "Good morning, Lord Hawkinge."

Henry smiled broadly. "It is a fine day, is it not?" he asked.

Gemma eyed Henry curiously. He was not one to be exuberant, making her wonder what he was about. "It is a fine day," she replied. "My aunt had said something similar just a short time ago."

"Seeing that it is such a fine day, would you care to take a tour around the gardens with me?"

Drats. She saw no way out of this without appearing rude. "What a lovely idea," she said, hoping her words sounded convincing enough.

Henry approached her and offered his arm. "May I escort you to the gardens?"

"Thank you," Gemma said, placing her hand on his arm.

Without asking for permission, he reached for her hand and moved it to the crook of his arm. "Have you become accustomed to the gardens here?" he asked.

"Not overly familiar, no," she replied.

"That is a shame," he said as he led her out of the drawing room. "You should always acquaint yourself with the state of the gardens to encourage conversation."

Gemma remained silent as he offered criticism. There was no reason to argue with him since it only incited his anger.

Henry stepped into the parlor and grew visibly frustrated. "This townhouse is a maze," he declared. "How in the blazes do we get to the gardens?"

Gemma resisted the urge to smile. Henry always liked being in control, but even he couldn't control the layout of the townhouse. "Would you like for me to show you, my lord?"

"I suppose, if you must," he grumbled.

She led them out of the parlor and down a hall that was lined with family portraits. As they came to the rear door, a footman opened it and proceeded to follow them outside.

Gemma went to move her hand, but Henry caught it. "I prefer when you are close, my dear," he said as he returned it to the crook of his arm.

"Have you had a chance to visit the House of Lords?" she asked.

Henry tsked. "A woman should not ask such things," he said. "It is much too serious of a topic for the weaker sex."

"What would you care to talk about then?" she asked, trying to keep the irritation out of her voice.

He led her towards a bench and assisted her as she sat down. Then he claimed the seat next to her. "I'm afraid I have some distressing news."

"Is that so?" she asked, uninterested.

Shifting in his seat to face her, he replied, "I wish to speak to you about Mr. Wycomb. He is not the man that he has led you to believe he is."

"I would prefer not to discuss Mr. Wycomb with you."

"You must, because he has been deceiving you this entire time," Henry said.

Gemma pressed her lips together. "I doubt that. He is a good man."

"No, it is true," Henry pressed. "After our meeting yesterday, I was so distraught by you spending time with Mr. Wycomb that I hired a Bow Street Runner to investigate him."

"Henry," she gasped. "You didn't? That was wholly unnecessary."

Henry placed his hand on her arm and said, "You are innocent in so many ways and you cannot possibly understand the debaucheries of men."

"Regardless, you had no right to investigate Mr. Wycomb—"

"He frequents gambling hells," Henry said, cutting her off.

Gemma's eyes grew wide. "You are lying!"

"The Bow Street Runner confirmed that he visited the Scarlet Lady a few nights ago, and he even spent his time flirting with one of the women serving drinks."

Gemma stared at Henry in disbelief. "I don't believe you."

"You have been tricked, Gemma," Henry said. "Mr. Wycomb is no better than your father. He may claim the part of an honorable gentleman, but he uses the darkness of light to show his true character."

"That is impossible."

"Why?" Henry asked. "Because you are friends?"

"I would like to speak to this Bow Street Runner."

"I can arrange that, but he won't tell you anything other than that I have already revealed."

Gemma had no reason to suspect Henry was lying, but it went against everything she thought to be true about Stephen.

Henry leaned closer to her and lowered his voice. "Mr. Wycomb has no interest in you," he said. "He just wants to lift your skirts."

"Henry!" she exclaimed. "Don't be crass."

"I know this must be difficult for you to hear, but there is more," Henry said as he removed a piece of paper from his jacket pocket. "When Mr. Wycomb was a first lieutenant, he engaged in a duel over a woman, seriously injuring the other officer, and participated in a court-martial."

"He couldn't have been found guilty if he continued to serve in the Royal Navy."

Henry glanced down at the paper in his hand. "You are right, but he was granted permission to keep the woman in his cabin with him."

Gemma placed a hand to her forehead. "That can't possibly be true. He wouldn't do something so dishonorable."

"I'm afraid it is," Henry said with pity in his eyes. "Mr. Wycomb is nothing more than a serial philanderer and he set his cap on you."

Rising, Gemma walked a short distance away and wrapped her arms around her waist. Could it be true? Had Stephen tricked her into believing he was something that he was not? Was that why he never spoke about his time in the Royal Navy?

Henry came up behind her and placed his hands on her shoulders. "You can't blame yourself, Gemma," he said, his warm breath on her neck. "Mr. Wycomb only let you see what he wanted you to see."

Gemma felt conflicted. She knew the disdain that Henry had for Stephen, and he only seemed too eager in sharing this damning news. After all, she wanted to believe the best in Mr. Wycomb but what if she was wrong to do so? He had only treated her honorably but was it all an act? If so, she had fallen for it, time and time again. One thing was certain, though, she would ask Stephen if these allegations were true. She owed him that.

"Given the circumstances, I have taken the liberty of clearing my schedule so I may escort you back to Hawkinge," Henry said.

She turned around to face him. "I am not ready to leave London. I need to speak to Mr. Wycomb about this."

"I think you leaving straightaway would be for the best," Henry remarked. "Mr. Wycomb has made you a laughing-stock of high Society."

"Who else knows about Mr. Wycomb's past?"

"Soon, everyone will," Henry replied. "I alerted the

morning newspapers, and they were more than eager to write a story on it."

Gemma felt herself growing angry. "How could you do such a thing?" she demanded. "I am ruined now."

Henry shook his head. "I paid off the newssheets not to mention your name."

"But that won't be enough to save my reputation," Gemma said.

"That is why we need to have you leave Town," Henry encouraged. "With any luck, the *ton* will forget about your liaison with Mr. Wycomb in a few years."

With a slight huff, Gemma said, "The *ton* is not known to be of a forgiving nature."

"True, but you are a lady and Mr. Wycomb is a commoner. I daresay that the *ton* will be much more favorable to you."

Gemma pursed her lips. "Why do you think I would go anywhere with you right now?" she asked. "It is because of you that I am in this situation."

"No, it is because of Mr. Wycomb. Need I remind you that he tricked you by hiding his true nature."

"But you alerted the newssheets without a care for my regard."

Henry reached for her hand but she stepped out of his reach. As his hand dropped to his side, he said, "I promised Baldwin that I would watch over you and the only way I could properly do that was by ruining Mr. Wycomb."

"Well, you thought wrong, Henry," Gemma responded. "You could have come to me rather than go to the newspapers. We could have sorted this out privately."

"If I didn't do something drastic, I was afraid you wouldn't see reason," Henry argued. "Don't you see that I am trying to help you?"

Gemma needed to be far away from Henry right now. Frankly, she needed to be away from everyone right now. Her thoughts were discombobulated, and she needed time to sort them out.

In a voice that was far more steady than she felt, Gemma said, "I need to be alone right now."

Henry took a step closer. "You don't need to be alone; you have me."

Gemma placed a hand on his chest, stilling him. "Quite frankly, I want nothing to do with you at the moment. You have placed me in an impossible position, and I am unsure of what to do."

Disappointment flooded his features and dripped from his voice. "I shall call upon you in two days' time to see if you've changed your mind about leaving Town."

"I would not hold your breath, Henry."

Henry held his hands up. "What will you do now?" he mocked. "You are ruined and all the invitations that you have received will be rescinded. The only logical course of action for you is to return home to Hawkinge and hope the *ton* will be more forgiving next Season. Unless you do not give a whit for your family's reputation and you want to drag their names through the mud, along with yours."

Gemma knew that he was right, but she didn't dare admit that to him. Her Season was over. Nothing would stop what Henry had set in motion.

With a smug look, Henry turned and headed towards the townhouse, causing Gemma to let out the breath she hadn't even realized she had been holding. She wanted to be alone, no, she *needed* to be alone. How had she allowed this to happen? Henry had made sure to ruin her, all in an attempt to keep her away from Stephen.

Was he protecting her by forcing her hand? It didn't feel that way. It felt vengeful, spiteful. Tears streamed down her face, but she made no effort to wipe them away. Regardless, she needed to learn the truth about Stephen before she even thought about running away.

# Chapter Twelve

Stephen had a lot of work to do but instead he found himself sitting on the settee with Bandit's head in his lap. He was pleased with the progress that he had made with Gemma. The more he spent time with her, the more he knew that she was the one for him. With just one smile, she had bewitched him, and he never wanted to go back to the way it was before she had walked into his life. He couldn't since he was truly and utterly happy. And he hadn't felt this way in a long time.

Bandit's head shot up and he turned his head towards the door.

A moment later, his butler shuffled into the room and announced, "Lord Hawthorne is here to see you, sir."

"Send him in."

"As you wish," the butler said before he left to do his bidding.

Stephen went to move from the settee, but Bandit wanted nothing to do with that. The dog stared up at him with his brown eyes and he reluctantly leaned back in his seat.

Hawthorne stepped into the room and asked, "Shall we depart for the docks?"

"I suppose so."

"You suppose so?" Hawthorne asked. "I thought you wanted to track down Benjamin?"

Rising, Stephen wiped off the dog hair from his trousers. "I do, but I got distracted."

Hawthorne gave him a knowing look. "I must assume that you are speaking of my cousin, Gemma."

"I am," Stephen admitted, seeing no reason to deny it. "I do not want to rush her, but I am hoping she will be open to my offer of courtship soon enough."

"Just be patient with her," Hawthorne encouraged.

"I have every intention to," Stephen said. "I will wait as long as it takes to convince her that I am the man for her."

Hawthorne smirked. "It wouldn't be such a terrible thing to welcome you to our family."

"Careful, that almost sounds like you approve."

"Then I must have said it wrong," Hawthorne joked. "I took the liberty of securing a hackney to take us to the docks. It is waiting out front."

"Let us depart before the driver grows tired of waiting and abandons us," Stephen said as he headed towards the door.

They didn't speak as they exited his townhouse and approached the hackney. Stephen opened the door for Hawthorne and waited until he was situated before he stepped inside.

Stephen brought a hand up to his nose as a foul odor permeated the coach. "Did you pick the most offensive smelling hackney you could find?"

Hawthorne shrugged. "You get used to the smell."

"I somehow doubt that to be true." He went to open the window but quickly realized that it was broken. There was little he could do but sit back and try to ignore the pungent smell. No amount of complaining would change his current situation.

Stephen stared out the window. The street was so crowded

with traffic that the coach wasn't moving much faster than the people walking down the pavement.

"At this rate, we will never get there," Stephen remarked.

"It is preferable to walking." As Hawthorne said his words, the hackney began to pick up some speed.

"The docks are extensive," Stephen pointed out. "Are you sure you know where to find Benjamin's wife… er… fake wife?"

"I do."

Stephen found himself curious about something and asked, "How is it that an earl is acquainted with the docks?"

"I have spent some time there."

"Do you not worry about your safety?"

Hawthorne reached down to his boot and retrieved a muff pistol. "That is why I carry two pistols and a dagger on my person."

"Isn't it uncomfortable having a pistol in your boot?"

"You get used to it," Hawthorne replied as he returned the muff pistol to his boot. "Besides, it is better to prepare for a fight than expect none."

"How often do you get into fights?"

Hawthorne chuckled. "That is a ticklish question."

"It shouldn't be."

"What I do with my time is none of your concern," Hawthorne said, his voice holding a warning.

Stephen knew it was best if he stopped asking questions. Hawthorne was entitled to have his secrets, even if he was the most perplexing man he had ever met.

They both retreated to their own thoughts as they traveled towards the docks since neither one of them seemed intent on conversing.

The hackney came to a stop and Hawthorne glanced out the window. "We are here," he said. "Be aware of your surroundings and follow my lead."

Hawthorne didn't wait for a reply before he opened the

door and stepped out onto the narrow pavement. He turned to address the driver. "Wait here," he ordered. "We will be back shortly."

"That will cost you," the driver shouted down.

Hawthorne reached into his waistcoat pocket and retrieved a coin. He extended it towards the driver. "I will double that amount if you wait here for us to return."

The driver clutched the coin in his hand. "I won't wait forever."

Hawthorne acknowledged the man's words with a tip of his head. Then, he met Stephen's gaze. "Follow me," he ordered.

Stephen followed Hawthorne down one of the worst sections of town that he had ever seen. The blackened buildings were collapsing in on themselves but somehow it appeared as if people were still living in those conditions. The people were dressed in dirty, ill-fitting clothing and their faces had streaks of dirt on them. Furthermore, their eyes all seemed to have the same hollowed-out looks.

Hawthorne came to a stop at an alleyway where five women were leaning against the brick wall.

A dark-haired woman with a brown, faded dress pushed off from the wall. "Are you looking for a good time, Mister?" she asked in a sultry voice.

"I am here to speak to Lavinia," Hawthorne said.

The dark-haired woman stepped closer to Hawthorne and purred, "You will find that I am much more preferable to Lavinia."

Hawthorne remained stoic. "Do you know where Lavinia is or not?"

"I do, but it will cost you," the dark-haired woman replied. "Information don't come cheap here."

A woman's voice came from deep within the alley. "Leave them alone, Patty. They aren't here to see you."

It was but a moment later when the redheaded lady from

the boarding house came into view and she came to a stop in front of them.

Her eyes lit up with recognition. "I know you two. You were the ones that knocked on Colin's door that day to see if he were home," Lavinia said as she tightened the threadbare shawl around her thin shoulders.

"We are," Hawthorne confirmed. "Thank you for agreeing to meet with us."

"I didn't have much of a choice, at least that is what the bloke told me." Lavinia glanced over her shoulder. "Can we do this somewhere more private?"

"Are you hungry?" Hawthorne asked.

Lavinia nodded slowly. "I am. I haven't eaten since yesterday," she replied. "I had been hoping that work would pick up."

"There is a tavern over on the next block. We could get you some food there," Hawthorne suggested.

"Thank you," Lavinia said. "I would like that very much."

Hawthorne put his hand out, indicating that she should go first.

The pavement was too narrow for them to walk side by side so Stephen trailed behind. It was a short distance until they arrived at the tavern. As they stepped inside, it grew silent and the men inside seemed to take that moment to size them up.

Hawthorne seemed unconcerned by the attention they were garnering and went to sit down at an empty table. Once they were all situated, a serving wench walked up to the table and said, "I'm afraid we don't serve women like her."

"You will today," Hawthorne said.

The serving wench frowned. "We have a reputation to uphold."

Hawthorne removed three guineas from his waistcoat pocket and placed them on the table. "Bring us whatever is available to eat."

Indecision crossed the serving wench's face. "I… uh…" Her voice trailed off before she glanced over her shoulder at a man in the corner. "Just eat quickly and we won't have a problem," she said as she grabbed the coins.

Lavinia gave Hawthorne a grateful smile. "That was kind of you to do."

"May I ask you a few questions?" Hawthorne asked.

"You may," Lavinia replied.

Hawthorne held her gaze as he asked, "Why did you lie to us about being Colin's wife?"

Lavinia glanced down at the table. "The boarding house does not rent to single people and Colin paid me to pretend to be his wife."

"If that is the case, why did you leave the boarding house?" Hawthorne questioned.

"Colin never came back after you came to see me and I didn't have the funds to pay the rent," Lavinia explained.

Stephen spoke up. "Did you know that Colin wasn't his real name?"

Lavinia's eyes shot up. "I did not," she replied. "But I had no reason to question it. He paid me real good to stay with him."

The serving wench approached with a tray and placed it down in front of Hawthorne. "I got you some bread, cheese and meat," she said. "Is that sufficient?"

"It will be," Hawthorne replied.

With a disapproving glance at Lavinia, the serving wench ordered, "Just be quick about it."

Hawthorne pushed the tray towards Lavinia and her eyes lit up. She eagerly reached for the bread and took a large bite.

"Can you tell us anything that might lead us to Colin?" Hawthorne asked.

Lavinia chewed her food thoughtfully. "He would frequent the Glistening Pigeon tavern and would stay out for all hours of the night," she replied. "I told him it wasn't safe to be walking on the streets that late at night but he gave me little heed."

Hawthorne leaned closer and lowered his voice. "Do you know if he was involved with any radical groups?"

"It is quite possible since he had some progressive views," Lavinia said before she picked up a piece of cheese. "He would go on and on about the war with Napoleon and he seemed to idolize the man."

Stephen interjected, "Did he ever speak about his time in the Royal Navy?"

Lavinia shook her head. "Not once," she replied. "He was tight-lipped about where he came from before he met me."

"Do you know why that was?" Hawthorne asked.

"I just assumed he didn't want me to know," Lavinia said. "It ain't uncommon in my line of work. No man wants to reveal too much to a light-skirt."

Hawthorne removed some coins from his waistcoat pocket and placed them down next to Lavinia. "Thank you for your time."

Lavinia stared down at the coins in astonishment. "What is this for?"

"Get yourself cleaned up and try to find respectable employment," Hawthorne replied.

"No one will hire a prostitute, Mister," Lavinia said dejectedly. "We are outcasts amongst even the most despised groups."

Hawthorne shoved back his chair and rose. "If you choose to, you can come to Lord Montfort's townhouse and there will be work for you. But it won't be easy work."

Lavinia's eyes grew wide. "Are you Lord Montfort?"

"I am not, but do not come if you don't want to make an honest wage," Hawthorne said. "Come around to the servants' entrance and I will let them know to be expecting you."

"Why are you doing this for me?" Lavinia asked.

Hawthorne gave her a brief smile. "Because everyone deserves a second chance."

The serving wench walked over to the table and said in a hushed voice, "Don't forget to take that whore with you."

The smile disappeared from Hawthorne's face and he addressed the serving wench. "This woman is not to be disturbed while she is eating," he ordered in a steely voice. "Do I make myself clear?"

"But, she is—"

Hawthorne cut her off. "You will allow her to stay or I will ask the magistrate to take a special interest in this tavern."

The serving wench's mouth snapped shut. "She may stay, but only until she finishes her meal," she muttered.

"Very good." Hawthorne tipped his head at Lavinia. "I do hope you will consider my offer most carefully."

"I will, Mister," Lavinia said.

Rising, Stephen followed Hawthorne out the door and asked, "How did you know the serving wench would let Lavinia stay by summoning the magistrate?"

"It wasn't hard, considering I would bet every man in that tavern has something to hide," Hawthorne said. "I doubt they would want a magistrate poking into their business."

"It was smart."

Hawthorne looked amused. "You sound surprised."

"No, it was just unusual for you," Stephen joked.

***

Gemma had never felt so alone before. She felt embarrassed, humiliated and angry. How dare Henry put her into this position! She needed to speak to Stephen to sort out the truth, and she hoped that Henry had been wrong. She was trying to be sensible about it all, but the doubt kept creeping back in. She hoped that she hadn't been so lonely that she had fallen for a man that gambled- a vice that corrupted even the best of men.

How she missed Baldwin at this precise moment. He would know exactly what to say to get her out of this predicament, but he wasn't here. And she didn't dare admit her folly to her family. Good heavens, they would feel pity for her and that was the last thing that she wanted. No, she was alone in this, and she didn't see another way out besides returning to Hawkinge in shame.

Her aunt's voice broke her out of her musings. "Gemma," she said. "Are you well?"

She brought her gaze up. "I am," she replied.

"You have a terrible habit of woolgathering at the most inopportune times," her aunt said lightly. "Lord and Lady Haddington were just announced."

"Wonderful," Gemma murmured.

Her aunt eyed her with concern. "Are you still suffering from the headache that has plagued you since Lord Hawkinge left?"

"I am," she lied, "but with any luck, it will go away shortly."

"Did Lord Hawkinge say something that upset you?" her aunt asked.

Gemma pressed her lips together, then replied, "No, we just spoke on polite conversational topics." She wasn't ready to confide in her aunt yet.

It looked as if her aunt wanted to say more on the subject but was interrupted by Lord and Lady Haddington stepping into the room.

Evie approached Aunt Edith and gave her a kiss on the cheek. "It is good to see you looking so well."

Her aunt smiled. "I was pleased when Dinah informed me that she invited you and Reginald to dine with us this evening."

Evie shifted her gaze towards Gemma. "Good evening,

Gemma," she greeted. "I do not believe my husband has had the pleasure of meeting you."

"I have not." The tall, dark-haired lord bowed. "My wife has spoken very highly of you, Lady Hawkinge."

"You have a kind wife," she replied.

Lord Haddington exchanged a look with his wife that was filled with love. "That I do," he said. "I hope one day that I will be worthy of her."

"Do you know why we were summoned here?" Evie asked.

"Summoned, dear?" Aunt Edith asked in a confused tone.

Evie smiled. "We were told in no uncertain terms that we were to join Dinah and Nathaniel for dinner this evening."

Aunt Edith's lips twitched. "I have a fairly good idea of what it is about, but I do not want to spoil the surprise."

"I assumed it was about Dinah increasing," Evie said plainly.

With a glance at the door, Aunt Edith lowered her voice. "The doctor did come to call today, and he was up with Dinah for quite some time."

"Not Nathaniel?" Evie asked.

Aunt Edith waved her hand in front of her. "You know how Nathaniel is," she said. "He disappears at all hours of the day, but he did go straight up to see Dinah when he arrived home."

"I do not know why it took Nathaniel so long to summon the doctor," Evie remarked. "It was evident that Dinah has been increasing for some time now."

Marielle and Hugh stepped into the room and the room went quiet.

"Dare I ask what was being discussed before we entered the room?" Marielle asked.

Aunt Edith took a step closer to Marielle and replied, "We were discussing Dinah's delicate condition."

Marielle laughed. "I am hoping that they will use this

dinner party to announce what we have all already suspected for so long."

"That is the hope," Evie said. "It has been rather tedious to pretend that all is well when it has assuredly been not."

"Why hasn't anyone told Dinah of their suspicions?" Hugh asked with a bemused look on his face.

Aunt Edith brought a hand to her chest. "We couldn't take away the surprise of them discovering it on their own."

"That sounds illogical," Hugh remarked.

Aunt Edith turned towards Evie and asked, "Will Mrs. Carter be joining us this evening?"

"I'm afraid my aunt is visiting a dear friend this evening, but she sends her greetings," Evie replied.

"Will Mr. Wycomb be joining us?" Aunt Edith asked Marielle.

At the mention of his name, Gemma grew hopeful that he would join them. It would give her an opportunity to speak to him.

Marielle shook her head. "I'm afraid that my brother had other plans this evening."

"Do you know what his plans are for tomorrow?" Gemma asked.

With a questioning glance at her, Marielle replied, "I do not, but I can make some inquiries."

Gemma felt a blush creeping up her neck. How forward his sister must think she was to ask such a brazen question. To make matters worse, she rushed out, "You don't need to trouble yourself. I am just disappointed that Mr. Wycomb will not be accompanying us this evening. It is a shame, a really big shame." Why did she keep rambling on?

"It is a shame, but I am sure that he will be coming to call on you tomorrow, if that is your concern," Marielle said with mirth in her eyes.

Gemma pursed her lips as she decided it would be best if she just told her family the truth- well, the partial truth. "I do hope so since I have decided it would be best to return to Hawkinge in a few days."

All eyes turned towards her, and her aunt's mouth parted in disbelief. "But, Gemma…" She stopped. "Why would you do such a thing, especially after everything you told me about Lord Hawkinge?"

"After tomorrow, I will be ruined and I do not want to besmirch your family's reputation by continuing to reside here," Gemma said.

Her aunt moved to sit down on an upholstered armchair. "I don't understand. Why do you believe you are to be ruined?"

Gemma's eyes darted towards Marielle before saying, "Lord Hawkinge leaked a story to the morning newspapers about Mr. Wycomb and his time in the Royal Navy. Apparently, Mr. Wycomb was involved in a duel over a woman, and she resided in his cabin with him while they were at sea."

"I know nothing of a duel," Marielle said, "or of this woman."

"It would appear that your brother has kept a part of himself hidden from you, as well," Gemma remarked.

Marielle's face turned determined. "There must be more to the story," she said. "I know my brother and he is methodical on what he does. He must have had a good reason for engaging in that duel."

Evie interjected, "I must side with Marielle. I do not believe Stephen has a dishonorable bone in his body."

"One cannot outrun one's past," Gemma stated.

"You can't just walk away, Cousin," Hugh asserted.

Gemma clasped her hands in front of her lap. "I cannot, in good conscience, remain here, knowing that my name is associated with Mr. Wycomb's," she said. "It wouldn't be fair of me; not after the kindness you have bestowed upon me."

Hugh approached her and asked, "What of Stephen? We

all would be blind if we did not notice your growing affection for him."

"A future with Mr. Wycomb seems highly improbable now," Gemma murmured.

"Why?" Hugh prodded.

Gemma bit the inside of her cheek to prevent her from crying. "I am not entirely sure I know Mr. Wycomb," she said. It hurt her to admit it, but until she knew the full truth, she couldn't possibly believe there could be a future for them. That is assuming Stephen even wanted a future with her.

The sound of Dinah's voice drifted in from the entry hall, and Gemma was grateful for the reprieve. Once her family read the newssheets tomorrow, they would all be in agreement that she should remove herself from London. She was sure of it. For how could they not? By continuing to reside here, she would open them up to gossip and ridicule. And she couldn't do that to them.

With a bright smile on her face, Dinah stepped into the room on Nathaniel's arm. "We are sorry that we are late, but we do have an announcement."

Nathaniel glanced at his wife for permission before saying, "Dinah is increasing."

Cheers erupted in the room as everyone rushed towards the couple to offer their congratulations. It was a happy moment for the family and Gemma found herself embracing her cousin.

Nathaniel leaned back and asked, "What is wrong, Cousin?"

Gemma smiled, hoping it was convincing enough. "Nothing is wrong," she lied. "I am just so happy for you and Dinah."

"Thank you," Nathaniel said as he released her. "It was unexpected, but we couldn't be happier."

"I am surprised that Dinah allowed a doctor to examine

her, considering she believes they are all quacks," Marielle said lightly.

Dinah let out a puff of air. "I did object at first, but I told the doctor that I refused to participate in bloodletting."

Evie embraced her sister warmly. "You are going to make a wonderful mother," she declared as she stepped back.

"I just wish that Mother was here," Dinah said softly.

Nathaniel reached for his wife's hand. "I know, my love," he responded as he brought her hand up to his lips.

Tears came to Dinah's eyes. "I must sound so ungrateful right now, especially since I have been blessed with such a loving family."

Aunt Edith smiled tenderly at her. "It is all right to miss your mother. I know I can't take her place, but I was most fortunate to have gained a daughter when you married Nathaniel."

Dinah smiled through her tears. "Thank you, Edith."

Balfour stepped into the room and announced, "Dinner is ready to be served."

Gemma stayed back as everyone filed out of the drawing room and she let out a sigh. She loved it here, but she didn't have a choice. She had to leave or else her family would be opened to ridicule, and that was something she was not willing to do to them.

# Chapter Thirteen

Stephen sat at the dining table as he ate his breakfast and read the newssheets. Bandit was resting next to the table and stared up at him with hopeful eyes.

He had just turned the page when Marielle stormed into the room. "What in the blazes have you done?"

Stephen's hand stilled. "Can you be more specific?"

Hugh stepped into the room with a look of uncertainty on his face. "Have you read the Society page yet?"

"I don't read that drivel," Stephen said.

"I think you should," Hugh encouraged.

Stephen rifled through the page until he got to the Society page. His eyes roamed the articles until he saw one about him.

"Botheration," he muttered as he started to read the article that referenced his duel with John Paulson.

He brought his head up. "I can explain."

"Can you?" Marielle asked. "Because Gemma is packing to return to Hawkinge as we speak."

Stephen shoved back his chair and rose. "For what purpose?" he demanded.

"You fought a duel over a woman and then you kept her in your cabin," Marielle said, giving him a pointed look.

"I did, but it is much more complicated than that."

Marielle walked over and removed the newssheets from his hand. "The article also mentions that you frequent gambling hells."

"That is not true," Stephen declared. "I abhor gambling hells."

"Do you deny going to the Scarlet Lady?"

Stephen winced. "I did go, but I can explain."

Marielle frowned. "It seems like you don't have an easy answer for anything and that is not going to bode well for you."

As he reached for his blue jacket that was draped behind his chair, Stephen said, "I know this looks bad, and I will gladly tell you everything, but I need to go stop Gemma from leaving Town."

Hugh came to stand next to his wife. "I would choose your words very carefully when speaking with Gemma. She seems to believe she is doing the honorable thing for our family by returning to Hawkinge."

Stephen shrugged on his jacket. "I must assume she has read the Society pages."

"She did this morning, but Lord Hawkinge informed her yesterday about your debauchery," Marielle said.

"What I did was hardly debauchery," Stephen said. "I merely assisted a young woman that was in need of assistance."

"Did she thank you by sleeping in your bed?" Marielle asked dryly.

"You know not what you are speaking of," Stephen said. "I can assure you that nothing untoward happened."

Hugh interjected, "It does look bad for you."

Stephen walked over to the door and stopped. It would take some time before his coach would be brought around front and he didn't want to wait that long. Every second was precious right now since he needed to see Gemma to explain everything.

"Did you bring a coach?" he asked.

"We did," Marielle replied as she followed close behind. "Would you care for a ride?"

"I would." Stephen walked over to the main door and opened it, not bothering to wait for his butler.

He followed Marielle and Hugh out the door and into the waiting coach. Once the door was closed, Marielle asked, "Why were you at the Scarlet Lady?"

"I was looking for someone," Stephen replied.

Marielle was not appeased by his vague response. "You will need to reveal more of yourself if you want to convince Gemma to stay."

Stephen sighed. "I was looking for my first lieutenant and I was told that he frequented the Scarlet Lady. I was only there long enough to discover what boarding house he was residing at and then I left."

"Did you find him at the boarding house?" Marielle questioned.

"I did not, but I won't stop searching until I find him," Stephen said.

Marielle exchanged a glance with Hugh before saying, "Perhaps he doesn't want to be found and you are on a fool's errand."

"Regardless, Hawthorne is helping me track the man down," Stephen shared.

If Hugh was surprised by his brother's involvement, he didn't show it. "If Nathaniel is helping you, then you will find him."

Marielle crossed her arms over her chest and asked, "Can you kindly explain the duel to us?"

"I had little choice in the matter," Stephen contended.

"That seems unlikely," Marielle muttered.

With a glance out the window, Stephen said, "It was

discovered that a seaman had disguised herself as a man and was working aboard our ship. One of the lieutenants started making lewd comments about her and I caught him trying to force himself upon her."

Stephen continued. "When I confronted him, he told me to mind my own business and that the captain had placed him in charge of the young woman. I knew by the time I spoke to the captain that it would be too late. So, I challenged him to a duel and he accepted."

"You had a duel on the ship?" Hugh asked.

"It wasn't my brightest idea, but we both found seconds and we met on the main deck," Stephen said. "My shot hit him in the side, and he almost died. We both were subjected to a court-martial, but we were both let off with a warning."

Marielle uncrossed her arms. "What happened to the young woman?"

"Since I won the duel, the captain assigned me to watch over her until we arrived back in England," Stephen explained. "I knew she wasn't safe on a ship full of men so I had her sleep on my hammock in my quarters while I slept on the ground."

"You expect me to believe that nothing happened between you two?" Marielle asked.

"I do, because it is the truth," Stephen said. "Once we arrived back in England, she was escorted off the ship and I have never seen her again."

Marielle considered him for a moment before saying, "I believe you."

"Thank heavens for that," Stephen muttered.

"But I am not the one that you need to convince," Marielle said. "I have no doubt that Gemma is really hurt and confused right now."

Stephen ran a hand through his hair. "How did the newssheets even discover my involvement in the duel?"

"It came from Lord Hawkinge," Hugh said. "Gemma had

mentioned that her brother-in-law doesn't exactly approve of you."

The coach came to a stop in front of Lord Montfort's townhouse and Stephen didn't wait for the footman to open the door. He hurried up to the main door and was pleased when it was opened by the butler.

"I have come to call on Lady Hawkinge," Stephen declared, reaching for his calling card.

The butler gave him an apologetic look. "I do apologize, but Lady Hawkinge is not available for callers at this time."

"Will you not at least ask her?" Stephen asked.

As the butler went to respond, Hugh spoke first. "I suspect my cousin is in the drawing room," he said. "I'm not going to let her dismiss you so easily."

Stephen followed Hugh into the drawing room, and he saw the window that led out to the gardens was open.

Lady Montfort was sitting on the settee with needlework in her hand. "You just missed Gemma," she informed them as she pulled the needle through the thread. "When she heard Mr. Wycomb's voice, she decided to leave by way of the window."

Stephen approached the window and asked, "Do you mind, my lady?"

"That depends," Lady Montfort said, bringing her gaze up. "Are you an honorable man, Mr. Wycomb?"

"I strive to be," Stephen responded honestly.

Lady Montfort lowered the needlework to her lap and considered him for a moment. "You may go speak to my niece, but we shall be watching you from the drawing room."

"I would expect nothing less," Stephen said before he stepped through the window.

As he came to stand in the plant bed, his eyes roamed the lush landscape and he saw no sign of Gemma. He stepped on the path and slowly made his way towards the rear of the gardens.

He practically breathed a sigh of relief when he saw Gemma. She was sitting on the center of a bench and her gaze was downcast.

Not wanting to startle her, Stephen kept his voice low and he said, "Gemma."

Her eyes slowly came up and he could see that she had been crying.

Stephen came to a stop a short distance from the bench. "Why did you try to run from me?"

"I was afraid."

"Of what?"

"The truth," she replied softly.

He took a step closer to her. "I can explain everything, Gemma."

"There is no need," Gemma said. "You lived your life, and I lived mine."

"Yes, but I now want to live them together."

Gemma's lips tightened into a flat line. "Is that an offer?"

"It is, if you are willing," Stephen replied.

Gemma shook her head. "I'm afraid I must decline," she said. "I want to believe the best in you, but I am scared. I am scared that you are not the man I thought you were; the man I have grown to care greatly about."

"I am that man!" he exclaimed. "Just give me a chance to prove it."

"Were you in a duel?" Gemma asked.

"I was, but—"

Gemma spoke over him. "And did you recently frequent a gambling hell?"

"I did, but I am no gambler."

"Your behavior suggests otherwise," Gemma said, rising. "I'm sorry but I cannot enter a relationship with a man that gambles. I have seen the destruction that it causes to a family firsthand."

As Gemma went to walk past him, he gently reached for

her arm, stilling her. "I was in a duel, but I did it only because no one else cared what happened to this young woman. I couldn't sit back and do nothing. My conscience wouldn't have allowed that," he asserted. "But I assure you that nothing untoward happened between us."

She met his gaze. "You risked your career, your reputation, for this young woman."

"I did, but if you give me a chance to explain, I will tell you everything."

Gemma's eyes showed hesitation. "I will hear you out," she finally said.

Stephen dropped his hand from her arm. "When I was a first lieutenant, I learned of a young woman that had disguised herself as a man and she was working as a seaman on my ship," he explained. "I wish I could say that it was uncommon, but it happened more times than you can imagine. In some cases, it is the difference between life or death for these women."

"What happened to the young woman when she was discovered?"

"The captain had little time on his hands and asked me to ensure she was being properly tended to," Stephen replied. "That is when I discovered one of the lieutenants was trying to force himself on her."

"How awful," Gemma murmured.

"Unfortunately, her fate would've been much more grim than that if I hadn't interceded," Stephen said. "Sailors can go years without seeing a woman and they would have no qualms with taking advantage of her. I couldn't stand by and let that happen to her. Challenging the lieutenant to a duel was the only way to keep her safe."

"You were court-martialed."

"I was, but I chose to do the right thing, regardless of the consequences."

Gemma went to sit down on the bench, a frown marring

her features. "Lord Hawkinge informed me that this young woman slept in your quarters with you."

Stephen bobbed his head. "That is right. She slept on my hammock, and I slept on the ground. It was the only way to ensure her safety until we docked," he said. "But I assure you that nothing happened between us."

"I want to believe you, but it just sounds so…" Her voice trailed off.

He took a step closer to her. "What does it sound like?" he prodded.

"Remarkable," Gemma replied as her eyes searched his.

Stephen gestured towards the seat next to her on the bench. "May I?" he asked.

Gemma nodded her approval.

As he sat down, he said, "We do have a problem."

"Which is?" Gemma asked.

He shifted to face her. "If you don't trust me, then what more do we have to discuss?" he asked.

Gemma's gaze left his and she stared straight ahead. He would have given everything that he had to know her thoughts at that precise moment.

---

Gemma knew that Stephen was right. Without trust, what did they have? And she did want to trust him, but something was holding her back. She was afraid of giving him her heart and not knowing if he would break it. She closed her eyes and wished she had a crystal ball that would tell her precisely what to do.

She felt Stephen place his hand over hers and she felt a sense of peace wash over her. And in that moment, she wasn't as afraid as she had been before.

Gemma opened her eyes and said, "I do believe you, Stephen."

A boyish grin came to his lips. "I am pleased to hear you say so."

"But that doesn't explain why you were at a gambling hell," Gemma said. "Are you a gambler?"

"I am not," he replied. "I abhor gambling."

Gemma lifted her brow. "Will you kindly explain why you were at the Scarlet Lady?"

"I was searching for someone." Stephen reached into his jacket pocket and pulled out a folded piece of paper. He unfolded it as he explained, "This list contains the names of the officers that died when my ship went down. For every name crossed out, I visited their families and have offered my condolences."

Stephen's voice grew hoarse as he continued. "They gave their lives fighting for the Crown, and I did not want their deaths to be in vain."

Gemma noticed that one name was not crossed out. "You only have one name left."

"That is the odd part," Stephen said. "When I went to visit his family, I discovered that Benjamin Heathcote is alive. He somehow evaded capture and death on that fateful day. I don't know how he managed such a feat."

"Didn't his family know where Benjamin was?"

"Unfortunately, not," Stephen replied. "His sister did inform me that he frequented the Scarlet Lady, hence why I went there. A tip there led to a boarding house where we met someone that was masquerading as his wife."

"It sounds as if Benjamin doesn't wish to be found."

"It does, which makes me wonder what he is about. Your cousin, Hawthorne, is helping me to track down Benjamin."

"My cousin?" Gemma asked. "What does an earl know about tracking down someone?"

Stephen chuckled. "You would be surprised. He is a man with many abilities and even more secrets."

"I'm afraid I do not see it."

"I didn't either until I needed use of his particular skill set," Stephen said. "He is not a man that I would want to cross."

Gemma wasn't convinced. Nathaniel was many years older than her, but he had always been kind to her. She may question his sense of fashion, with his tattered clothing, but he had never been secretive around her.

"I see that you don't believe me," Stephen remarked lightly.

Gemma gave him a questioning look. "How did you know?"

Stephen smiled. "A line in your brow appears when you are deep in thought."

"Oh," she murmured. "I hadn't realized."

In a low voice, Stephen said, "It is just one of the many things that I have noticed about you."

She felt a slow burn crawling up her neck, suffusing her face. "I'm afraid to ask what else you have noticed," she said, pleased her voice sounded steady.

"There is no reason to be afraid," Stephen said as he leaned closer to her. "You are the perfect mix of everything that I have ever desired."

Gemma felt a smile come to her lips at his words, but it quickly disappeared when she saw her father approaching them with a disgruntled look on his face.

"Gemma!" her father shouted. "What is the meaning of this?"

Stephen removed his hand from hers and rose. "It was entirely my fault—"

Her father cut him off. "Do you mean to compromise my daughter, Mr. Wycomb?" he growled.

"I do not," Stephen replied.

"Yet you are alone with Gemma in the gardens, unchaperoned, holding hands," her father said. "What were you hoping to do?"

Stephen swallowed slowly. "I was hoping to press my suit with Lady Hawkinge."

"Absolutely not!" her father exclaimed. "You are not worthy of her."

"I would agree, sir, but——"

Her father huffed. "There are no 'buts'," he said. "You shouldn't even be here, not after what I just read in the morning newspaper." He waved his hand. "Leave us and do not return."

Gemma had just about enough of her father, and she wasn't going to stand by and let him treat Stephen so horribly.

"Father," Gemma started, rising, "you will not talk to Mr. Wycomb that way."

"Or what?" her father challenged. "You seem to have overlooked that he is nothing but a shipbuilder."

"I know perfectly well what kind of man he is, and he is not defined by his profession," Gemma said.

Her father's eyes narrowed. "I raised you to be a lady, not a light-skirt."

Stephen clenched his jaw so tightly a muscle below his ear started pulsing. "You will not treat Lady Hawkinge so disrespectfully."

"I am her father. I will speak to her however I choose to," he said haughtily.

As Stephen took a commanding step towards her father, Gemma stepped in between them and placed a hand on his chest. "I think it is best if you go, Father," she urged.

"You would choose this commoner over your own father?" he asked in disbelief.

Gemma shifted to face her father. "You have never been, and never will be, a father to me," she said.

Her father didn't show any reaction to her words, but his

next words caught her by surprise. "If it is permissible to you, I would like to speak to you privately... please."

Gemma had never heard her father say "please" to anyone, causing her to wonder what he was about.

Stephen spoke up from behind her. "Would you care for me to stay close by?" he asked, earning a scoff from her father.

"I haven't agreed to speak to him yet," Gemma replied.

Her father's eyes grew sad, if that was even possible. Her father was not one to show emotion of any kind and it softened her stance towards him.

Gemma turned towards Stephen and said, "It is all right. I will speak to him privately."

"Are you sure?" Stephen asked.

"I am."

Her father interjected, "For heaven's sakes, will you not allow me to speak to my daughter?"

Stephen glared at her father. "If you say or do anything that disrespects her in any way, I will..."

"You will what?" her father asked, uninterested.

A dangerous gleam came into Stephen's eyes, and she feared that her father had pushed him too far.

Stephen's voice grew hard. "You do not want to cross me, my lord," he drawled. "I will not stand for anyone disrespecting Lady Hawkinge."

Her father opened his mouth to respond so Gemma spoke first. "My father will behave." She gave him a pointed look. "Won't you?"

He nodded. "I will."

Gemma met Stephen's gaze. "You do not need to worry," she said. "I assure you that I can handle my father."

"Very well," Stephen responded, albeit reluctantly. "I will go, but I shall call upon you tomorrow."

"I will be looking forward to it."

Stephen's gaze shifted towards her father's and they stared

at each other. After a tense moment, Stephen started walking back towards the townhouse.

Gemma turned and faced her father. "What is it that you want, Father?"

"What?" he asked. "No pleasantries?"

"I'm afraid not."

Her father watched as Stephen stepped into the townhouse. "What are you thinking, Gemma?" he asked. "That man is not worthy of your time or notice."

"How I spend my time is not your concern."

"I am still your father."

"I believe I let my feelings be known on that."

Her father walked over to the bench and sat down on one side. "I understand that Kitty came to visit you," he said.

"She did."

"I wish Kitty hadn't done that, but she thought she was helping," her father shared.

Gemma crossed her arms over her chest. "Helping with what?"

Her father met her gaze as he admitted, "I'm dying, Gemma."

She felt the breath leave her lungs and she moved to sit down on the bench. "How?"

"The doctor says I have cancer."

"Have you gotten a second opinion?"

Her father nodded. "I have gone to various specialists, and they all told me the exact same thing."

Gemma hesitated before asking, "How long do you have?"

"Months, weeks…" He shrugged. "I was told to get my affairs in order sooner rather than later."

Unsure of what to say, she settled on, "I'm sorry."

"I have come into some money lately, and I was hoping that you would consider coming to live with me during this final stage of my life."

"I don't think that is such a good idea."

Her father stared blankly ahead. "I know I haven't been the best father to you, but I did do the best that I knew how."

Gemma bit her tongue, knowing it was not the time or place to contradict him.

"I did set some money aside for you in my will," he shared.

"That was thoughtful of you."

Her father sighed. "With the short time I have left, I want to try to make amends with you," he said. "Please say that it is not too late."

It didn't escape her notice that he said "please" again. She could send him on his way as retribution for how he had treated her, but she knew she would come to regret it. Maybe not today, or tomorrow, but at some point in her life.

"It is not too late, but I can't promise anything," Gemma said.

"I understand."

Her father turned his head towards her. "You shouldn't be wasting your time on Mr. Wycomb."

Gemma rose. "I do not care to discuss Mr. Wycomb with you."

"Your marriage prospects will be dim now that your name is associated with him," her father said. "That article did no favors to you or Mr. Wycomb."

"I have weathered worse storms than this," Gemma remarked.

"Promise me that you won't marry Mr. Wycomb."

Gemma let out a puff of air. "I cannot promise that, Father."

"But you are a lady and he is—"

Speaking over him, she replied, "He is an honorable man, and I care for him."

Her father looked displeased as he lowered his voice. "A widow can have some indiscretions, assuming they are discreet."

"Are you suggesting that I take Mr. Wycomb as a lover?"

"It is better than being married to him."

Gemma's mouth dropped. "You are unbelievable."

"I am being realistic," her father said. "If you marry Mr. Wycomb, you will never be welcome in high Society."

"I will take my chances."

Rising, her father asked, "May I call upon you soon?"

"You may."

He offered his arm. "Allow me to escort you back inside."

"I would prefer to remain where I am."

Her father withdrew his arm. "As you wish."

As her father walked back towards the townhouse, Gemma lowered herself onto the bench and found herself in quiet contemplation. Her father was dying, and what scared her the most was that she wasn't quite sure how to feel about that.

# Chapter Fourteen

After learning of her father's dire condition, Gemma found that she was in no mood to converse with anyone. All she wanted to do was retire to her bedchamber and be left alone with her thoughts. Voices drifted out of the drawing room as she crossed through the entry hall. There would come a time that she would need to discuss what had been said between her and her father, but now was not the time.

As she placed her foot onto the first step, Nathaniel stepped into the entry hall and acknowledged her with a tip of his head. "Gemma," he greeted.

"Cousin," she responded.

Nathaniel stepped closer to her and lowered his voice. "Stephen mentioned in passing that he told you I was aiding him in his search for his first lieutenant."

"He did."

"I would prefer if you would keep that to yourself," Nathaniel said.

Gemma cocked her head. "May I ask why?"

"My mother would not be pleased if she discovered that I was visiting gambling hells," he replied.

"But not Dinah?"

"Dinah already knows how I spend my time," Nathaniel shared. "We have no secrets between us."

"That is admirable and a rarity amongst the *ton*."

"There was a time I kept secrets from Dinah, before we were married, and I quickly discovered that my wife is not one to tolerate being left in the dark."

"Is any woman?"

Nathaniel chuckled. "Touché."

Gemma bit her lower lip before asking the one question that she dreaded the answer to. "Do you think I would be foolish to marry a man so far below my station?"

"I take it that Stephen has offered for you."

"He did, but I declined it."

Nathaniel grew pensive. "I see," he said. "And why did you do that?"

"I was angry that he hadn't told me about the duel or how he visited a gambling hell," Gemma replied.

"I was with him when he visited the Scarlet Lady and I can testify that he was entirely out of place there."

"I believe you but engaging in duels is illegal."

"That doesn't stop them from happening," Nathaniel said. "To a man, honor is everything. It determines if one is worthy of respect and admiration."

"Did Stephen tell you why he fought the duel?"

Nathaniel shook his head. "The reason doesn't matter to me. I know Stephen to be an honorable man and I wouldn't hesitate to be his second, assuming he asked."

"You cannot be in earnest," Gemma stated.

"Sometimes the good outweighs the bad," Nathaniel said. "A courageous man will not stand by and let fear win. He will do what is right, every time, without fail, no matter the consequences."

"And you believe Stephen is a courageous man?"

Nathaniel lifted his brow. "You don't?"

"I just want to make sure I am doing the right thing," she admitted.

"There is no certainty in life, or in love," Nathaniel advised. "It takes but a moment to fall in love, but it takes years to truly understand what love is."

Gemma tensed. "I said nothing about love."

Nathaniel's face softened. "You didn't have to."

"Regardless, Stephen will never be accepted in high Society," Gemma said.

"Is that what troubles you?"

"No," she said with a shake of her head. "I care little if Stephen is ever accepted by the *ton*."

Her cousin placed a hand on her shoulder. "Don't let anyone tell you who you should love. That isn't fair to you or Stephen."

"Thank you," Gemma murmured.

Nathaniel dropped his hand. "I hope I didn't lecture you too much."

"Not at all," Gemma responded. "It was greatly appreciated."

Taking a step back, Nathaniel said, "If you will excuse me, Stephen and I have an errand that we need to see to."

"Will this errand take you into the rookeries?" Gemma asked.

"Perhaps."

"Do be safe, Cousin," Gemma said.

Nathaniel tugged down on the lapels of his brown, tattered jacket. "You need not concern yourself with me. I am very familiar with the rookeries."

"And that is what concerns me the most."

"Good day, Cousin," Nathaniel said as he headed towards the main door.

As Gemma started up the stairs, Hugh exited the drawing room and said, "A word, Gemma."

She stifled the groan that was on her lips and descended the few stairs that she had managed to scale. What now?

Hugh came to a stop in front of her. "My mother and Marielle were hoping that you would join them in the drawing room."

"Can it wait?" she asked.

Marielle's voice came from inside the drawing room. "No, it can't."

Hugh chuckled. "As you can see, they are rather eager to speak to you."

With great reluctance, she said, "Very well, then."

Gemma walked the short distance to the drawing room and noticed that Hugh wasn't following her. She stopped and turned back around. "Aren't you coming?"

"I think it is wise if I leave you all to it," Hugh replied.

"Coward," Gemma teased.

Hugh grinned. "I wish you luck," he said before heading up the stairs.

Gemma knew that it would be best if she got this over with. She headed into the drawing room and saw her aunt and Marielle sitting on the settee with teacups in their hands. They both were eyeing her with interest as she came to sit across from them.

Marielle spoke first. "May I ask how your meeting with my brother went?"

"It went well," Gemma replied, not wanting to give too much away.

It was evident that Marielle was not pleased by her vague response by her next question. "Did my brother grovel?"

"There was no need to grovel," Gemma said. "He informed me of the circumstances around the duel and I found his explanation to be satisfactory."

"I see," Marielle murmured. "Are you two engaged now?"

"We are not," Gemma replied.

Marielle let out a dramatic sigh. "That is most unfortunate."

Her aunt took a sip of her tea, then said, "I find myself more curious as to why your father came to call."

Gemma shifted uncomfortably in her seat. "He informed me that he has cancer and that his death is imminent."

Her aunt let out a soft gasp. "That is terrible news," she said. "But I daresay that my brother is too surly to die."

"I hope that is the case," Gemma responded.

Leaning forward, her aunt placed her teacup down and picked up the teapot. She poured a cup of tea and extended it towards Gemma.

She accepted it and murmured her thanks.

Her aunt gave her a look that was filled with compassion. "Is there anything that I can do for you?"

"Not at this time," Gemma replied. "I am still just trying to process what my father told me."

"That is to be expected."

Gemma sipped her tea before lowering it to her lap. "I know this may sound foolish, but I find myself angry at my father," she said. "Even after he told me about his diagnosis, he spent his time berating me about associating with Stephen."

"Your father is a complex man," her aunt attempted.

"He has never been a father to me so why should I care if he lives or dies?" Gemma asked.

"Because you are nothing like him."

"Thank heavens for that," Gemma declared. "He even had the ridiculous notion that I should go reside with him until his death."

"Would that be so terrible?" her aunt asked.

Gemma stared at her aunt in disbelief. "It would be awful," she said. "I refuse to live under the same roof as my father and stepmother."

"It might be your only chance at reconciliation," her aunt pointed out.

With a shake of her head, Gemma said, "My father may claim he wishes things were different, but I know better. He just wants one more opportunity to control me."

Marielle spoke up. "Do you still intend to depart for Hawkinge?"

"I think it would be best if I stayed," Gemma hesitated, shifting her gaze towards her aunt, "assuming that is all right?"

"Why wouldn't it be?" her aunt asked.

"I assume you read the morning newssheets this morning," Gemma started.

Her aunt bobbed her head. "Your uncle and I did read the article about Mr. Wycomb this morning, but we found it to be a little underwhelming."

"Are you not worried about the scandal, considering my association with Stephen?" Gemma asked.

"I am not," her aunt replied. "You are family, and that means something to us. Besides, Marielle is Mr. Wycomb's sister. Do you suggest we send her away?"

"Of course not, but she has the protection of Hugh's name," Gemma replied.

"And you have the protection of ours," her aunt asserted. "Your uncle is a powerful man, and he will not stand by and let our names be dragged through the mud."

"I did not mean to cause trouble," Gemma said.

Her aunt gave her an amused look. "This is hardly trouble," she responded. "You must stop worrying about what is best for everyone else and focus on what is best for *you*."

Gemma gave her a sheepish smile. "I'm afraid that does not come naturally to me."

"I know, dear, but it is okay to be selfish at times," her aunt counseled. "If we spend all of our energy on others, what is left for us?"

Dinah stepped into the room and asked, "Did I miss the intervention?"

"There was no intervention," her aunt replied. "We just had ourselves a nice little chat, did we not?"

Gemma's lips twitched. "It was an intervention."

"I knew it," Dinah declared as she came to sit down next to Gemma. "Did the intervention work?"

Her aunt sighed. "Again, it wasn't an intervention."

"I have decided not to return to Hawkinge," Gemma said.

Dinah clasped her hands together. "What wonderful news!"

"Edith has assured me that my presence here won't cause a great scandal," Gemma shared.

Marielle interjected, "Which is a good thing for Stephen. How could he possibly press his suit if you left Town?"

Dinah arched an eyebrow. "Does this mean you have finally accepted Mr. Wycomb as a suitor?"

"I am not as opposed to it as I once was," Gemma replied.

"That is vague, and not at all helpful," Dinah joked.

Gemma laughed. "I would prefer if we spoke about something else," she said. "How are you feeling?"

Dinah let out an unladylike groan. "I feel awful. Who knew having a baby would be so miserable?"

"It will all be worth it the moment you hold the baby in your arms for the first time," her aunt responded. "It is a feeling unlike any other."

"Until then, I feel like I am going mad," Dinah said. "I can go from starving to nauseous in a matter of moments."

"You should drink more tea. It will help calm your stomach," her aunt suggested.

Dinah's eyes lit up when she looked down at the tray. "I would prefer biscuits," she said as she reached for one.

Gemma leaned forward and placed her teacup onto the tray. "If you will excuse me, I would like to rest before dinner."

Her aunt gave her an understanding nod. "We shall talk more over supper."

Stephen stood outside his townhouse at the precise time that Lord Hawthorne had requested him to do so. The sun was beating down on his neck and he could feel the sweat dripping down the middle of his back.

He had just pulled out his pocket watch to check the time when a hackney came to a stop in front of him.

The door opened, revealing Hawthorne, and he ordered, "Get in."

As Stephen stepped inside, he saw that Lord Haddington was sitting next to Hawthorne. He stifled the groan on his lips as he sat across from them.

The hackney jerked forward, merging into traffic, and an awkward silence descended over them. Stephen found he had little to say to Haddington, but he was curious as to why he was there. If the annoyed look on Haddington's face was any indication, he wasn't pleased to see him either.

Stephen removed his top hat and wiped the sweat off his brow. The hackney was stuffy, and the open window was doing little by the way of circulating the air.

Hawthorne spoke up. "I invited Haddington to accompany us," he said. "I hope you do not take issue with that."

Stephen forced a smile to his lips. "Not at all," he lied.

"Haddington is familiar with the Glistening Pigeon, and he informed me that it is a known gathering place for radicals," Hawthorne shared.

"How exactly did Haddington come by this information?" Stephen questioned. How would a marquess know such a thing?

Haddington shrugged his shoulders nonchalantly. "It is common knowledge."

Stephen knew that Haddington had no intention of answering his question truthfully. Not that he blamed the man. He would do the same thing to Haddington. It wasn't as if he didn't trust the man; he just didn't like him.

Hawthorne glanced out the window before saying, "I do have unfortunate news about the man that attacked you at the museum."

"Which is?" Stephen asked, turning his attention towards Hawthorne.

"Upon the threat of transportation, the man confessed that he had no idea who paid him to attack you," Hawthorne said. "His job was just to rough you up and scare you into leaving Gemma alone."

"How is it possible that he doesn't know who hired him?" Stephen asked.

"A note was slipped under his door, along with a few coins," Hawthorne replied. "If the man succeeded in keeping you away from Gemma, he would have received additional payment."

"How lovely," Stephen muttered. "So we are no closer to discovering who wants me to stay away from Gemma?"

"That would be correct," Hawthorne said.

"Should we hire a Bow Street Runner?" Stephen asked.

Haddington huffed. "Bow Street Runners are useless," he said. "It would be better if we hired a child to handle the investigation."

"Surely they are not that bad?" Stephen questioned.

"If you want to waste your time and money, then by all means, hire a Bow Street Runner," Haddington replied.

Stephen turned his attention towards Hawthorne. "Do you share the same disdain for Bow Street Runners?"

"I do believe Bow Street Runners serve a purpose, but they tend to just get in the way," Hawthorne responded.

Hawthorne's words gave him pause, causing him to ask, "Have they gotten in your way before?"

"On occasion," Hawthorne replied.

Stephen stared at the earl and tried to make sense of what he was saying. Why would a Bow Street Runner get in his way? How exactly did he spend his time? These were questions that he knew he would never get a straight answer from Hawthorne.

The hackney came to a jerking stop in front of a dilapidated building. The windows were broken, the bricks needed tending to and there were men that were loitering out front. This did not look like a tavern, but more like a hovel.

"We are here," Haddington announced.

"We are?" Stephen asked.

Haddington chuckled. "Trust me, it is worse on the inside," he said. "Come along."

They exited the hackney and stood on the narrow pavement. A pungent odor emanated from the ground, and he heard someone retching in the alley.

Haddington gave him a pointed look. "I would be careful where you step," he advised before he headed towards the door.

Before he had taken a step, Hawthorne said, "Let us do the talking."

"I can handle myself," Stephen asserted.

"Not here, not now," Hawthorne remarked. "These are dangerous men and they do not take kindly to gentlemen."

"Is that why you wear those clothes, to blend in?" Stephen asked.

Hawthorne tugged down on the tattered sleeves of his brown jacket. "Quite possibly."

Stephen followed Hawthorne into the tavern and his steps faltered once he was inside. There were small, round tables spread throughout the tavern. The men that were sitting around these tables all had dirty faces and the smell that wafted off them was more poignant than what he had smelled outside.

Some of the men glanced his way and grunted. One man pushed back his chair and walked slowly towards him. He had a long scar that protruded from the side of his forehead to his jawline.

"What are you looking at?" the man demanded.

Stephen didn't cower in front of the man, but challenged him, instead. "I was looking at no one in particular."

The man stepped closer to him. "It almost seems that you came here looking for trouble."

"I didn't come here looking for trouble, but it would appear that it found me," Stephen said.

As the man reared his arm back, Haddington grabbed the man's fist and jerked his arm behind his back.

"Is that any way to treat a newcomer?" Haddington asked, his voice stern.

The man turned his head towards Haddington. "Do you know this man, Daventry?"

"I do, sadly," Haddington replied as he released the man's arm. "He is with me."

"Why didn't you say so?" the man asked.

"Well, I would have thought it was obvious since he walked in with me," Haddington replied with a smile.

The man rubbed the back of his neck with his hand. "Why are you friends with some fancy bloke?"

Haddington slapped the man on the back. "Because he is buying me drinks tonight."

"If that is the case, I want to be friends with him, too," the man joked.

With a chuckle, Haddington asked, "Is there a meeting in the back?"

All humor was stripped from the man's face. "You don't mean to take that bloke in there with you, do you?"

"I was thinking about it," Haddington said.

The man shook his head vehemently. "Peter would never allow it," he declared. "It would be best if you just had a drink and be on your way."

Haddington removed his hand from the man's shoulder. "That sounds like a fine idea." He held his hand up to get a serving wench's attention. "I think I will start now."

With a parting glare at Stephen, the man walked back over to the table and slumped down onto his seat.

Haddington leaned closer to him and warned, "Do not make eye contact with any of these men. They would sooner kill you than befriend you."

"Understood," Stephen said.

They walked over to an empty table and pulled out the rickety chairs. It was a far cry from what he was used to at White's.

A serving wench walked up to the table and placed three tankards down in the center. Haddington removed a coin from his pocket and extended it towards her.

"Will there be anything else?" the serving wench asked.

As he reached for his tankard, Haddington replied, "Not at this time."

The serving wench fluttered her eyelashes. "It would be no trouble to stay with you and keep you company."

"No, thank you," Haddington replied as he brought the tankard to his lips.

A disappointed look came to the serving wench's face. "If you change your mind, you know where to find me," she said before walking away.

Stephen picked up one of the tankards and took a sip of the tepid, watered-down ale. It wasn't the worst drink he had ever had, but it was close. He wanted to ask Haddington about being called "Daventry", but he knew that he wouldn't get a straight answer.

Hawthorne leaned over the table and asked, "Do you see Benjamin?"

Stephen's eyes roamed over the room but he saw no sign of Benjamin. "No, he is not here."

"He might be in the back." Haddington turned his attention towards the door along the back wall. "That is where the rebels meet."

"Do you think Benjamin is involved with rebels?" Hawthorne asked.

"I don't rightly know," Stephen replied. "There was a time when I would have said no, but now I don't know what he is truly capable of."

Haddington shoved back his chair and rose. "Come along," he ordered. "Keep your mouth closed and do precisely as I say."

Rising, Stephen placed the tankard down and followed Haddington. He wasn't sure what Haddington intended to do and it worried him.

Haddington stopped in front of the back door and rapped it four times. Then he paused before repeating it.

The door opened a crack and Haddington leaned closer to say something. It was too loud in the tavern for Stephen to hear what had been said.

After a long moment, the door opened wide, and Haddington stepped through it. He gave Stephen a pointed look, indicating he should follow.

Stephen stepped into the dark room and saw the worn drapes had been pulled closed. A fire was in the hearth and a lone candle sat on each of the six round tables.

His eyes perused the room until they landed on a man that was sitting down, his back towards him. His long brown hair was tied with a string and he was wearing a green jacket. There was something familiar about him.

"Do you see Benjamin?" Haddington asked.

"Possibly." Stephen pointed towards the man. "Do you recognize him?"

Haddington shook his head. "I do not."

Stephen walked along the back wall until he saw the profile of the man's face. *Benjamin.* As he put his hand up to get his attention, Benjamin turned his head and met his gaze. Panic registered on his expression.

Benjamin shoved back his chair and ran towards a side door, throwing it open.

Without the slightest hesitation, Stephen chased after him. He wasn't going to let Benjamin go until he answered a few questions.

Stephen raced into the alleyway and came to an abrupt stop. He wasn't sure which way Benjamin had gone and the only sound was a cat meowing in the distance.

"Blazes," he muttered under his breath. He had been so close to finally getting the answers he sought from Benjamin.

He had just turned around when he heard the sound of a pistol cocking.

"Turn around, slowly," the familiar voice said.

Stephen put his hands up and did as he was instructed. He saw Benjamin stepping out of the shadows with a pistol in his hands.

"What is the meaning of this?" Stephen demanded.

Benjamin smirked. "You do not get to ask the questions, Captain," he replied. "I'm in charge here."

"Then what is it that you want to know?" Stephen questioned.

Benjamin came to a stop a short distance from him. "Why have you been looking for me?"

"That is simple- you were supposed to be dead." He paused. "How did you survive the onslaught?"

"I have my ways."

"And somehow you avoided capture," Stephen said.

Benjamin's smirk disappeared. "I don't want to kill you, but you are leaving me with little choice in the matter."

"Why is that?"

"You were never supposed to return home," Benjamin said. "I watched you die."

"I was merely wounded."

Benjamin's face grew hard. "This time, I will ensure you are dead," he said as he took aim with his pistol.

## Chapter Fifteen

Stephen didn't flinch as he stared into the barrel of Benjamin's pistol. He wasn't going to give the man the satisfaction of showing any fear. If it was his time to die, then so be it.

He had many regrets, but the only one that stood out was not telling Gemma how he truly felt about her. He loved Gemma. He knew it, and he could deny it no longer. But she would never know how deeply he cared for her.

Benjamin sneered. "Any last words, Captain?" he asked as his finger twitched on the trigger.

"None that I wish to share with you," Stephen replied.

As he braced for being shot, Haddington's voice came from behind him. "Put the pistol down," he ordered.

"Why would I do that?" Benjamin asked as he shifted his gaze towards Haddington.

Haddington came to stand next to Stephen, a pistol in his hand. "Because if you shoot Stephen, then I will have no choice but to kill you."

Benjamin's expression grew hard. "Why do you care if Stephen lives or dies?"

"Quite frankly, I can't stand the man, but I don't want him dead," Haddington replied.

"Thank you for that," Stephen muttered.

Haddington shrugged. "It is merely the truth," he said. "You are a nuisance, but my wife thinks highly of you. I just don't quite see it."

Benjamin's eyes narrowed. "Just go inside," he stated. "This doesn't concern you."

"I disagree," Haddington countered. "I find myself curious as to why you are trying to kill Stephen."

"I have my reasons," Benjamin said.

"Which are?" Haddington pressed.

Benjamin adjusted the pistol in his hand. "I don't have to explain myself to you."

"That is true," Haddington agreed. "But you will have to explain yourself to my friend. While I was distracting you, he was able to sneak up behind you."

Stephen heard the gun cocking before he saw Hawthorne step out of the shadows behind Benjamin.

"Kindly put your gun down," Hawthorne commanded.

Benjamin's hand wavered. "If I do that, I am a dead man."

"Look around you. You will be a dead man if you pull that trigger," Haddington said. "But you will live another day if you put the pistol down."

"How do I know you won't kill me once I lower my pistol?" Benjamin asked.

"I guess you are going to have to trust us," Haddington replied.

Benjamin huffed. "I don't trust anyone."

"That is your mistake," Hawthorne said.

"You are just going to let me walk away?" Benjamin asked.

Hawthorne shook his head. "No," he replied. "We are going to escort you to Newgate."

Benjamin's face paled. "Why?"

Hawthorne kept his pistol aimed at Benjamin's back as he said, "I have been thinking, and I can't help but wonder how it is possible that you were able to escape when your ship was attacked."

"I was lucky," Benjamin attempted.

"No, there is more to it than that," Hawthorne said. "I came to the conclusion that you were working with the French."

Benjamin shifted in his stance, looking deucedly uncomfortable. "That is rubbish."

"Is it?" Hawthorne asked. "You avoided capture, avoided death, and then you go into hiding once Stephen returns to Town."

"I was not hiding," Benjamin declared.

"You were using an alias," Haddington pointed out. "Only guilty men try to disguise their identities."

"You are wrong," Benjamin spat out.

"Then why kill Stephen, unless you want to tie up loose ends?" Hawthorne asked.

"My reasons are my own," Benjamin responded.

"That isn't good enough," Haddington said. "If you don't answer our questions now, the next time we ask we won't be as accommodating."

Benjamin glared at Stephen. "This is all your fault," he declared. "Why did you have to come looking for me?"

"I needed answers," Stephen replied.

"You should have left well enough alone," Benjamin said.

"I couldn't do that, not knowing the truth."

Benjamin scoffed. "What is the truth, exactly?" he asked. "You and I can have a different version of the truth."

Hawthorne interjected, "This is not a philosophical debate. Just tell us the truth and be done with it."

"Why?" Benjamin asked. "So I can get transported? No, thank you."

"It is better than being killed," Hawthorne responded.

Benjamin lowered his pistol to his side. "I have done nothing wrong. I was merely a victim of happenstance."

"Regardless, you tried to kill Stephen," Hawthorne said as he came to relieve Benjamin of his pistol.

"I wouldn't have killed Stephen," Benjamin attempted. "I just wanted answers; same as you."

"You think you are so clever but you will falter when we interrogate you at Newgate," Hawthorne remarked.

Benjamin didn't appear concerned. "I have nothing to hide."

"We shall see." Hawthorne handed over the pistol to Stephen. "Keep this on you when you are in the rookeries."

Stephen accepted the pistol. "Thank you."

Hawthorne addressed Haddington. "Will you join me in accompanying our new friend to Newgate?"

Haddington nodded. "I would be honored."

"Can I come along?" Stephen asked.

Hawthorne exchanged a look with Haddington before saying, "I do not think that is a wise idea."

"Why is that?" Stephen pressed.

"We are much more forceful when it comes to rooting out the truth," Hawthorne replied.

Stephen lifted his brow. "You don't intend to interrogate Benjamin, do you?"

With a glance at Benjamin, Hawthorne replied, "We do."

"Why not let the guards at Newgate handle it?" Stephen asked.

Haddington gave him a smug look. "I assure you that we are much more proficient at discovering the truth than the guards are."

"Why would you sully your hands with this?" Stephen prodded. "Why not leave it to the magistrate?"

"Because we don't have time to ask politely," Haddington said. "Not when we are dealing with a French spy."

Benjamin put his hands up. "I am no spy," he asserted. "Furthermore, there is no need to torture me. I will tell you what you want to know, assuming you don't take me to Newgate."

"We shall see," Hawthorne said.

"Listen, I did nothing wrong," Benjamin stated. "The French threatened my family if I didn't cooperate with them. I had no choice."

Hawthorne turned to face Benjamin. "Everyone has a choice. You chose poorly."

"What was I supposed to do?" Benjamin asked. "I couldn't let my family die because of me."

Hawthorne grabbed Benjamin's arm. "We will continue this conversation at Newgate."

Benjamin jerked back his arm. "I am not going to Newgate. I did nothing that any sane person wouldn't do."

"I doubt that," Hawthorne responded.

Benjamin reached into his boot and pulled out a dagger. "If I go to Newgate, my family will be ruined," he said, holding it up.

Hawthorne glanced at the knife, appearing unconcerned by the threat. "What is your plan?" he asked. "You have a knife, and we all have pistols."

Benjamin's eyes grew panicked. "You don't understand. I was forced to give up the route our ship was heading. I had no idea they were going to attack us."

"*You what?!*" Stephen exclaimed.

"I had no choice, Captain," Benjamin said. "They threatened me and my family. What was I supposed to do?"

"You could have come to me," Stephen replied.

"And what could you have done?" Benjamin asked. "I was approached by a man before our ship was deployed and I wasn't in a position to say no."

Stephen took a commanding step. "Your actions caused the death of your comrades."

"I know, and I live with that realization every day," Benjamin said. "Don't you think I regret my actions?"

"You are not the man that I thought you were," Stephen declared. "You are a traitor and deserve a traitor's death."

"I am no traitor!" Benjamin exclaimed. "I was forced to do it."

Stephen pointed his pistol at Benjamin and cocked it. "I should kill you for what you've done."

"It wasn't my fault—"

"It was!" Stephen exclaimed, speaking over him. "You gave the French our coordinates. You put us in the position to be attacked."

"I didn't know they would attack," Benjamin said.

"What do you think they wanted our route for?" Stephen demanded.

Benjamin lowered his gaze to the ground. "I never asked."

Stephen's finger twitched on the trigger. It would be so easy to kill Benjamin. It was because of him that so many of his crew were dead.

Haddington's calm voice broke through his musings. "I know what you are thinking. But killing him will solve nothing."

"He must pay for what he has done," Stephen said.

"And he will," Haddington responded. "But it must not be by your hand."

Stephen pursed his lips together as he stared at Benjamin. His shoulders were hunched and he looked defeated. There would be no victory in shooting this man. Haddington was right, as much as it pained him to admit it.

Stephen lowered the pistol to his side. "I want him to suffer for what he has done."

"You can be assured of that," Haddington said.

Before anyone could react, Benjamin shoved the dagger into his own stomach and twisted it. He staggered back until he fell to the ground.

Stephen rushed over to Benjamin and crouched down next to him. "What in the blazes have you done?"

Benjamin's face grew pale as he laid his head onto the ground. "I couldn't go to Newgate. I know what they do to people like me."

"You don't know that for sure," Stephen attempted.

Benjamin's hand pulled out the bloody dagger and said, "My family will be better off without me."

"I will see to them," Stephen said.

Benjamin looked at him in disbelief. "You would do that, even after everything I've done?"

"Your family members are innocents in all of this," Stephen replied.

"Thank you," Benjamin said softly. "I can now die in peace."

Stephen watched as Benjamin's eyes closed and he took his last breath. How had it come to this?

Hawthorne placed a hand on Stephen's shoulder. "It would be best if we departed now to seek out the magistrate."

Stephen rose slowly, his eyes remaining fixed on Benjamin's body.

"It is better for him that he died this way then being hanged in the square," Hawthorne said.

"You are right, of course," Stephen murmured.

Hawthorne gestured towards the end of the alleyway. "Come on," he encouraged. "Nothing good will come from loitering around his body."

As Stephen followed Hawthorne and Haddington out of the alleyway, he didn't know quite what to feel. He felt relief at knowing the truth, but he also felt some blame for Benjamin's death.

Gemma closed the door to her bedchamber and headed towards the drawing room on the main level. The dinner bell hadn't chimed yet, but she intended to take advantage of the time and work on her embroidery. She had just turned the corner when she saw Nathanial approaching from the opposite direction with a frown marring his features.

Nathanial came to a stop in front of her and the frown disappeared. "Good evening, Cousin," he greeted.

"Good evening," she said. "Is everything all right?"

A lazy smile came to Nathaniel's lips. "Everything is just as it should be."

Knowing that her cousin was just trying to appease her, Gemma decided to prod a little and hoped he would confide in her. "How did your meeting in the rookeries go?"

"It went well."

Gemma waited for Nathaniel to expand, but when no additional information was forthcoming, she asked, "You don't intend to tell me, do you?"

"I do not."

"That is infuriating."

Nathaniel chuckled. "It might please you to know that I invited Stephen to dinner this evening, and he is waiting in the drawing room."

A thrill of excitement coursed through her at her cousin's words. She smoothed down her dark blue gown with a square neckline as she tried to appear indifferent.

"I suppose I should not keep him waiting," Gemma said.

Nathaniel did not look fooled by her lackluster response. "It is all right if you are anxious to see him," he said as he went to walk past her.

Gemma continued down the hall until she reached the grand staircase. She descended the stairs with quick steps and arrived at the drawing room. She was anxious to see Stephen, which was absurd since she had seen him earlier that day.

As she stepped into the room, she saw Stephen was staring

out the window, his hands clasped behind his back, and he had a solemn look on his face.

"Good evening, Stephen," she greeted.

Stephen unclasped his hands and turned to face her. "Good evening, Gemma." His tone was cordial enough, but it sounded strained.

Gemma took a step closer and asked, "How did Nathaniel convince you to join us for dinner?"

"It wasn't that difficult to convince me, considering it gave me an opportunity to see you again," Stephen replied.

She felt the familiar blush come to her cheeks. "That is kind of you to say."

"It is merely the truth."

They stared at one another for a long moment and Gemma knew that she would never tire of looking into the depths of his eyes. For in them, she saw love, deeply embedded. It both scared and terrified her.

A maid stepped into the room and went to sit in the corner.

Gemma gestured towards the settee. "Would you care to sit while we wait for the dinner bell to be rung?"

"I would."

She walked over to the settee and sat down, leaving more than enough space for Stephen to sit next to her. To her disappointment, he sat across from her.

With a wave over the tray, Gemma said, "I would offer you some tea, but I daresay I already know that answer."

"I am sorry to disappoint you."

Gemma smiled. "I do not care one whit if you enjoy tea."

Stephen returned her smile, but it didn't quite meet his eyes. It was a sad smile and that concerned her greatly.

"Whatever is the matter?" she asked.

"Nothing that I wish to burden you with."

Gemma felt her back go rigid. "Do you think of me as a simpering miss that cannot handle the harsh realities of life?"

"I did not mean to imply that."

"Then what did you mean?" Gemma pressed.

Stephen sighed. "You have a light about you that I never want to be responsible for dimming," he said. "I can assure you that I mean it as the greatest compliment."

Gemma felt herself relax at his words. "Where do you think I got that light from?" she asked as she moved to sit on the edge of her seat. "You brought it back into my life, and I want to share it with you."

"I will only drag you down."

"I do think you underestimate me."

Stephen moved to the edge of his seat, bringing him closer to her. "Never," he said. "Only a fool would do so."

Gemma could reach out and touch Stephen if she wanted, but she kept her hands clasped firmly in her lap. But, heaven help her, she wanted to. There was something about him that drew her in, making her feel safe and protected.

Stephen glanced at the maid in the corner before saying, "I found him."

"Your first lieutenant?" she asked.

He nodded. "Aye."

"Where is he?"

"Dead."

Gemma's hand flew up to her mouth. "How did he die?"

A pained look came into his eyes. "He killed himself, but not before he admitted to betraying us all," he murmured. "He told the French the route our ship was taking."

Gemma gasped. "Why would he do such a thing?"

"He claimed that they threatened his family to do so."

"You don't believe he was being truthful?"

Stephen shrugged. "I don't know what to believe anymore," he said. "He could have come to me. I would have helped him."

"What would you have done?"

"I don't know, but he never gave me the opportunity to

try," Stephen replied. "Instead, he caused the slaughter of my crew."

Gemma knew she was being brazen, but she reached for Stephen's hand, encompassing it in her own. "What happened was not your fault."

"How could it not be?" Stephen demanded. "Benjamin was my first lieutenant. I should have known—"

"Known what?" she asked, speaking over him. "That he would betray you."

"There had to be some signs that I missed. There must have been."

Gemma tightened her hold on his hand. "You cannot blame yourself for things you had no control over."

"I was the captain. I am ultimately responsible for what happened on my ship."

"Those deaths are not your fault."

Stephen lowered his gaze to their hands. "I wish I could believe you, but every time I close my eyes, I hear the screams of my men. I failed them. I should have had the decency to have died alongside them."

Gemma could hear the profound sadness in his voice, and it grieved her deeply. She knew he meant what he said, and she didn't quite know what to say to make him feel better. How could she make him understand how empty her life would be without him in it?

Stephen pulled his hand back and abruptly rose. "It was a terrible idea for me to come this evening."

"Then why did you come?"

He met her gaze, his eyes holding a raw vulnerability. "To see you," he admitted softly.

Rising, she said, "You should stay."

"I'm afraid I won't be very good company."

"That matters little to me."

Stephen huffed as he shook his head. "How is it fair that I

am with you, right now, and so many of my men died?" he asked. "I should not have been so lucky."

"There is no shame in living."

"For me there is," Stephen said. "A captain always goes down with his ship, but I was wounded. I had blacked out, and when I woke up, I was being tended to by our doctor in an enemy's cell. Only a small group of us had survived and we were taken to a dank and dreary French prison. If not for the prisoner exchange, we would all have most likely succumbed to death."

"I'm sorry," Gemma murmured, knowing her words were wholly inadequate.

Stephen's eyes grew moist with tears. "All of those men died, and I was powerless to stop it. I am weak."

Not caring about the repercussions of her actions, Gemma stepped forward and wrapped her arms around him. "You are not weak, Stephen," she said. "You are the strongest man that I know."

Stephen's arms went around her, pulling her close. "Those men..." he started, his voice hitching.

"Are dead because of your first lieutenant, not you," she asserted.

The maid in the corner cleared her throat.

Gemma felt no urgency to leave the comfort of Stephen's arms as she turned her attention towards the maid and ordered, "Leave us."

The maid's eyes grew wide. "But, my lady, what will Lady Montfort say?"

"Let me deal with my aunt."

With great hesitation, the maid rose and departed the room.

Gemma looked up at Stephen and said, "There are advantages to being a widow."

"I do not wish to get you in trouble with Lady Montfort."

"There are some things worth getting in trouble for," Gemma said.

Stephen held her gaze. "How is it possible that you have such faith in me?"

"Because I know you, Stephen. You are an honorable man."

"I want to believe you, to believe that the attack was not my fault, but my heart is heavy with the burden of the living."

"You did the best that you could."

"It wasn't enough." He paused. "I wasn't enough." His words were no louder than a whisper, but they were filled with regret.

Gemma took her right hand and cupped his cheek. "You are enough," she assured him. "You did not fail those men. You fought until you could fight no more. Those are not the actions of a coward."

"All of those men died," he murmured.

"Yes, and their deaths will not be in vain," Gemma said. "You must live as if your life is a gift. Embrace it. Never take it for granted."

"But how many of my men died that I may live?"

Gemma saw that Stephen was blinking back the tears that were threatening to fall from his eyes. "You need to prove to yourself that you were worth saving."

"How do I do that?"

"Live a good life, one that honors them through your actions."

Stephen leaned into her hand. "It is not that simple."

"Why can't it be?" she asked. "You can't change the past, no matter how much you want to, but you can learn from it and change your future."

"I don't know where to begin."

"Then let me help you."

Stephen reached up and encompassed her hand in his. "I can't burden you with this. It wouldn't be fair of me."

"Let me worry about that."

"Thank you."

Gemma smiled. "You are welcome."

As they stared at one another, she barely acknowledged that Marielle had stepped into the room and announced, "Edith is on her way."

Stephen dropped his hand and took a step back. "Thank you, Sister," he said as he adjusted his cravat.

Marielle lifted her brow. "I would be remiss if I did not tell you that what I witnessed was both encouraging and inappropriate."

"Gemma and I were merely conversing with one another," Stephen attempted.

"I see," Marielle said, not appearing convinced by Stephen's explanation. "You might want to come up with a better story when Edith asks why you dismissed the maid from the drawing room."

Marielle walked over to the settee and continued, "I think it might be best if I remain here until Edith arrives."

"Suit yourself," Stephen said as he stole a glance at Gemma.

## Chapter Sixteen

Later that evening, Stephen sat hunched over at a table in the corner of White's as he nursed the drink in his hand. He wanted to forget all these blasted memories that haunted him every time he closed his eyes. But he was unable to do so. They kept reappearing, reminding him of how he had failed his crew.

His hand tightened around his glass as he raised it to his lips. No matter how much Gemma tried to convince him that it wasn't his fault, he knew differently. It was his job to keep his crew safe. Yet he had allowed a traitor to permeate the highest folds of the crew.

How had he not seen Benjamin for what he was- a traitor? He had been so distracted by doing his job that he failed to see what was right in front of him. And it had cost him everything.

Stephen lowered the glass to the table, keeping his gaze downcast. He would never be able to convince himself that he was worthy of Gemma. She had endured hardships, but the goodness inside of her had never left her. She had fought her battles and had come out stronger because of it. Sadly, he could not say the same.

If Gemma knew how troubled he truly was, she would leave him be. It was no less than he deserved.

Hugh's voice broke him out of his grumblings. "I assumed we would find you here."

"Go away," he muttered, not bothering to look up.

With a chuckle, Hugh pulled out a chair and sat down. "I see that you are being your usual pleasant self this evening," he joked. "We are here on Marielle's behest."

"Why am I not surprised?" Stephen mocked.

Hawthorne spoke up as he came to sit down next to his brother. "We couldn't help but notice that you were rather despondent during dinner."

Stephen looked over at the earl. "Don't you have anywhere else to be but here, bugging me?" He knew he was being rude, but he wasn't in the mood to converse.

"There are many places that I could be, but I feel I am needed here the most," Hawthorne replied.

"Do you take pity on me, then?" Stephen asked.

Hawthorne shook his head. "I do not pity you."

"No?" Stephen asked, his voice rising. "Perhaps you think me a fool."

"My opinion of you has not changed," Hawthorne responded in a calm, nonengaging manner.

Stephen scoffed. "How can it not?" he asked. "I was trained to engage with our enemies, but apparently I can't even do that correctly."

Hawthorne leaned closer to him and lowered his voice. "You are being much too hard on yourself."

"You would have spotted the traitor," Stephen declared. "One look, and you would have known."

"Stephen..." Hawthorne started. "You are grieving and aren't thinking clearly."

"I am not grieving that traitor. He was a man that I had thought was my friend for all those years," Stephen declared. "I am glad that he is dead. He got what he deserved."

Hugh glanced between them with a curious expression and asked, "I take it that something transpired between you two?"

Stephen saw no reason not to take Hugh into his confidence and learn of his shame. "Right before my first lieutenant killed himself, he confessed to giving the French our ship's route, allowing them the element of surprise when they attacked us," he explained.

Hugh stared at him with a look that could only be construed as pity. "I'm sorry…"

He put his hand up, stilling Hugh's words. "I do not want your sympathy," he said. "If I had been a better captain, I would have known."

"Your logic is faulty," Hawthorne remarked. "You couldn't have predicted that one of your own would have turned on King and Country."

"I keep replaying every conversation that I had with Benjamin, but I still can't find any indication of his devious nature," Stephen shared.

"A person's true nature is revealed when they are faced with great adversity," Hawthorne said. "Regardless, no one faults you for what happened."

"I fault myself."

Hawthorne gave him a knowing look. "Were you disciplined by the Royal Navy for the loss of your ship?"

Stephen shook his head. "I was not," he said. "The day we were attacked it was foggy and visibility was poor. We didn't even see the French frigate until they were right upon us."

"If no one else finds you to be at fault, when will you forgive yourself for the things that you cannot change?" Hawthorne asked.

"Gemma said something similar," Stephen said. "But I don't think I can."

A server approached the table and placed two glasses of brandy onto the table. "Will there be anything else?"

Hawthorne reached for a glass as he replied, "Not at this time."

"Very good, my lord," the server said before he walked off to a nearby table.

Hugh took a sip of his drink, then said, "I was once where you are now."

Stephen huffed. "I doubt that."

"I defended a murderer, and I was able to get him acquitted by a jury of his peers," Hugh started. "After he was released, he went on to murder his wife and his daughter."

Unsure of what to say, Stephen remained quiet.

Hugh leaned forward in his seat and continued. "I couldn't come to terms with what I had done, so I turned to gambling. I ran away from my problems, instead of facing them head on. In doing so, I was spiraling out of control, and I pushed everyone away."

"What changed?" Stephen asked.

A smile came to Hugh's lips. "Marielle came into my life, and she believed in me."

"Surely it can't be that simple."

"I'm afraid it was," Hugh said. "She disrupted my life, but in a good way, causing me to rethink everything I knew to be true."

Hawthorne interjected, "Never underestimate the power of love and the woman that wields it."

Hugh raised his glass. "Well said, Brother."

"I can't just forget what transpired and move on," Stephen said.

"Nor should you," Hugh agreed. "You can't change the past, but you can choose whether or not to learn from it."

"What about all the people that died?" Stephen asked in a harsh tone. "They don't have the luxury of learning from anything."

"No, they don't, but that doesn't mean you throw away

your life because of it," Hugh counseled. "Live life to the fullest."

Stephen tossed back his drink and slammed the empty glass onto the table. "I'm afraid I can't do that."

Hawthorne exchanged a concerned look with Hugh before saying, "Then you will lose Gemma."

Stephen let out a sigh. "I can't lose what I never had."

"I know you care for her," Hawthorne pressed.

"I do," Stephen readily replied. "I have never cared for another as much as I do for Gemma."

"Then you have to decide if the trouble of your past is more important than your future," Hawthorne said.

"How is that possible?" Stephen asked, half-hoping.

"Bad things happen, you must accept that," Hawthorne said. "No one is immune to heartache and sorrow, but you decide how to respond."

"I don't think I can just put a smile on my face and pretend all is well," Stephen remarked.

"Nor should you," Hawthorne agreed. "But remember what you are fighting for. That makes all the difference."

The image of Gemma came to his mind and Stephen knew precisely what he was fighting for. He was fighting for a future with Gemma. He loved her and always would. She was the one good thing in his life that he knew he couldn't live without. His reality with Gemma was far better than any dream he could have concocted.

Stephen pushed his glass away from him. "Even if, by some chance, I can convince Gemma to marry me, you must know that I am not worthy of her."

Hugh bobbed his head. "We know, but it is Gemma's decision. Not ours."

"What if she does not want to take a chance on a broken man?" Stephen asked.

With a smirk, Hawthorne said, "I daresay that you underestimate Gemma. She is not like most women of the *ton*."

"No, she is not," Stephen agreed. "Most women wouldn't even give me a second look because of my lowly connections."

"You are still quite wealthy in your own right," Hawthorne said.

"I am, but how would you know such a thing?" Stephen asked.

Hawthorne chuckled. "Now it is me that you have underestimated," he said. "I made some inquiries to ensure you were the man I thought you to be."

"When did you make these inquiries?" Stephen questioned.

"The moment you started showing interest in my cousin," Hawthorne said.

"I should have known," Stephen muttered. He wasn't offended by Hawthorne's admission, but, rather, it demonstrated how much he cared for his cousin's welfare.

Hawthorne caught the eye of a passing servant and held his empty glass up, indicating he wished for another drink. "Shall we celebrate your upcoming nuptials with Gemma?" he asked as he lowered his glass.

"She hasn't agreed to be my wife."

"Yet," Hawthorne said. "But she will."

"How can you be so confident?" Stephen asked.

"Because I see the way she looks at you, as if you were the only thing that could possibly matter," Hawthorne said.

Feeling the emotions stirring inside of him, Stephen found himself admitting, "I love her."

Hawthorne grinned. "We know, but why are you telling us?" he asked. "You should be confessing this to Gemma."

Stephen glanced over at the darkened window. "It is too late to call upon Gemma, but I will do so tomorrow."

Hugh spoke up. "You might want to work on your speech," he advised. "I rehearsed mine, over and over, but my words became fumbled the moment I stood in front of Marielle."

"But you convinced her to marry you," Stephen said.

"I did, but that was because I spoke from the heart," Hugh shared.

A server came over with a tray of drinks and placed them into the center of the table. Then he collected the empty glasses and stepped back.

Hawthorne retrieved a glass and held it up. "To Stephen," he said. "May you say the right words and not botch it up with Gemma."

"Thank you for the vote of confidence," Stephen remarked.

Lord Grenton approached the table and pulled out a chair. "Are we celebrating something?" he asked, glancing between them.

Hawthorne lowered his glass and shared, "Stephen is going to offer for Gemma."

"It is about time," Grenton said. "It was evident by the way he spoke of her that he cared for her deeply."

"I encouraged Stephen to work on his speech because it is easy to get befuddled when you confess your feelings to the woman you love," Hugh shared.

Grenton bobbed his head. "I second that sentiment," he said. "There is nothing more nerve wracking."

"But it worked out splendidly for both of you," Stephen remarked.

"Only by the grace of God," Hugh said.

Stephen reached for a glass. "I daresay you both are exaggerating. I will just say what needs to be said and be done with it."

Hugh gave him an amused look. "Good luck with that."

As Stephen took a sip of his drink, he started to think of everything that he wished to say to Gemma. He didn't want to botch up the proposal… again.

With the morning sun streaming into the windows, Gemma sat on the settee and worked on her embroidery. She was content, which was something she hadn't felt in a long time. And she knew the source of what her contentment was- Stephen. He had a way to make her feel valued and- dare she believe- loved.

Her heart had been broken when Baldwin died, and she thought it could never be happy again. But she had been wrong. She knew without a doubt that all the broken, shattered, forgotten pieces of her heart were worth putting back together again, because she had found love once more.

Marielle spoke up, breaking the silence. "You are awfully quiet this morning," she said.

"I suppose I am," Gemma responded.

"Anything you wish to talk about?"

"Not particularly."

Marielle pulled the needle through the fabric. "We could discuss the fact that you were about to kiss my brother yesterday when I walked in on you."

Gemma's eyes shot towards the door. "Shh," she admonished. "What if Edith hears you?"

"Perhaps she will finally acknowledge what we all know."

"Which is?"

Marielle lowered the needlework to her lap and replied, "That you and Stephen are meant for one another."

Gemma knew there was no point in arguing with Marielle. "I do care for Stephen, but I do not presume to know his feelings for me."

"My brother is not one to toy with a woman's affections."

She reached over and placed her needlework onto the table. "I know, which is one of the many things I adore about him."

Marielle grew solemn. "My brother deserves to be happy, and I do believe that you are his best chance at that."

"I want nothing more than for Stephen to be happy."

Marielle smiled, but it didn't quite reach her eyes. "I assume that my brother has shared some of his past with you."

"He has," she replied, seeing no reason to deny it.

"I'm glad, because everyone needs someone to talk to, to confide in," Marielle said. "It is not good to walk this earth alone."

Gemma cocked her head. "Doesn't he confide in you?"

"He has shared a few things with me, but he tries to protect me from the truth." Marielle paused. "He always has."

"Stephen seems to be a good brother."

"He is," Marielle rushed to say. "I thought my heart would never recover once I heard his ship went down."

"You had already suffered so much with the loss of your parents."

"It is true, but everyone has their shares of heartache and sorrow."

"That doesn't make it easier."

"No, it doesn't," Marielle agreed softly.

Balfour stepped into the room and met Gemma's gaze. "Lord Hawkinge has requested a moment of your time, my lady."

Gemma forced a smile to her face, hoping it appeared cordial enough. "Please send him in," she ordered.

Balfour nodded his understanding and left to do her bidding.

Marielle leaned closer and whispered, "You do not seem pleased by Lord Hawkinge's arrival."

"Is it so obvious?"

"It is to me."

Before she could reply, Henry stepped into the room and

his eyes quickly fell to her. There was a seriousness to them that she found to be disconcerting.

"Good morning," he greeted before executing a bow.

"Morning, my lord." Gemma rose and gestured towards Marielle. "Have you been introduced to Lady Hugh Calvert?"

Henry smiled at Marielle. "I have not had the pleasure."

Marielle tipped her head in response. "My lord," she murmured.

Turning his attention back towards her, Henry asked, "May I speak privately with you for a moment?"

Gemma hesitated. She no more wanted to speak privately to him than she wanted a thorn in her boot. But it would be intolerably rude of her to refuse him.

"We could take a turn around the gardens," she finally suggested.

Henry looked pleased by her response. "That sounds wonderful." He offered his arm. "Shall we?"

With reluctance, she placed her hand onto his arm and resisted the urge to snatch her hand back when he moved it to the crook of his arm.

They walked in silence as they headed towards the rear of the townhouse. A footman opened the door, then proceeded to follow them outside.

Once they started walking down a path, Gemma went to remove her hand, but Henry held firm to it.

"I prefer when you are close, my dear," Henry said, glancing at her.

Gemma didn't quite know what to say to that and remained silent. The endearment on his lips grated on her ears, but she didn't dare admit that to him.

"I have decided that it is time for you to return home," Henry remarked. "I indulged you by allowing you to stay as long as you have, but now you are in a position to do irreparable harm to my reputation."

"I disagree…"

Henry spoke over her as if she hadn't said anything. "My coach will arrive this afternoon and you should be home before nightfall."

"That is a kind offer, but…"

Henry stopped and turned to face her. "This is not open to negotiation," he declared. "You will do what I say."

"Do I not get a say in all of this?" she asked defiantly.

"Not any longer," Henry replied. "I have tried to be patient with you but you are intent on ruining your reputation and mine."

"That was never my intention."

"Then what was?" Henry asked. "You are consorting with a shipbuilder for heaven's sake. That man is not even worth your attention."

"I disagree."

Henry looked bored. "What was your intention?" he asked. "Marry a shipbuilder and be shunned by high Society?"

"So be it."

Henry scoffed. "Baldwin would be so disappointed in you right now. He valued duty above all else and you are throwing away everything you have worked for."

"Baldwin did value duty, but he believed in following your heart."

"Your heart?" Henry asked. "What does love have to do with this?"

"Everything."

Henry took a step closer to her. "You are so weak, Gemma," he said. "How can you claim you loved Baldwin as deeply as you did if you fall for the first man that shows you interest?"

"I loved Baldwin."

"Clearly, you did not."

"That is not fair of you to say," Gemma said. "You do not know my heart."

Henry placed his hands on her shoulders and leaned in. "You are fooling yourself," he said. "You don't have to settle for a shipbuilder."

"I am not settling."

"If you are worried about your future, I will continue to care for you, assuming you agree to a few changes to our current situation."

Gemma hoped she had misheard Henry. "Pardon?"

A slow, possessive smile came to Henry's lips. "I have not failed to notice what a beautiful woman you are, and I would be happy to share a bedchamber with you."

She blinked. "You wish for me to be your mistress?"

"I didn't want to rush you, but I can see you are ready now."

Gemma stepped out of his arms. "I am no man's mistress."

Henry looked displeased. "Yet you are whoring yourself with a shipbuilder," he spat out.

"I am doing no such thing!" she exclaimed. "Stephen has been nothing but honorable to me, unlike you."

"Stephen?" Henry asked. "You are calling each other by your given names now?"

"We are," Gemma said.

Henry narrowed his eyes. "I thought you were a sensible woman, but I can see that I was wrong," he said. "You have nothing to your name and have lived off my good graces since my brother died."

"For which I have been most grateful—"

Henry cut her off. "You have a funny way of showing that," he growled. "Does Mr. Wycomb know that you have nothing to your name?"

"I haven't told him that exactly, but I daresay it wouldn't matter."

"No?" Henry asked. "Because you would be a drain on his finances, just as you have been a drain on mine."

"I am still the Countess of Hawkinge."

"That you are," Henry said, grabbing her arm, "and you will do what I say."

Gemma attempted to yank her arm back, but Henry wouldn't release his hold on her. "You are hurting me, Henry," she cried out.

Henry pulled her closer towards him. "It isn't just me that is appalled by your behavior," he said. "Your father has expressed his concerns as well."

"I do not care a whit what my father thinks about me or my behavior," she declared.

Henry's face grew hard. "What happened to you, Gemma?" he growled. "You used to be such an agreeable woman."

As she went to reply, Nathaniel's commanding voice came from behind her. "Release my cousin," he ordered.

Henry dropped his hand, and his face grew expressionless. "We were just having a friendly conversation."

Nathaniel came to stand next to her. "It didn't appear so friendly." He turned to address her. "Are you all right, Gemma?"

Gemma rubbed her reddened arm. "I am now."

Nathaniel frowned as he glanced down at her arm. "This goes without saying, but you are no longer welcome in our home."

"But Gemma is my countess!" Henry declared. "You have no right to keep her from me."

"She is family and will continue to reside with us."

Henry took a menacing step towards Nathaniel. "That means little to me since she belongs to me."

Gemma's mouth dropped open. "I belong to no man."

Nathaniel put his hand out and ushered her behind him. "You heard her," he said. "Gemma is a widow and I do believe has earned the right to answer for herself."

"Where were you this past year and a half?" Henry

demanded. "I was the one that cared for her and gave her a roof over her head."

"That was your duty since she was your brother's wife," Nathaniel said.

"If my brother had cared for her at all, he would have given her a jointure," Henry remarked. "But he didn't. He didn't care for her well-being."

Nathaniel's voice held a warning. "You are out of line."

"I don't think I am," Henry responded. "To prove to Gemma how unimportant she was to him, Baldwin left her a worthless piece of property."

Gemma felt tears burn in the back of her eyes. "What a cruel thing to say," she said as she remained behind Nathaniel.

"It is about time that someone said it," Henry responded.

Nathaniel went to stand toe to toe with Henry. "It is time for you to leave," he ordered.

"Or, what?" Henry huffed. "You will make me?"

Stephen's voice came from further down the path. "We will be happy to assist Lord Hawthorne in removing you from the premises."

Gemma glanced over and saw Stephen and Hugh approaching with purposeful strides. Henry must have realized he was outnumbered because he took a step back.

"Ah, the shipbuilder and gambler have arrived to save the day," Henry mocked.

Stephen came to stand next to her and Gemma felt buoyed by his nearness.

Henry put his hands up. "I am a smart enough man to know when to bow out," he said before turning his attention towards her. "But this is not a goodbye, Gemma."

He didn't bother to wait for her reply. He turned on his heel and walked back towards the townhouse, as if he didn't have a care in the world.

All the men shifted to face her with concerned looks on their faces.

"I am all right," she rushed to assure them. "I am just thankful you arrived when you did."

Nathaniel put his hand on her shoulder. "You will remain here, under our protection, assuming that is what you want."

"It is," Gemma responded.

Her cousin removed his hand. "Very good," he said in approval. "May I walk you back inside?"

Gemma snuck a glance at Stephen. "If it is permissible, I would like to take a turn around the gardens with Stephen."

Nathaniel bobbed his head. "Be mindful that Marielle and my mother are watching you from the drawing room window."

Turning her head towards the window, she saw Marielle waving at her, showing no sign of remorse at being caught staring.

Hugh followed her gaze and chuckled. "My wife is a delight," he said, his words filled with pride.

As her cousins started walking back towards the town-house, Gemma turned her attention towards Stephen and saw that his jaw was clenched.

# Chapter Seventeen

Stephen had never been so furious before. Lord Hawkinge had the nerve, no, the audacity, to hurt Gemma. That could not go unanswered. He wanted to chase after Lord Hawkinge and beat him to a bloody pulp.

As his chest heaved, he felt Gemma's hand on his sleeve. "Are you all right, Stephen?" she asked, her words soft.

"No," he replied honestly. "I want to challenge Lord Hawkinge to a duel for hurting you."

"I am not hurt."

"He had no right to even touch you."

Gemma took a step closer to him. "I agree with you, but no good would come from challenging Lord Hawkinge to a duel."

He shrugged one shoulder. "It would make me feel better."

"Do I need to remind you that duels are illegal?"

"Only if you get caught."

Gemma shook her head. "You are impossible," she said lightly.

Stephen glanced at the drawing room window and saw his sister and Lady Montfort were still watching them with smiles on their faces. He wanted to speak frankly with Gemma, but he didn't want an audience when he did so.

Gemma followed his gaze and suggested, "Perhaps we should take a tour of the gardens, away from prying eyes."

"Precisely what I was thinking."

Gemma removed her hand from his sleeve and he immediately missed the contact. She turned and started walking down the path.

He met her stride and asked, "Has Lord Hawkinge ever hurt you before?"

"No, he hasn't."

Stephen felt relief at her words, but it was short-lived.

Gemma kept her gaze straight ahead. "Henry was always kind to me, too kind, and it made me uncomfortable."

"How can someone be too kind?"

"It never felt genuine to me," she replied. "It only got worse after Baldwin died, but I had little choice in the matter."

"Why was that?"

"The property that Baldwin left me was worthless so I was forced to rely on Henry's good graces."

"How do you know the property is worthless?"

"Henry told me," Gemma replied.

"And you trusted him?"

Gemma glanced over at him. "I had no reason to believe he was lying to me," she said. "Besides, most of the property was entailed so it went to Henry on Baldwin's death."

"I just don't trust the man."

Gemma gave him a weak smile. "I do owe him a debt of gratitude since he took care of me when I was in mourning."

"You owe him nothing, Gemma," Stephen asserted.

"I was so lost after Baldwin died," Gemma said. "I could scarcely get out of bed and I had to force myself to eat."

"That is to be expected."

Gemma felt the familiar tears forming in her eyes and she

blinked them back. "One day he was there, and the next he was gone."

Stephen came to a stop on the path and reached for her arm. As he gently turned her to face him, he said, "You don't have to be brave for me, Gemma."

A tear escaped her eye and rolled down her cheek. "I'm sorry," she murmured. "I thought I had put this behind me."

Stephen reached up and wiped the tear away. "A part of you will always mourn for Baldwin, and I would have it no other way."

"You wouldn't?"

He felt his face soften. "I am pleased to know that you and Baldwin loved each other so dearly. I would never want to take that away from you."

"Henry told me that Baldwin didn't truly love me," Gemma said, her words ending on a sob. "If he had, he wouldn't have given me such a worthless property."

"He was wrong to say that."

Tears filled Gemma's eyes. "But what if he was right?"

Stephen placed his hands on her shoulders and leaned closer. "Do not doubt that Baldwin loved you," he said. "You are worthy of being loved."

Gemma nodded slowly. "I know I sound foolish..." she said, her words trailing off.

"You could never sound foolish to me." He leaned back but he didn't remove his hands. "I just don't want you to give any heed to Lord Hawkinge's words."

"I try not to, especially when he asked for me to be his mistress."

Stephen tensed. "Pardon?" he growled.

Gemma looked unsure. "He wanted me to return back to his country estate with him and be his mistress."

"What did you say?"

Gemma tilted her chin. "I refused him, of course."

Stephen removed his hands and took a step back. "This

cannot go unanswered," he said as he started walking towards the townhouse.

Gemma caught up to him and stepped in front of him. "What do you intend to do?" she asked, placing a hand on his chest.

"I have no choice but to challenge him to a duel."

"And what if he kills you?"

Stephen chuckled. "I doubt that."

"So you would kill him?"

The humor left his face. "What would you have me do?" he asked. "He dishonored you by asking you to be his mistress."

Gemma removed her hand and asked, "Then shouldn't I be the one that challenges him to a duel?"

"But you are a woman."

Placing her hand on her hip, she said, "I can fight my own battles."

"I never meant to imply that—"

She spoke over him. "Henry may be despicable, but he is still my brother-in-law. I do not wish for any harm to come to him."

Stephen let out a heavy sigh. "I will respect your wishes... for now," he said. "I cannot promise that he won't say or do something in the future that will demand satisfaction."

"Most likely he will, but he isn't all bad."

"How can you defend the man?"

A reflective look came to her eyes. "He ordered his servants to place fresh flowers on Baldwin's grave every morning for a whole year. He didn't have to do that but he said it would help ease my burden of picking flowers for Baldwin's grave."

Stephen grated his teeth as he admitted, "That was thoughtful of him."

"It was," Gemma whispered.

He took a step closer to her. "How is it possible that you can see good inside of everyone?" he asked.

"It is easy, if you are looking."

"I must not be looking very hard then."

Gemma held his gaze as she said, "Some people neglect the good that is inside of them, but it is still there."

"Some might call you naive for saying so."

"What would you call me?"

He stepped closer so she had to tilt her head up to look at him. "I would say you are brilliant."

A bright smile came to Gemma's lips. "Careful, your flattery might go to my head."

His eyes dropped to her lips, and he fought the urge to kiss her. This was not the time or place, despite every fiber of his being wanting to pull her into his arms and kiss her senseless.

With great reluctance, he took a step back and cleared his throat. "I was hoping to speak to you about something important."

"It sounds serious," Gemma teased, her smile intact.

"It is." He paused. "I'm afraid I don't know your middle name."

Gemma gave him a curious look. "It is Oleve."

"Oleve?" he asked. "That is an odd middle name."

"It was my mother's surname," Gemma explained. "It was her way of ensuring I would always remember her family."

"It is fitting, then."

Stephen took a deep breath as he found the courage to say his next words. As he opened his mouth, Gemma asked, "What is your middle name?"

"James," he replied. "I was named after my father. With any hope, I will be half the man that he was."

"I didn't know your father, mind you, but I daresay he would be proud of the man that you have become."

"I hope that is the case."

Gemma took a step closer to him. "You are a good man, Stephen. I wish you could see how extraordinary you are."

"I am not extraordinary."

"In my eyes, you are," Gemma said as a faint blush appeared on her cheeks.

Stephen swallowed slowly, knowing this would be the perfect time to offer for her. But he couldn't seem to form the words, not when she was looking at him like that.

How was that possible? He had commanded a crew of hundreds of men, but he couldn't ask the woman he loved a simple question. Although it wasn't a simple question. It was a question that would change the direction of both of their lives.

But he wanted Gemma by his side, always. He couldn't live, not knowing if she was happy. He was the one that wanted to make her happy.

As he opened his mouth, Lady Montfort's voice came from behind them. "It is a lovely day we are having, is it not?" she asked politely but there was a firmness to it.

Stephen took a step back and that is when he noticed how close he had been to Gemma. No wonder why Lady Montfort had injected herself into the conversation.

"It is," he rushed to agree.

Lady Montfort clasped her hands together. "I fear that Gemma has tarried long enough in the gardens and could use a cup of tea."

Gemma nodded. "That sounds delightful."

"Would you care to join us, Mr. Wycomb?" Lady Montfort asked.

Before he could reply, Gemma interjected, "Mr. Wycomb doesn't like tea."

Lady Montfort gave him a bemused look. "I have never heard of such a thing. But we do have biscuits, if that is more your fancy."

"Thank you for that kind offer, but I'm afraid I must depart," Stephen said.

"How disappointing," Lady Montfort remarked. "Will we be seeing you at Lady George Wilcox's soiree this evening?"

As much as Stephen wanted to stay in for the evening, he would rather see Gemma again. If it meant that he had to endure the agony of polite talk for hours, then so be it. Perhaps he could even get her alone in the gardens for long enough to offer for her. His earlier attempt had been rather pathetic, and he knew he would need time to collect his thoughts.

Botheration! Hugh had been right, and that was infuriating. He should have spent more time practicing his speech, knowing his heart was on the line. He didn't want to botch the proposal.

Stephen brought a smile to his lips. "I intend to be there this evening."

Lady Montfort tipped her head. "Very well," she said before turning to address Gemma. "Shall we return to the comfort of the drawing room?"

Gemma offered him a private smile before saying, "That is a fine idea, Aunt Edith."

***

After Stephen had said his goodbyes, Gemma followed her aunt into the drawing room, where Marielle and Dinah were both waiting with smiles on their faces.

Marielle spoke first. "Did my brother finally offer for you?" she asked enthusiastically.

She shook her head. "He did not."

Her face fell. "Whyever not?"

Gemma laughed. "It will happen in due time." At least she hoped it would happen, but she didn't dare admit that.

"It is obvious that you two care for one another," Marielle pressed. "I shall have a word with my brother."

"You will not," Gemma said. "I never want to wonder if the offer was coerced."

Marielle let out an exaggerated sigh. "Have it your way, but I don't know how you can just sit around and wait for Stephen to offer for you."

Dinah gave her sister-in-law an amused look. "It hasn't been very long since Stephen was first introduced to Gemma."

"It feels like forever," Marielle said dramatically.

"Perhaps you need a cup of tea to soothe you," Dinah encouraged.

Marielle nodded. "That is a fine idea," she responded. "Although I don't know how you are so calm about this situation."

"There is no 'situation'," Dinah said.

"I contend there is." Marielle walked over to the settee and sat down. Then she reached for the teapot on the tray and poured herself a cup of tea. "I just want to see my brother happily settled down with Gemma."

Her aunt added, "Trust me, no good would come from you interfering."

Marielle brought the cup to her lips. "All right. I will just sit back and wait an inordinate amount of time for an offer to come," she said dramatically.

"Thank you," Gemma responded.

Her aunt went to sit down next to Marielle before asking, "Now what had Lord Hawkinge so upset with you?"

"He wanted me to return home with him and be his mistress," Gemma revealed.

Stunned faces stared back at her and her aunt was first to recover. "He came out and told you this?" she asked slowly.

"I'm afraid so," Gemma replied.

"The blackguard," her aunt muttered. "You are his brother's wife. The mere thought of that is inconceivable."

Gemma bobbed her head. "I was rather repulsed by the idea myself."

"As well as you should be," Marielle declared. "Does my brother know what Lord Hawkinge asked you?"

"He does, and he wanted to challenge him to a duel," Gemma said.

"It would be no less than he deserved," Marielle stated. "The man has some nerve to even ask you such a question."

"I do agree, but Nathaniel nicely asked Henry to leave and never come back," Gemma said.

Dinah lifted her brow. "That doesn't sound like my husband."

"I daresay I was worried that Nathaniel was going to take matters into his own hands before Hugh and Stephen arrived," Gemma remarked.

"Now that sounds more like my husband," Dinah said with a grin.

Gemma glanced down at her arm and the memory of Henry's touch caused her to shudder. "I am just glad that Nathaniel intervened when he did."

"As am I," Dinah said.

Her aunt leaned forward and retrieved her teacup and saucer. "We will send the coach to collect your things from the Dowager House and you will reside here."

"At least until she marries my brother," Marielle muttered under her breath.

Gemma smiled. "You are incorrigible."

Marielle gave her an innocent look. "Did I say something wrong?"

Her aunt took a sip of her drink, then said, "I do wonder why Mr. Wycomb is biding his time on offering for you."

"Et tu?" Gemma asked.

"It is obvious that you two care for one another," her aunt responded.

Gemma walked around an upholstered armchair and sat

down. "Can we talk about something else… anything else, perhaps?"

Dinah took pity on her and asked, "Who will be attending Lady George Wilcox's soiree this evening?"

"I believe we all are, especially since it is to be the event of the Season," her aunt replied.

Marielle placed her empty teacup onto the tray. "I do not care for Lady George."

"Neither do most people, but she is well connected in high Society," her aunt said. "You would be wise to hold your tongue around her. She is known to be quite a gossip."

"I am well aware," Marielle said. "I have heard that she was rather vocal of her disapproval that a daughter of a ship-builder managed to marry the son of a marquess."

"I wouldn't give it much heed," her aunt advised.

"I don't put much stock in other people's opinions about me," Marielle said.

Her aunt nodded approvingly. "That is most fortunate."

Balfour stepped into the room and announced, "Lady Haddington has come to…"

Before the butler could finish his sentence, Evie stepped into the room with a smile on her face. "Good morning," she greeted.

"You appear to be in a fine mood," Dinah remarked.

"I am," Evie replied as she removed the blue bonnet off her head. "I was able to get Lord Easton to donate a substantial sum to Georgie's orphanage."

"How were you able to do such a feat?" Dinah asked.

"Would you believe me if I said that I asked nicely?" Evie smirked.

Dinah gave her sister a knowing look. "I would not."

Evie waved her hand dismissively in front of her. "Regardless, the orphanage has enough funding to run for many years to come."

Dinah turned towards Gemma. "Georgie is always looking for more patrons, if you are interested."

"I'm afraid I wouldn't have anything to contribute," Gemma said reluctantly.

Evie gave her a curious look. "Did your husband not leave you a jointure?"

"He did not," Gemma replied. "Henry said that proves that Baldwin didn't care for me as much as he claimed."

"That is poppycock!" her aunt declared. "Baldwin adored you."

"I know, but Henry was just trying to get a rise from me," Gemma said.

"Why was he trying to do that?" Evie asked.

Gemma winced. "He was trying to convince me to be his mistress," she admitted.

Evie visibly tensed. "What a cod's head!"

"I won't disagree with you," Gemma said.

Dinah interrupted, "None of us will, but, dear sister, do try to be less vulgar."

With a laugh, Evie came to sit down on an armchair. "I did not mean to hurt your delicate constitution."

Dinah went to address Gemma. "You must excuse my sister," she started, "she was raised in a barn."

"I find her to be a delight," Gemma admitted.

Her aunt reached for the teapot and asked, "Would you care for a cup of tea, Evie?"

"I would, thank you," Evie replied.

Dinah shifted in her seat to face Evie. "Not that I am complaining, but what brings you by today?"

"I wanted to ensure you were well," Evie said as she accepted the teacup from her aunt.

Dinah placed a hand on her stomach. "Today has been a good day," she shared. "I have only thrown up once."

"That is wonderful news," Evie said.

Dinah seemed to beam with pride as she shared, "Nathaniel has been so attentive of me as of late."

"As well as he should," her aunt said. "His life will never be the same once your baby is born."

A yawn escaped Gemma's lips and she rushed to cover it with her hand before anyone noticed. But she was not so lucky.

Her aunt gave her an odd look. "Did you not sleep well, Gemma?"

"I'm afraid not," Gemma replied.

"Then you must go rest before Lady George's soiree," her aunt counseled. "Her social events go well into the morning."

Gemma rose. "I do believe I will heed your advice."

As she walked out of the drawing room, she heard a knock at the main door and watched as Balfour hurried across the entry hall. The door was opened, and she heard Balfour say, "You are no longer welcome here, my lord."

Henry's disgruntled voice came from the threshold. "I demand to see Lady Hawkinge."

"I'm afraid that is impossible," Balfour said. "Lord Hawthorne gave strict orders that you were to be denied entry."

"That is unacceptable!" Henry exclaimed. "Lady Hawkinge is family!"

Gemma knew that Henry wouldn't leave without a fight and she saw no harm in speaking to him at the door.

She walked over to the door and said, "It is all right, Balfour. I will speak to Lord Hawkinge."

Balfour frowned. "But, my lady, Lord Hawthorne gave strict orders to turn him away."

"I am well aware, but it would be best if I spoke to him before he makes a scene."

A reluctant look came to Balfour's face before he took a step back. She was grateful that he remained close.

Gemma turned to face Henry. "What is it that you want, Henry?" she asked bluntly.

Henry gave her an apologetic look. "I wanted to apologize for my disreputable behavior earlier and do hope you will forgive me."

"You hurt me," she said, crossing her arms over her chest.

"That was not my intention," Henry insisted. "I was just trying to get your attention."

"And you got it, but I was not interested in what you were offering."

Henry had the decency to look ashamed. "That is why I have come here with a peace offering."

"Which is?"

Reaching into his jacket pocket, Henry pulled out a piece of paper. "Considering the circumstances, I thought it would be prudent if I bought your property for five thousand pounds."

"Five thousand pounds," she repeated back in surprise. "I thought the property is worthless."

"It is, but consider it a gesture of goodwill," Henry said.

Gemma uncrossed her arms and accepted the paper that Henry extended towards her. "Why would you even want the property?" she asked as she reviewed the contract in her hand.

"I don't, but I want to help you," Henry replied. "When, and if, you marry, I want you to have funds at your disposal."

"That is most thoughtful of you."

"Are we in agreement, then?"

Gemma brought her gaze up and saw that Henry was smiling like he was offering her a grand treat. But she wasn't ready to give up the one thing that Baldwin had given her, even if it wasn't worth anything.

She handed him the paper back. "I'm sorry, but I do believe I will keep the property."

Henry's brow shot up. "Why would you do something so foolish?" he demanded.

"I just feel—"

He cut her off. "You won't get a better offer than mine!" he exclaimed.

"It is the only thing I have left of Baldwin."

With a scoff, Henry declared, "I hadn't taken you for the sentimental type, considering you have already forgotten Baldwin."

"I have not forgotten Baldwin," she asserted.

Henry tightened his hold on the paper in his hand. "You would be a fool not to take this offer," he said. "Baldwin would be rolling over in his grave, knowing you turned down all that money."

Gemma tilted her chin. "My answer is no."

Henry's right eye twitched. "You will regret this, Gemma," he said in a low, menacing voice.

"I don't think I will." Gemma reached for the door. "Good day, Henry."

Before he could say another word, she took a step back and closed the door. Only then did she let out the breath of air that she had been holding.

"Are you all right, my lady?" Balfour asked with a concerned look on his face.

Gemma bobbed her head. "I will be."

## Chapter Eighteen

Gemma sat in the darkened coach as she kept her gaze firmly on the window. She wasn't in a mood to converse. Her mind kept reeling as to why Henry was so angry about her not selling the property to him. What was he about? Was it truly a generous offer or was there more to the property than Henry had let on? What if it wasn't as worthless as he had led her to believe? Could Henry be keeping other things from her, as well? Perhaps it was time to seek out Baldwin's solicitor and make some inquiries.

She adjusted the sleeves of her primrose-colored ballgown and resisted the urge to sigh. She was dressed in a gown that she could scarcely afford, her hair was neatly coiffed, and she had every reason to be happy. But Henry's last words still haunted her. Would she regret not selling the property to him? Was she a fool to pass up such a large sum of money?

Nathaniel's voice broke through her musings. "You are quiet this evening, Cousin."

Gemma met his gaze. "I'm afraid I have a lot on my mind."

"Anything you wish to share?"

"Not at this time."

Nathaniel exchanged a look with Dinah before saying, "I understand that Lord Hawkinge returned to speak to you."

Gemma shifted uncomfortably in her seat. "He did."

"May I ask what he wished to speak to you about?" Nathaniel pressed.

"He wanted me to sell my property to him, but I didn't think it was prudent of me to do so," Gemma said.

"Why is that?" Nathaniel asked. "I thought the property was worthless."

"It is, at least that is what Henry told me," Gemma responded.

"You have reason to doubt him?"

Gemma winced. "I never did before, but I think it might be best if I become well-acquainted with the property."

"Would you care for me to make some inquiries?" Nathaniel asked. "I can speak to Baldwin's solicitor and see if he has any insight into this."

Gemma nodded. "I had the same thought."

Nathaniel smiled. "Great minds think alike."

"Thank you, Nathaniel," Gemma said.

Dinah spoke up. "Do you have any desire to sell the property?"

Gemma shook her head, causing the curls that framed her face to sway back and forth. "I do not," she replied. "It was the last thing that Baldwin gave me, and he did so for a reason."

"You have never visited the property?" Dinah asked.

"I have not," Gemma admitted. "I know I should have, but I couldn't quite bring myself to do so."

Dinah's face softened. "You do not have to explain yourself to me."

"But I feel as if I must," Gemma said.

"Perhaps you are just trying to convince yourself," Dinah responded.

The coach came to a jerking stop in front of a grand

townhouse and Gemma saw the line of people slowly making their way inside.

"This is a *crush*," Gemma said.

"Lady George's social events do not disappoint," Dinah shared. "She usually invites the highest echelon of high Society."

Gemma had to wonder if that was the case then why was Stephen invited. Not that she was complaining, but he didn't exactly hail from the aristocracy.

The coach door opened, and Nathaniel exited first. After he had assisted them out of the coach, he offered his arm to Dinah.

Gemma tugged on the ends of her long, white gloves. For some odd reason, she was rather anxious about this evening. Which was absurd. What did she have to be nervous about? Furthermore, Stephen would be here, and his presence always set her at ease.

"Cousin?" Nathaniel said.

Gemma brought her gaze up and saw that Nathaniel and Dinah were both watching her with concerned looks on their faces.

"I'm afraid I was woolgathering… again," Gemma said.

Nathaniel didn't look convinced by her explanation. "Shall we go inside?"

"That is a wonderful idea," Gemma replied.

They walked towards the main door and saw that Lady George was there to greet them in the entry hall. She was a tall woman with beady eyes that seemed to follow you wherever you went.

Lady George's eyes lit up when she saw Gemma. "Lady Hawkinge," she greeted cheerfully. "I am so glad that you could attend this evening."

Gemma dropped into a curtsy. "I do thank you for inviting me."

Lady George leaned closer but didn't lower her voice. "Mr.

Wycomb already arrived, and I can see why you have expressed interest in him. He is quite handsome, is he not?"

Not liking the direction of this conversation, Gemma forced a smile to her lips and attempted to change the subject. "You have a lovely home," she said.

Unfortunately, Lady George did not take the bait. "I am pleased that you have overlooked his lowly status. Every man should be judged according to his works."

"I agree," Gemma said.

"You agree that you overlooked his lowly status or that he should be judged according to his works?" Lady George pressed.

"The latter."

Lady George looked pleased by her words. "I, for one, would never marry a man so below my station, but I applaud you for following your heart. Although, it doesn't hurt that Mr. Wycomb is quite wealthy and you will not lack for anything."

Gemma did not like the fact that Lady George was prying into her personal life, knowing that she was quite the gossip-monger amongst the *ton*. She had little doubt that anything she said would be repeated so she needed to choose her next words carefully.

"Mr. Wycomb and I do not have an understanding," Gemma said. There. That was the truth.

"Yet," Lady George said smugly, taking a step back.

Tired of this line of questioning, Gemma gestured towards Dinah and asked, "Are you acquainted with Lady Hawthorne?"

Lady George tipped her head. "I am."

Gemma took the opportunity to slip away, and her eyes roamed over the room until they landed on Stephen. He was conversing with Hugh and Marielle near the rear of the room. He was dapperly dressed in a black jacket with a white cravat. His dark hair was brushed forward and his sideburns had recently been trimmed.

A smile came to her lips. Stephen was her future; she was sure of it. She had only loved two men in her life. One she had lost to illness, and she refused to lose the other by not being bold. He had offered for her once and she'd turned him down. Perhaps it was time for her to offer for him.

As she took a step towards Stephen, her stepmother broke through the crowd and approached her, wearing a gown that left little to the imagination.

"I am glad that you are here," Kitty said. "Your father wishes to speak to you in the gardens."

Gemma furrowed her brow. "May I ask why?"

Kitty stepped closer and lowered her voice. "He said it was of utmost importance," she asserted.

Gemma had no real desire to speak to her father, but she thought it would be best to get it over with. Most likely, he intended to lecture her on who she associated with.

"Where is he?"

Kitty looked pleased. "He is in the rear of the gardens, by the oak tree."

"Pray tell, why couldn't we have spoken in here?" Gemma asked.

"He didn't want any prying ears around," Kitty replied, shifting her gaze towards Lady George.

Gemma had to admit that her father wasn't wrong. It would be much more private if they spoke in the gardens.

"Will you inform him that I will be out in a moment?" Gemma asked.

Kitty frowned. "You intend to make your father wait?"

Gemma glanced over at Stephen and noticed that he was watching her with a curious look on his face. She offered him a weak smile before she turned back to her stepmother.

"I suppose I will go now," Gemma said.

Kitty took a step back and announced, "I shall wait for you here."

"You aren't joining us?"

With a shake of her head, Kitty replied, "He wanted to speak to you privately."

Gemma thought that was rather odd, but then again, her father did a lot of things that she didn't quite understand.

As she started walking towards the French doors that led into the gardens, she saw that Stephen was approaching her from the opposite direction.

He came to a stop in front of her. "Where are you going?"

Gemma glanced outside as she replied, "My father wanted to speak to me in the gardens."

"Now?"

She shrugged. "He claims it is of 'utmost importance'."

"But you aren't sure?"

"My father tends to exaggerate things," Gemma replied. "I am sure he just wants to chastise me about spending time with you."

Stephen perused the length of her. "You look lovely, Gemma."

Gemma smiled. "As do you."

He returned her smile. "A man generally does not like being called 'lovely'."

"My apologies," she replied. "Would you have preferred it if I had said 'handsome'?"

"That is much more preferable." He took a step closer and asked, "Will you sit by me during the music number?"

Gemma pretended that she was being put out. "I suppose I have to sit somewhere. It might as well be by you."

Stephen chuckled. "You are most kind." His eyes shifted towards Lady George. "It would appear that Lady George is watching us."

"I do believe we were both invited to be the entertainment for the evening," Gemma said, following his gaze to see Lady George was, in fact, staring at them with a knowing smile on her lips.

"It appears that way."

Gemma let out a sigh as she brought her gaze back to meet his. "I best go speak to my father."

"Would you care for me to escort you?"

"I would, but it is better if I go alone," Gemma replied. "My father doesn't exactly approve of you."

Stephen grew solemn. "I care little of what your father thinks of me. I only care what *you* think of me."

Gemma brought her gaze back to meet his. "I find you to be tolerable," she said lightly.

"Just tolerable?" he asked.

She smirked. "More than tolerable."

Stephen's eyes dropped to her lips. "I was hoping for 'more than tolerable'," he said in a hoarse voice.

Gemma's breath hitched. He already had her heart, but she didn't dare admit that, not here, not now.

Taking a step back, Stephen asked, "Would you care to take a turn around the gardens after you speak to your father?" He paused. "There is something that I wish to ask you."

Gemma nodded, not trusting her voice. She wanted nothing more than to remain here with Stephen, but she had her father that she had to attend to first.

Stephen's lips twitched as he watched her. "If we keep standing here, staring at one another, I have no doubt that gossips' tongues will start wagging."

His words caused her to snap back to reality. "You are right," she said, pleased she'd found her voice. "I shall be back in a moment."

"I will be waiting," Stephen responded.

Gemma headed out onto the veranda and down the path towards the rear of the gardens. She arrived at the giant oak tree but she saw no sign of her father.

Where was he? Perhaps he grew tired of waiting for her and went back inside.

The snap of a twig came from behind her, but before she could turn around, everything went black.

———⟶———

Stephen remained rooted in his spot as he watched Gemma walk down the path in the gardens. He wished that she would have allowed him to escort her to her father, but he knew it wasn't his place to do so. Once Gemma was out of his view, he walked over to the drink table and picked up a glass of champagne. He took a long sip before he placed it on the tray of a passing servant. Then he made his way through the crowd towards his sister and Hugh.

As he came to a stop next to Marielle, she asked, "Where is Gemma?"

"She went to speak to her father in the gardens," Stephen replied.

Hugh gave him an odd look. "Are you sure she was meeting with her father?" he asked. "I only ask because I saw Lord Winsley enter the card's room just a short time ago."

"That is what she told me," Stephen said as his eyes darted to the French doors that led to the gardens. "Perhaps I should go check on her."

"That might be for the best," Marielle encouraged.

Stephen didn't need to be told twice. He made his way towards the French doors and even the cool night air did little to squash the growing unease that was forming in the pit of his stomach. He hurried down the path, his eyes roaming over the gardens, but he saw no sign of Gemma.

Where was she? She couldn't have just disappeared.

As he arrived at the fence in the back, Stephen saw that a gate was slightly ajar but there were no obvious signs of foul play. He asked himself if she had left willingly.

No. She wouldn't have done such a thing. He was sure of

that. Which meant that someone forced her to go with them and he had a pretty good idea of who was involved with this- Lord Winsley. Why else would he have arranged a meeting with his daughter in the gardens under the darkness of night?

With determined strides, Stephen passed through the gardens and stepped into the ballroom. He pushed his way through the crowd as he headed towards the card's room.

As he was about to head inside, Hugh stepped in front of him and asked, "What has happened?"

"Gemma is gone," Stephen replied as he tried to sidestep Hugh, "and I am going to go speak to Lord Winsley."

Hugh stepped to the side and continued to block his path. "Come with me," he ordered.

"Why would I do such a thing?" Stephen asked. "Lord Winsley knows something about Gemma's disappearance. I am sure of it."

"We should go speak to Nathaniel before we do anything," Hugh encouraged.

Stephen knew that Hugh made a good point, but he wasn't thinking clearly. He just wanted to get Gemma back and he refused to let Lord Winsley get away with abducting his daughter.

Hugh must have anticipated what he intended to do because he said, "You can't go into the card's room and accuse Lord Winsley of abducting his daughter without proof. You will be thrown out of the soiree."

"I don't care," Stephen grumbled. "I only care that Gemma is returned, unharmed."

"Then we must go speak to Nathaniel. He will know what to do," Hugh asserted. "Besides, he is only a short distance away. What is the harm in speaking to him?"

Stephen glanced over his shoulder and saw Hawthorne and Dinah were conversing with Lord and Lady Haddington. Normally, he would groan at the sight of Haddington, but he might prove himself useful this evening.

Turning on his heel, Stephen approached Hawthorne with a resolute stride.

Hawthorne had a smile on his lips, but it slipped when Stephen came to stand next to him. "What is wrong?"

"Gemma is missing," Stephen admitted.

"Missing?" Hawthorne asked, his eyes scanning the room. "But we only just arrived."

Stephen nodded. "I spoke to her and she informed me that her father wished to speak to her in the gardens, but Hugh saw Lord Winsley enter the card's room," he explained. "When I rushed outside, Gemma was nowhere to be found."

Lady Haddington stepped forward and lowered her voice. "I will go see if I can see any signs of a struggle."

"I looked, but I didn't see any," Stephen said. "The gate door was slightly ajar, though."

Lady Haddington acknowledged his words with a tip of her head. "I understand, but I want to see for myself."

As Lady Haddington walked off, Hawthorne turned his attention towards Haddington. "We need to go speak to Lord Winsley."

"I agree," Haddington said.

Stephen glanced between them, having no intention of staying back. "I want to go."

"I don't think that is a good idea," Hawthorne said. "I daresay that you are too close to this."

"And you aren't?" Stephen asked.

Hawthorne gave him a pointed look. "If we allow you to accompany us, you must let us do the talking."

Stephen would agree to just about anything if it meant he could help Gemma. "I can agree to that."

Hawthorne shifted his gaze towards Hugh. "Would you care to join us, as well?"

Hugh shook his head. "I will see to escorting Dinah and Marielle home this evening. I believe that will be a better use of my time."

"Very good, then," Hawthorne said before he started walking towards the card's room.

Once they stepped inside the square room, Stephen's eyes roamed the room until they landed on Lord Winsley. He was playing at a table near the front, and by the looks of it, he was losing.

Stephen didn't wait for Hawthorne or Haddington as he had promised but quickly skirted the tables until he stopped next to Lord Winsley.

Lord Winsley glanced up at him and annoyance flashed on his features. "What do you want?" he grumbled.

"We need to talk," Stephen growled.

With a huff, Lord Winsley said, "I think not." He turned his attention back to the cards in his hand. "Go away. I have nothing to say to you."

Stephen remained rooted in his spot. "It wasn't a request."

Lord Winsley tossed down his cards and shoved back his chair. Rising, he narrowed his eyes. "If you want my permission to marry my daughter, I will never grant it. Ever!"

"That is not what I need to speak to you about," Stephen said.

Hawthorne's voice came from next to him. "Forgive us, Winsley, but we were hoping for a moment of your time."

Lord Winsley shifted his gaze towards Hawthorne. "What is this about, Hawthorne?" he asked.

Hawthorne gave him an apologetic smile. "It will make sense soon enough, but we need to speak privately."

"Does he have to come?" Lord Winsley asked, gesturing at Stephen.

"I'm afraid so," Hawthorne said.

Lord Winsley looked like he was going to refuse Hawthorne's request, but to Stephen's pleasant surprise, he nodded. "We can speak in the parlor."

No one said anything as they followed Lord Winsley out of

the card's room and down the hall. Once they arrived at the parlor, Hawthorne closed the door behind them.

Haddington crossed his arms over his chest. "Where is your daughter?" he asked bluntly.

Lord Winsley gave him a blank look. "How should I know?"

Stephen took a step closer to the disgruntled lord. "Gemma informed me that she went out into the gardens to speak to you."

"That is absurd. I have been in the card's room since I arrived," Lord Winsley said.

"Then how do you explain her disappearance?" Stephen pressed.

Lord Winsley scoffed. "Perhaps she was trying to get away from you," he said. "It would have been the first sensible thing my daughter has done since she arrived in Town."

Stephen clenched his jaw. "Gemma has no reason to run from me."

"Doesn't she?" Lord Winsley asked. "You are just a ship-builder, and you aren't worthy of her time or notice."

As he took a commanding step towards Lord Winsley, Hawthorne moved towards him and placed a hand on his shoulder. "Let us handle this, Stephen," he ordered. His tone brokered no argument.

"Very well," Stephen grumbled. The only reason why he relented was because he knew what Hawthorne and Haddington were capable of.

Hawthorne removed his hand from Stephen's shoulder and addressed Lord Winsley. "You are going to have to do better than that. Where is she?"

"Why are you asking me?" Lord Winsley asked. "I'm afraid I haven't spoken to my daughter in days."

"If you didn't arrange to meet with Gemma in the gardens, then someone must have lured her out there under the guise of speaking with you," Hawthorne said. "Do you know who would do such a thing?"

"I do not," Lord Winsley said.

Haddington uncrossed his arms. "You are trying my patience," he stated. "We need answers, and we need them now."

Lord Winsley grew defiant. "I do not have to answer your questions."

"You do," Haddington said as he retrieved a pistol from behind him. "It is simple- tell us the truth or you won't leave this room alive."

Lord Winsley stared at Haddington in disbelief. "You cannot be in earnest!"

"Lady Hawkinge is missing, and we don't have time for games," Haddington said. "Every moment we waste in here is a moment that we lose trying to find her."

Lord Winsley put his hands up. "I know nothing about her disappearance. In fact, I am as outraged as you are."

"Are you?" Hawthorne asked. "You don't seem outraged."

"Well, I assure you that I am," Lord Winsley said. "Gemma is my only child and I cannot lose her."

Stephen interjected, "Your actions speak otherwise."

Lord Winsley glared at him. "You know not what you are speaking of."

"You abandoned her when she needed you the most," Stephen asserted.

"She abandoned me!" Lord Winsley spat out. "I may not have been the most attentive father, but she was the one that decided to cut ties with me."

Stephen opened his mouth to object but Hawthorne spoke first. "We are not here to rehash the past," he said. "We just need to know where Gemma is."

Lord Winsley tossed his arms up in the air. "I do not know!" he exclaimed. "And I resent the accusation."

"I resent everything about you," Stephen said.

"The feeling is mutual," Lord Winsley shouted.

A knock came at the door before it was opened and Lady Haddington and Lady Winsley stepped into the room.

Lady Haddington closed the door behind her and said, "I had the most intriguing conversation with Lady Winsley." She turned towards Lady Winsley. "Would you like to tell them or should I?"

"Tell us what?" Lord Winsley asked, confusion on his face. "What is she talking about, my dear?"

Lady Winsley pressed her lips together. "I don't rightly know."

"It would appear that your wife was involved with your daughter's disappearance," Lady Haddington announced.

"I think not," Lord Winsley said. "Kitty would never do something so underhanded. Isn't that right?"

With a slight wince, Lady Winsley replied, "I had to do something before Gemma threw her life away by marrying a shipbuilder."

Lord Winsley's expression grew crestfallen. "Say it isn't so."

Lady Winsley tilted her chin stubbornly. "Lord Hawkinge came to me and explained everything," she said. "If we didn't intercede when we did, then our names would be dragged through the mud."

"So you arranged for Lord Hawkinge to abduct her?" Lord Winsley asked.

"With good reason," Lady Winsley said. "They are going to get married."

Lord Winsley lifted his brow. "It is illegal to marry your brother's wife or had you forgotten that detail?"

"Only in England," Lady Winsley responded. "They are going to sail to France and get married."

"But we are at war with France," Lord Winsley pointed out.

Lady Winsley bobbed her head. "Lord Hawkinge has found a merchant that has agreed to take them to France."

Lord Winsley stared at his wife in astonishment. "You are mad."

"I am not," Lady Winsley responded. "I did this for us."

"No, you did it for *you*," Lord Winsley declared. "Did you not consider the scandal that would ensue when Gemma marries Lord Hawkinge?"

"It is far more preferable than marrying a shipbuilder," Lady Winsley stated.

Hawthorne interrupted, "Where is Gemma?"

Lady Winsley clasped her hands in front of her. "I won't say."

"Oh, dear," Lady Haddington sighed. "Do you truly think I won't force you to talk?"

Fear shone in Lady Winsley's eyes. "There is no need for threats… again."

"I think there is," Lady Haddington said. "You see, Gemma is a friend of mine, and I won't allow her to be forced into an unwanted marriage."

"She is far better off with Lord Hawkinge than with Mr. Wycomb," Lady Winsley spat out.

"I disagree," Lady Haddington said as she removed the pistol from the folds of her gown. "I will only ask once and I expect the truth. Where is Gemma?"

Lady Winsley glanced down at the pistol, her face growing white. "You wouldn't kill me," she said, her words lacking conviction.

Lady Haddington smiled. "You are right. I won't kill you, but I will shoot you until you confess the truth."

"People will come running when they hear the pistols discharging," Lady Winsley said.

"Then I shall strive to shoot you quickly." Lady Haddington cocked her pistol and pointed it at Lady Winsley's leg. "Shall we begin?"

Lady Winsley threw her hands up. "Wait!" she exclaimed. "I will tell you where they are, but you must promise not to shoot me."

Lady Haddington lowered the pistol to her side. "I can agree to that."

"They are at the docks, near Whistleton Street," Lady Winsley said. "Lord Hawkinge is keeping Gemma on the *Swiftsure* until they depart, but I daresay you are too late. The ship should have departed by now."

As Lady Haddington slipped the pistol back into the folds of her gown, she said, "If I find that you lied to me, I can promise you won't like what happens next."

"I didn't lie," Lady Winsley rushed out.

Lord Winsley went to stand in front of his wife. "Why, Kitty?" he demanded. "Why would you betray me like this?"

"I was tired of one scandal after the next," Kitty murmured, lowering her gaze.

Haddington placed his pistol into the waistband of his trousers. "It would be best if we depart at once for the docks," he said as he walked towards the door. "We will formulate a plan in the coach."

## Chapter Nineteen

Gemma felt the rocking of the ship before she even opened her eyes. The throbbing in her head only seemed to intensify with every movement. She reached up to the back of her head where she felt a large bump and her hair was matted with dried blood. What had happened? The last thing she remembered was waiting for her father in the gardens at Lady George's townhouse. Had he abducted her? If so, for what purpose?

With great reluctance, she opened her eyes and saw that she was inside of a cabin. It was dark and dank, but the moonlight did stream through the porthole window, casting shadows around the room. A lone desk sat against the other wall.

Gemma shifted uncomfortably on the thin straw mattress as she tried to find the strength to sit up. She had to find a way out of here. Although, she didn't quite know where "here" was.

As she sat up, she heard the sound of booted footsteps coming from behind the closed door. She hoped this meant she was going to get some answers.

The door was opened, and Henry walked in with a candle

in his hand. He wore no jacket and the sleeves on his white shirt were rolled up. She had never seen him in such a state of undress before, especially since he prided himself on his appearance.

Henry approached the bed and smiled down upon her. "I am glad to see you are awake," he said. "I have never hit anyone over the back of the head before, and I feared I had hit you too hard."

"What am I doing here?" she asked.

"Isn't it obvious?" he asked. "I abducted you and we are to be wed."

Gemma shook her head, and she instantly regretted the motion. "I think not," she said. "I won't marry you."

"You will," Henry pressed. "You have no choice in the matter."

"It is illegal for us to marry."

"Not in France," Henry said. "I hired a nice merchant to take us there so we can be wed."

"But we are at war with France."

Henry gave her a smug look. "I assure you that his documentation is in order."

Gemma rested her back against the wall and winced slightly at the motion. "Regardless, I will never marry you."

The smile on Henry's face dimmed. "I had hoped you would be reasonable about this," he said, "but I see that you will need some convincing."

Henry placed the candle down on the desk. Then he retrieved the chair and positioned it near the bed. As he sat down, he continued. "You will marry me or else I will kill your beloved Mr. Wycomb."

Gemma gasped. "You wouldn't dare."

"I would, gladly," Henry said. "That man has been nothing but a nuisance to me. I even tried to warn him off of you by sending that ruffian to threaten him, but he wasn't smart enough to heed my warning."

"Why would you even wish to marry me?" Gemma asked.

Henry leaned forward and tucked a strand of her hair behind her ear. As his finger lingered on her skin, she resisted the urge to shudder. "Because you are mine," he finally said.

"I belong to no man," she said as she jerked back.

He chuckled. "I will take great pleasure in taming you, my dear. You will fall in line or there will be dire consequences for you."

"I don't understand why you are doing this," Gemma said. "You are an earl, and you could have your pick of women."

Henry studied her for a moment before saying, "You should have been mine, but my brother tricked you into marrying him."

"He did no such thing," Gemma asserted. "I loved Baldwin."

"If I had been the one to dance with you that evening, you would have fallen in love with me instead," Henry said.

"Do you take me to be so fickle with my heart?"

"You weren't interested in me because I was a second son," Henry said. "You wanted a title, just as all women do."

Gemma frowned. "I did not marry Baldwin for a title."

Henry huffed. "I doubt that," he said. "I was upset at first, but then I noticed you flirting with me."

Her eyes grew wide. "I did no such thing."

"You can deny it, but you would offer me private smiles," Henry said. "I knew it was your way of telling me how you truly felt about me."

Gemma let out a soft sigh. "You are confused—"

Henry spoke over her. "No!" he shouted. "It is you that is confused. You can pretend that you didn't seduce me with your eyes, but I know the truth."

"I loved your brother," she attempted.

"Not as much as you loved me," Henry declared. "Which is why I knew I had to get rid of him."

Fearing she'd misheard him, Gemma asked, "I beg your pardon?"

Henry reached for her hand and gripped it tightly. "Baldwin was in the way of our happiness," he said. "I did this for us so we could finally be together."

Gemma felt dread in her stomach as she asked, "What did you do?"

"I poisoned Baldwin," Henry admitted proudly.

"That is why you rushed his burial and refused to let a doctor examine him," Gemma said.

Henry brought her hand up to his lips. "That is one advantage of being an earl. No one even dared to question me when I requested an immediate burial."

"You are mad."

Henry's face grew hard as he dropped her hand. "I am no such thing," he said. "You wanted this; you wanted me!"

Gemma knew that she had to proceed cautiously or else she would push Henry too hard. She didn't want to make him more upset than he already was. He had already admitted to killing Baldwin and he had no qualms about it. It made her wonder if he would kill her just as easily.

"Henry..."

In a swift motion, Henry grabbed her arm and jerked her forward. "Do not attempt to pacify me, Gemma!" he exclaimed, his foul breath on her cheek. "You belong to me now."

"I won't marry you, no matter what you do to me."

Henry scoffed. "You would rather marry a common ship-builder."

Gemma remained silent.

He shook her. "Answer me!"

"I would, assuming he asks," Gemma said.

Henry released her and leaned back. "Then you leave me little choice in the matter." He rose. "Mr. Wycomb must die."

"Please, you mustn't hurt him."

Henry glared down at her. "I know you care for him, but your affection is misplaced. We are now free to be together and I won't lose you to someone that isn't even worthy to lick my boots."

Gemma knew she should bite her tongue, but she couldn't stand by and let Henry insult Stephen. "Stephen is twice the man that you are."

Henry reared his hand back and slapped her hard across the face. "Why do you make me hurt you?" he asked.

Gemma brought her hand up and placed it over her throbbing cheek. "You murdered my husband," she said. "I will never be with you."

The lines around Henry's lips tightened. "You will come to terms with it and then we will be blissfully happy. You will see."

A knock came at the door and a look of annoyance flashed on Henry's face. He walked over to the door and tossed it open. "What do you want?"

A lanky man in ill-fitting clothes stood at the doorway. "The captain says we can't leave until tomorrow morning."

"That is unacceptable!" Henry shouted. "We need to leave tonight."

"But the tide is not in our favor," the man replied.

"That matters little to me."

The lanky man glanced over Henry's shoulder at her with a look of mild curiosity. "A few hours won't make a difference, will it?"

Henry grew irate. "Inform the captain that I wish to speak to him."

"The captain doesn't like being summoned."

"I am paying him a lot of money and he will do what I say."

The man shrugged. "I will tell him, but I don't know if it will make a lick of difference."

"Just do as I say," Henry growled before slamming the door shut.

Gemma watched as Henry started to pace the small cabin with a furrowed brow. She knew once the ship departed she would have no chance of escape. She would be completely at Henry's whim, and she couldn't abide by that. Not after what he had just revealed.

Henry stopped pacing and glared at her. "This is all your fault!"

"My fault?" she repeated back in surprise.

"You should have never gone to London for the Season," Henry said. "Everything was just the way it should be in Hawkinge."

"In what way?"

"You would have become my mistress and you would never have learned the truth of your property."

"What truth?"

Henry ran a hand through his hair. "The property that Baldwin left you actually produces about ten thousand pounds a year."

Gemma's mouth dropped open. "But you told me it was worthless."

"What else was I supposed to do?" Henry asked. "I could barely keep the estate afloat and Baldwin left you the most valuable piece of property he owned."

"You could have told me the truth."

Henry gave her an amused look. "And lose out on the money the property produced?" he asked. "I think not."

"I would have helped you."

With a wave of his hand, Henry said, "It is a moot point. Once we are married, the property will belong to me, as it rightly should have from the beginning."

Gemma stared up at Henry with disdain. He had wanted her to believe that Baldwin had left her with nothing, proving that he cared little for her. But the opposite was true. Baldwin had willed her a valuable piece of property; one that would ensure she was well taken care of.

"You are a horrible person," Gemma said.

Henry's eyes narrowed. "You will watch your tongue."

"I will not!" Gemma exclaimed. "Baldwin loved me, and he proved it by leaving me that property."

"My brother was blinded by his affection towards you." Henry came to stop in front of the bed. "He should have never left you that property."

"But he did."

Henry leaned forward, causing her to shift on the bed to create more distance between them. "It won't matter soon enough," he said.

Gemma tried to keep her face expressionless, but she was afraid of Henry. She thought she had known him, but she was wrong. She had no idea that he was capable of such terrible things.

Henry's eyes roamed over her face, and they landed on her lips. "Once we depart from London, I intend to take what is mine."

"I am not yours," she said in a firm voice.

A cruel smile appeared on his lips. "We shall see."

A knock came at the door and the smile disappeared. Henry leaned back and walked over to the door. As he opened it, he asked, "What is it?"

The same lanky man stood there. "The captain will see you now."

"It is about time." Henry turned to face her. "Do not fret. I will return shortly, my dear."

After Henry departed from the cabin, Gemma jumped up from the bed and walked over to the desk. She pulled out the drawers but saw nothing that would help defend herself from Henry's advances.

Gemma walked over to the porthole window and stared out. They were still docked, but for how long? She knew that

Stephen would be looking for her, and she hoped that he would find her in time.

------

Stephen felt every rotation of the wheels as the coach moved closer to the docks. This was all his fault. He should have challenged Lord Hawkinge to a duel when he discovered he had asked Gemma to be his mistress. Then, Lord Hawkinge wouldn't have been in a position to abduct Gemma.

He would do whatever it took to get Gemma back. He would fight for her, harder than he had ever before. She had changed his life, every aspect of it for the better. He couldn't lose her. He wouldn't. She was the reason why he didn't quite feel so broken anymore.

Hawthorne's voice broke up the silence in the coach. "What is the plan?"

"We need to rescue Gemma," Stephen replied.

Haddington huffed. "Great deduction. How do you propose we do that?" he asked dryly.

Lady Haddington swatted at her husband's sleeve. "Be nice to Mr. Wycomb," she chastised lightly.

"Yes, dear," Haddington said.

Lady Haddington turned her attention towards Stephen. "Are you familiar with the docks?" she asked.

"I am not," Stephen replied.

"The docks are a lawless place, and people there would just as soon as kill you as rob you of your coins," Lady Haddington said. "You cannot be complacent when you are there. It could get you killed."

Stephen gave her a curious look. "Pray tell, how are you so accustomed to the docks?"

"We do not have time to delve into that," Lady

Haddington said. "You will just need to trust that I know what I am doing."

"I do trust you," Stephen revealed. That was the truth.

Lady Haddington nodded in approval. "Then everything will go much smoother this evening."

Hawthorne leaned over and pulled out a metal box. He opened it and retrieved a pistol. "I assume you can shoot," he said.

"I was a captain of my own ship," Stephen reminded him.

"That was lost to you," Haddington muttered under his breath.

Stephen didn't want to dignify Haddington's words with a response, so he opted to ignore them. He accepted the pistol from Hawthorne and took a moment to adjust to the weight of it.

"There is a chance that we won't live through this," Hawthorne said, giving him a pointed look. "I just want you to know the odds before we go in."

"I know what is at stake, but I can't risk losing Gemma," Stephen responded. "She is my life, my love."

Lady Haddington smiled. "You love her?"

"I do," Stephen admitted. "She is the only woman that I have ever known that has convinced me to fall in love with her."

"Then we won't lose her," Lady Haddington said.

"No, we won't," Stephen said as he held the pistol up. "I will do whatever it takes to get Gemma back."

Hawthorne frowned. "Perhaps you should wait in the coach."

"Why would I do that?" Stephen asked.

Haddington interjected, "You are emotional and that can get you killed."

"You do not need to be concerned with me. I have been in battles before and have come out the victor," Stephen said.

"This is different," Haddington argued.

"In what way?"

Haddington reached for his wife's hand. "You are fighting for the one that you love and that is much more nerve racking."

"I will be fine," Stephen said.

The coach came to a jerking stop and Stephen didn't wait for the footman to open the door. He stuck his hand out the window, ignoring the foul stench that wafted off the River Thames, and opened the door.

He stepped out onto the slick cobblestone and tucked the pistol into the waistband of his trousers. His eyes roamed over the docks, and he saw the *Swiftsure* secured a few yards down.

As he took his first step towards it, Hawthorne placed a hand on his shoulder and said, "Not yet. We can't go in pistols blazing. If we do, Gemma might get shot."

"Then what do you propose?" Stephen asked.

Lady Haddington spoke up. "I will go first and see what I can discover."

"You?" Stephen asked.

Haddington turned towards his wife. "Do be careful," he encouraged.

Stephen glanced between them. "You can't be in earnest!" he demanded. "Lady Haddington could be killed."

Lady Haddington pressed her lips together, clearly displeased by his words. "I thought you were going to trust me."

"I am... I do..." Stephen stammered out, "but I don't want you to get killed."

"Oh, ye of little faith," Lady Haddington said lightly. "Wait for my sign before proceeding to the ship."

Stephen watched as Lady Haddington walked along the fog-lined dock as if she didn't have a care in the world, despite being dressed in a gold ballgown in a rough section of town.

"Should we follow her?" Stephen asked.

Haddington shook his head. "My wife knows what she is

doing," he said. "I have learned it is much easier to do precisely what she says."

"Even if it could get her killed?"

"Evie is a formidable woman," Haddington said. "She is capable of great things."

"I didn't mean to imply…"

Haddington put his hand up, stilling his words. "You want Evie advocating for you," he said, "but whatever happens here, must stay between us. It is imperative that it does."

"I understand."

"Good, because I would hate for a reason to kill you," Haddington remarked in a firm tone, leaving little doubt to the sincerity of his words.

Hawthorne came to stand next to him. "I don't want a reason to kill you either," he said. "But I will if it comes to it."

Stephen glanced between Hawthorne and Haddington and it was evident that they would do anything to protect Lady Haddington, making him wonder what they were all involved in. But he had no intention of prying into their business. They were entitled to their secrets; just as he was entitled to his.

Haddington's stern gaze left his and turned towards his wife. She had just come to a stop in front of a man that was guarding the gangway of the *Swiftsure*.

Stephen held his breath as he watched Lady Haddington converse with the man. He wondered what she was saying to him.

Judging by the look on the man's face, he appeared enamored with Lady Haddington, but he made the mistake of turning away from her. Lady Haddington promptly pulled out a pistol and hit him on the side of the head, causing him to fall to the ground in a heap.

"That was the sign," Haddington said as he rushed to aid his wife.

Stephen followed closely behind Haddington and Hawthorne as they approached Lady Haddington.

Lady Haddington held the pistol in her hand as she informed them, "Most of the crew is either below deck or at The Frenzied Rabbit pub."

"Were you able to determine if Gemma was on board?" Stephen asked eagerly.

Lady Haddington nodded. "According to the sailor, a dandy brought an unconscious woman on the ship a short time ago, and they are ferrying them to France."

Hawthorne addressed Lady Haddington. "Where is Gemma being kept?"

"In the captain's quarters."

Stephen retrieved his pistol and growled, "Leave Lord Hawkinge to me."

"I worry that you aren't thinking clearly," Lady Haddington said. "Why don't you stay here and keep watch for the other sailors?"

"You honestly expect me to stay back and stand guard?" Stephen asked.

Lady Haddington gave him an encouraging smile. "We will bring Gemma back to you."

"I'm not going to do nothing when Gemma is being held captive by a madman," Stephen asserted.

"Don't bungle this, then," Haddington said. "Even though we have had our differences, I don't wish you dead."

"I am a trained soldier. I can handle this."

Haddington didn't look convinced. "Do not go in ill-prepared. Do as we say, and we might survive this."

Lady Haddington grinned. "That was quite the motivational speech."

Hawthorne glanced down at the unconscious man. "We need to get him back on the ship and hide his body," he ordered.

Stephen tucked his pistol away before he assisted

Hawthorne with carrying the unconscious man over the gang-way. Once they stepped onto the ship, they made quick work with hiding the man under some ropes.

Hawthorne held his pistol up and whispered, "I will go downstairs and hold off the rest of the crew while you find Gemma."

"The captain's cabin is always at the stern of the ship," Stephen informed them. "I will go retrieve Gemma."

Lady Haddington reached down and ripped the bottom of her ballgown. When she straightened, she said, "That is much more comfortable."

"There goes another perfectly good gown," Haddington grumbled.

With a smile at her husband, Lady Haddington said, "I will go with Mr. Wycomb to ensure he doesn't kill himself."

"Then I will guard the gangway," Haddington stated.

With a purposeful stride, Stephen headed towards the stern of the ship and came to a stop in front of the captain's cabin. He reached for the handle on the door, and he tried to turn it. *Locked.*

"It's locked," he whispered over his shoulder.

Lady Haddington pushed him out of the way and crouched down in front of the door. She pulled out two long metal hair pins from her hair, slipping them into the locking mechanism, and twisted them until a distinctive click could be heard.

Lady Haddington rose and encouraged, "After you."

Stephen didn't need to be told twice. He opened the door and stepped inside. It took a moment for his eyes to adjust to the darkness of the room, but he saw that the cabin was empty. Where was Gemma being held if not here?

"She is not here," Stephen said as he turned to leave.

A hesitant voice spoke up from inside of the room. "Stephen?"

"It is me." Relief flooded over him as he recognized the soft voice. "Where are you, Gemma?"

He watched as Gemma crawled out from under the desk and rose. Her hair was terribly disheveled and her gown was ripped, but to him, she had never looked more lovely.

Gemma closed the distance between them and said, "I didn't think you would find me in time."

As he reached for her hand, he responded, "It doesn't matter. I would have never stopped looking for you."

Gemma smiled up at him and he thought he would burst with happiness that she was here with him.

Lady Haddington's voice came from behind them. "We should go," she encouraged in a hushed voice. "Gemma isn't safe yet and neither are we."

"Evie?" Gemma asked as she glanced over his shoulder.

"Hello, Gemma," Lady Haddington replied.

"What are you doing here?" Gemma asked.

Stephen interjected, "It is best if you don't ask questions."

"I don't understand," Gemma said.

"As far as we are concerned, Lady Haddington was never here and played no role in your rescue," Stephen shared.

Gemma nodded her head in understanding. "Can we please get off this ship?"

"I think that is a grand idea," Stephen said.

Stephen tightened his hold on Gemma's hand and followed Lady Haddington out of the captain's cabin.

As they headed towards the gangway at the front of the ship, Lady Haddington came to an abrupt stop.

"What is it?" Stephen asked, following her gaze.

Lady Haddington didn't have to answer because Stephen saw why she had stopped. Lord Hawkinge was holding a pistol at Haddington's head, and he wasn't alone. Two stocky men stood behind him with their pistols drawn.

Lord Hawkinge smirked. "This is the part where I tell you to put down your pistols or Lord Haddington is a dead man."

# Chapter Twenty

Gemma watched the scene in front of her in stunned silence. Henry was leveling a pistol at Lord Haddington's head, and she had little doubt that he would make good on his promise to kill him. After all, he had killed his own brother without showing any hint of remorse. She didn't even know what he was capable of anymore.

Henry cocked the pistol and pressed it up against Lord Haddington's temple. "Drop your pistols, now!"

Evie leaned over and placed the pistol onto the ground. "Do as he says," she urged.

"If we do, then we are dead men," Stephen responded.

"You must trust me," Evie said in a hushed voice.

Stephen hesitated for only a moment before he dropped his pistol to the ground. "I hope you know what you are doing," he muttered under his breath.

Henry lowered the pistol in his hand. "You insult me, Mr. Wycomb," he said. "You actually thought you could stage a rescue with the help of Lord and Lady Haddington."

Stephen shrugged. "It seemed like a good idea at the time."

"You brought them to die."

"This fight is far from over," Stephen asserted.

Henry chuckled dryly. "You have lost!" he exclaimed. "Admit it. You were outplayed."

"I will admit no such thing."

"You were always too cocky for your own good," Henry said. "I will take great pleasure in killing you."

Gemma gasped. "You will do no such thing," she said as she went to stand in front of Stephen. "You will have to kill me first."

"Gemma…" Stephen started from behind him.

She turned and spoke over him. "Henry killed Baldwin. I refuse to let him kill you, too."

Stephen's jaw clenched. "How do you know he killed Baldwin?"

"He confessed it to me," Gemma replied. "He poisoned him so he could marry me and get the land that Baldwin left me."

"I thought that property was worthless," Stephen said.

"Henry lied to me, about everything," Gemma responded. "None of it was true."

Stephen shifted his gaze towards Henry. "Is this true?"

"It is," Henry replied in a bored tone. "But I do not know why it matters to you. You will be long dead when I marry Gemma."

"I think you are underestimating me," Stephen said.

Henry put his hands up. "You boarded the ship with the help of a useless lord and lady," he said. "What did you think would happen?"

"They are far from useless," Stephen pressed.

Henry pointed the pistol at Gemma. "I don't want to kill you, my dear," he said. "But I will if you do not step out of the way."

Gemma felt panic well up inside of her. She couldn't just

let him kill Stephen. She needed to think of a plan, and quickly.

"What if I willingly marry you?" Gemma asked. "Will you let Stephen and Lord and Lady Haddington live?"

Henry shook his head. "I'm afraid not. They know too much."

Haddington interjected, "I think Gemma is asking the wrong question."

"What do you mean?" Henry asked.

"Well, from where I stand, you are bound to lose this fight and will most likely be killed," Haddington said. "I think a better question is- will *we* let you live?"

Henry lifted his brow. "Surely you cannot be this delusional?"

"I have been called much worse," Haddington replied. "But you seem to be under the impression that we have come alone."

Henry's eyes darted around the main deck. "Who else did you bring?"

"A skilled marksman," Haddington said.

"You are lying," Henry declared.

Haddington shrugged. "Why don't you put your finger on the trigger and find out?"

Henry's expression grew clouded with doubt. "You are just trying to buy yourself more time," he said. "It won't work."

"I am many things, but I am not a liar," Haddington stated in a firm tone.

In a swift motion, Henry pointed the pistol at Haddington's head. "Come out!" he ordered. "Or else I will kill Lord Haddington!"

*Silence.*

Gemma's eyes roamed the deck but she saw no one make themselves known. What game was Haddington playing?

Henry pressed the barrel of the pistol into Haddington's head. "This is your last warning," he said.

"Is your finger on the trigger?" Haddington asked, appearing unconcerned by the threat on his life. "He won't reveal his location until he knows that you aren't bluffing."

Gemma watched as Henry's finger twitched on the trigger. He was going to shoot Lord Haddington, right here, in front of her.

A shot rang out and Henry's pistol dropped to the ground with a clang. He cradled his right hand in his left and shouted, "Shoot them! Shoot them all!"

As one of the men brought up his pistol, Evie reared her hand back and released a dagger. It lodged in the man's chest, and he collapsed to the floor.

The other man leaned down and put his pistol onto the floor. Then he put his hands up and said, "There is no reason anyone else has to die here."

Haddington went to retrieve Henry's pistol. "That is the first smart thing that has been uttered all evening."

Henry's eyes narrowed. "There is a whole crew below deck and they will have heard the gunshot. You will be outnumbered and outgunned in mere moments."

Nathaniel stepped out from the shadows, holding a pistol in his hand. "You have lost, Hawkinge."

Henry stared at Nathaniel, dumbfounded. "How many lords did Wycomb bring with him?"

"Enough," Nathaniel replied. "You should know that I have spoken to the crew and they don't have a vested interest in helping you."

"You are lying!" Henry shouted.

"I'm not," Nathaniel said. "They agreed to take you to France, but they never agreed to fight your battles for you."

Henry turned towards the man with his hands up. "You are the captain of this ship. Order your men to help me!"

The captain glanced down at the dead man on the ground. "You are on the losing end of this," he said. "It would be in your best interest to walk away with your life, while you still can."

"I will pay you," Henry stated.

"Money isn't any good to a dead man," the captain responded.

Henry released his right hand and blood dripped from the tips of his fingers. "Gemma is mine," he exclaimed. "I knew it from the moment I saw her."

Stephen spoke up. "Shouldn't Gemma decide who she wants to be with?"

With a scoff, Henry said, "She is merely a woman. She doesn't truly know what she wants."

Gemma frowned. "I know my own mind, and I want to be with Stephen."

"No!" Henry exclaimed. "You belong to me!"

"As I have told you before, I belong to no man," Gemma said.

Henry took a step towards her, and Stephen attempted to usher her behind him. But this was something that she had to do. This was her fight.

"It is all right, Stephen," she said. "Lord Hawkinge can't hurt me now."

Henry's eyes burned with fury as he asked, "Do you know what I had to do to be with you?"

"That was your doing, not mine," Gemma replied.

"I killed Baldwin for you… for *us!*"

Gemma shook her head. "No, you killed Baldwin for you. I loved Baldwin."

"You love me!" Henry shouted. "I can see it in your eyes. You have always loved me."

"I'm sorry, but I do not love you."

Henry gestured at Stephen. "Yet you love a shipbuilder? A commoner. A nobody."

"I do," she admitted.

A crestfallen look came to Henry's face. "Why don't you love me?" he demanded.

"I have only ever considered you as a brother."

Henry's face contorted in rage and he reached down to pick up the pistol that the captain had dropped.

Haddington cocked his pistol as he pointed it at Henry. "Put the pistol down, Hawkinge," he ordered. "You need to see a doctor, not the mortician."

Henry lowered his gaze towards the pistol in his hand. "Gemma is the only woman that I have ever loved. How can I go on without her?"

Nathanial kept his pistol aimed at Henry. "If you would like, we can have a frank conversation after you put down your pistol."

Henry brought his gaze up and a blank look was on his face. "If I can't have her, then no one can."

As Henry went to take aim, Stephen moved to stand in front of Gemma, shielding her with his body, and the sound of pistols discharging could be heard echoing throughout the night.

The next thing she heard was Stephen's calm, comforting voice next to her ear. "It is all right," he said softly. "It is over now."

"Is he dead?"

"He is," Stephen replied.

Gemma knew it was terrible of her, but all she could feel was relief that Henry was dead. She knew that as long as he was alive, she would never have been free of him.

Stephen took a step back and Gemma saw that Haddington was standing over Henry's sprawled out body.

Evie eyed her with concern. "We should get you home."

"I won't disagree with you," Gemma said with a shudder.

"You are cold." Stephen promptly removed his jacket and slipped it over her shoulders. "This should keep you warm enough."

"Thank you," Gemma murmured.

Nathaniel approached her with a solemn look on his face. "How are you faring?" he asked. "I only ask because it is all right if you are not okay."

Gemma pulled the jacket closer to her body. "I am much better now that I know Henry can't hurt me again."

"It is a terrible thing to watch people die in front of you," Nathaniel said.

"It is something that I do not want to make a habit of," Gemma remarked lightly.

Nathaniel tipped his head before turning his attention towards Evie. "Will you escort Gemma home?" he asked. "I need to see to a few things before I can return home."

"It will be my pleasure," Evie said.

Haddington came to stand next to his wife. "It would be best if we departed before we attract any further attention to ourselves."

Stephen cleared his throat. "I would like to escort Gemma home, assuming it isn't too much of an imposition," he said. "I daresay I won't be able to get much sleep until I know she is back home with her family."

"I assumed as much," Evie remarked.

Stephen gave Gemma an encouraging smile. "Let's get you home."

Home.

Gemma came to the realization that home wasn't a place, but rather, a feeling. And when she was around Stephen, she felt at home.

---

Gemma felt no need to converse in the coach as they traveled back to her family's townhouse. And she wasn't alone. No one had spoken since they had left the docks. Everyone seemed to be lost in their own thoughts.

Stephen's shoulder brushed up against her and Gemma wished that they were alone. She just wanted to be held by him and hear him tell her that everything would be all right. She would believe him, too.

The coach jerked to a stop in front of the townhouse and it dipped to the side as the footman stepped off his perch. Then the door opened and the footman extended his hand to assist her out of the coach.

Once she was on the pavement, she removed her hand from the footman's and readjusted Stephen's jacket over her shoulders. She was pleased to see that Stephen had followed her out and had come to stand next to her.

Lord Haddington's voice came from inside of the coach. "Shall we wait for you?"

Stephen shook his head. "I will see myself home."

"Very good," Lord Haddington said. "We will wait here until Lady Hawkinge has stepped inside."

Stephen offered his arm to her. "May I escort you to the door?"

"Thank you," Gemma said as she placed her hand onto his proffered arm.

They walked up the few steps towards the main door and Stephen went to open it for her. Fortunately, it was unlocked.

As they stepped inside the entryway, she saw her aunt rushing out from the drawing room with her arms out wide. "You are home!" she exclaimed as she embraced Gemma. "We have been so worried."

Gemma returned her aunt's firm embrace. "I am fine."

Her aunt leaned back and perused the length of her. "You look awful, Child," she declared. "You require a bath at once."

"It is much too late for a bath."

"Nonsense," her aunt said with a wave of her hand. "I shall see to the preparations at once."

Gemma watched as her aunt walked off and sighed. She felt bad for the servants that would be required to leave the comfort of their beds to prepare her bath.

Stephen spoke up. "I, for one, do not think you look awful," he said. "I don't believe you have ever looked more beautiful to me."

"You are being much too kind."

"It is merely the truth."

Gemma turned to face him and slipped his jacket off her shoulders. "Thank you for this," she said as she extended it back to him.

"You are most welcome," Stephen said as he shrugged the jacket on. "How are you faring, Gemma?"

"I am well," she lied.

Stephen's eyes filled with compassion. "I would prefer the truth, if you don't mind."

Gemma sighed as she admitted, "All I feel is relief that Henry is dead." She hesitated. "Is that awful of me?"

"Not at all," Stephen said. "You are allowed to feel however you feel. There is no shame in that."

"Everything Henry had told me was a lie," Gemma said as she felt tears burn at the back of her eyes. "Why did he have to murder Baldwin?"

"I do believe that Henry was mad. He saw only what he wanted to see, nothing more."

A tear slipped out and ran down her cheek. "He stole everything from me," she said as she reached up to wipe it away.

"Not everything, Gemma," Stephen said, taking a step towards her. "I may be presumptuous in saying this, but you still have me."

"And I am most grateful for that."

Stephen reached for her hand. "What Henry did was inexcusable, but I am here for you. I will always be here for you."

Gemma stared deep into his eyes, and she didn't just see him, but she saw her today, her tomorrow and her future for the rest of her life.

Her father's voice came from the doorway of the drawing room. "Release my daughter, Wycomb!" he growled.

Stephen slipped his hand out of hers and turned to face her father. "Lord Winsley," he started, "as always, it is a pleasure."

Her father narrowed his eyes and he closed the distance between them. "You will stay away from Gemma. I command you to," he barked, coming to stand toe to toe with Stephen.

"Here is the thing, my lord, I have never dealt well with taking orders," Stephen said in a dry voice.

"Well, you will need to start, because you are no good for Gemma. You are nothing—"

Stephen grabbed her father's cravat and leaned closer to him. "You are a pompous jackanapes, and your opinion means very little to me."

"How dare you talk to me in such a high-handed manner!" her father shouted. "Do I need to remind you that you work for a living."

"You seem to forget that I was a captain in the Royal Navy."

Her father huffed. "Not a very good one."

Gemma gasped. "Father!"

Stephen's voice turned ominous. "You know not what you are speaking of, and I would strongly encourage you to choose your next words wisely."

Her father took a step back and Stephen released his grip on Lord Winsley's cravat. "I don't know what you intended to prove with that spectacle, but you failed to impress me."

"I wasn't trying to impress you," Stephen responded.

"No?" her father asked. "Do you think Gemma would appreciate your lack of composure?"

Stephen glanced at her and she could see questions in his eyes. She offered him an encouraging smile before turning back towards her father. "Why are you here?"

Her father frowned. "To ensure you were safe."

"Well, I am home now," Gemma responded. "You may go back to Kitty."

With a shake of his head, her father said, "You are not home. You need to come live with me and Kitty."

Gemma let out a disbelieving laugh. "You cannot be in earnest?" she asked. "Kitty was the reason I was abducted. If it wasn't for her, I would have never gone into the gardens."

"Kitty was just trying to help you," her father attempted.

"Henry was trying to force me into marriage. How was that trying to help me?" Gemma demanded.

Her father sighed. "I knew you would be difficult about this."

Gemma's mouth dropped open. "You think I am being difficult?" she asked. "I almost died tonight, and Kitty played a role in that."

"You must see that Lord Hawkinge would have been a better fit for you than Mr. Wycomb." Her father paused. "Where is Lord Hawkinge?"

"He is dead," Gemma replied. "He was shot while trying to kill me."

Her father pursed his lips together. "That is most unfortunate. Now we will need to find you another suitor."

"There is no need for that." Gemma walked over to the main door and opened it. "I want you to leave, and never come back."

Her father stared at her in surprise. "Surely you don't mean that."

"I do," Gemma said. "It is time that we both move on, without one another."

"But, Gemma…" His voice stopped and he pointed his finger at Stephen. "This is all your doing!"

Stephen put his hands up. "I may think you are a terrible, vile person, but this is not coming from me."

Gemma interjected, "My whole life you made me think that I wasn't good enough. But I am good enough. Stephen has helped me see that."

Her father adjusted his cravat as he said, "I do believe recent events have muddled your thinking. Once you are in your right mind, we can speak again."

"There will not be another time," Gemma insisted. "I am going to live my life how I see fit."

"If you marry Mr. Wycomb, then you will be a social outcast," her father declared. "Do you want to live your life on the outside of the life you were born into?"

Gemma took her hand off the door and approached Stephen. "I feel bad for you, Father," she said. "I don't believe you have ever experienced love."

"Love?" her father scoffed. "Love has nothing to do with marriage in our circles."

"Love has everything to do with marriage," she asserted. "I have loved two men in my life. The first died by Henry's hand, and the second is an honorable man that rescued me in more ways than one."

"You will be a shipbuilder's wife. Have you no shame?"

She boldly reached for Stephen's hand. "Goodbye, Father."

Her father glanced down at their hands and his face went hard. "If you marry Mr. Wycomb, then I will disown you. I will leave you nothing in my will."

"That is your choice, not mine."

Her father stormed over to the door and stopped. Then he turned on his heel and said, "When I die, you will regret treating me like this."

"I will take my chances," Gemma replied.

She watched as her father departed the townhouse, slamming the door behind him.

Stephen's compassionate eyes turned towards her. "I know that must have been hard for you."

"No, it was the easiest decision I have made in a long time," Gemma replied.

Her aunt's voice came from the stairs. "Good heavens, it was about time that you stood up to your boorish father," she said.

Hugh and Marielle stepped out of the drawing room, holding hands. "I'm afraid we were shamelessly eavesdropping," Hugh revealed. "We didn't want to make our presence known."

Stephen went to release her hand, but she held firm. "I'm done hiding," she said in a hushed voice.

He smiled. "I'm glad to hear that."

Her aunt came to a stop in front of them. "I heard what Kitty had done but was Lord Hawkinge truly shot when he tried to kill you?"

Gemma nodded. "Frankly, I don't know who shot him, but I am grateful that it happened."

"As am I," her aunt said. "Lord Hawkinge turned out to be a terrible excuse for a human being."

"I won't disagree with you there," Gemma remarked.

Balfour stepped into the room and announced, "Lady Hawkinge's bath is ready in her bedchamber."

"Thank you, Balfour," Gemma said.

He tipped his head before he turned and departed from the entry hall.

"You should go," Stephen encouraged.

Gemma turned to face him. "Thank you for what you did tonight," she said.

His eyes crinkled around the edges. "I would do anything for you. You must know that."

"I do," Gemma replied.

Stephen brought her hand up to his lips. "If it is permissible, I would like to call upon you tomorrow," he said. "There is still the matter of the question that I must ask you."

"I shall be looking forward to it."

He released her hand and said, "As will I."

After Stephen murmured his goodbyes, Gemma watched as he walked out of the door and into the night.

Her aunt came to stand next to her. "Your father was right about one thing."

"Which is?"

"You will lose your place in Society if you marry Mr. Wycomb."

Gemma bobbed her head. "I'm afraid I have no choice," she said. "I already lost my heart to Stephen."

Her aunt placed a hand on her shoulder. "Then you are doing the right thing."

Marielle let out a shriek. "We are going to be sisters!" she exclaimed as she rushed over to Gemma and embraced her.

"Your brother hasn't asked yet," Gemma pointed out.

"He would be a fool not to," Marielle said.

Her aunt interrupted, scrunching her nose, "It is time you have a long soak. I'm afraid you smell quite awful."

"Stephen didn't seem to mind much," Marielle remarked.

Her aunt perused the length of Gemma. "We will also need to throw out that ballgown. I'm afraid it is beyond saving."

"Then I shall buy a new one since I have the funds to do so now," Gemma said.

"I'm afraid I don't understand," her aunt said.

Gemma clasped her hands in front of her. "It turns out that the property that Baldwin left me produces an income of ten thousand pounds a year."

Marielle's brow shot up. "You are an heiress."

"I am," Gemma said. "That was just one of the things that Henry lied to me about."

"Oh, dear," her aunt stated. "It sounds as if we have much to discuss tomorrow. But, first, you need to take a bath and wash that stench off you."

"I agree," Gemma said as she walked towards the stairs.

# Chapter Twenty-One

With a drink in his hand, Stephen sat in the corner of White's as he attempted to pass the time before it was a respectable time to call upon Gemma. He had a few fitful hours of sleep since he was wrestling with his thoughts of what he could say to Gemma to convince her to marry him. She completed him in a way that he never thought possible.

A part of him was always going to struggle with the loss of his crew, but Gemma gave him hope that he was more than the sum of his past mistakes. He was better with her by his side, and he would be a fool to let her go.

The door of the club opened, drawing his attention, and he saw Lord Winsley step into the main hall. His eyes proceeded to roam the hall until they landed on him.

To his surprise, Lord Winsley approached his table with a solemn look on his face. He came to a stop next to the table and asked, "May I sit?"

Stephen wanted to refuse him, to send him on his way, but something compelled him to nod his approval. He found he was curious to see what Lord Winsley wanted.

Lord Winsley glanced down at his drink. "Do you usually drink this early?" he asked disapprovingly.

"I am biding my time until I can call on Gemma," Stephen replied with a glance at the window.

Lord Winsley looked displeased by his remarks. "Do you intend to offer for her?"

"I do," he replied.

"If you do, I am of the mind that she will accept," Lord Winsley said. "For the life of me, I can't figure out why she favors you."

Stephen decided to speak frankly with the infuriating lord. "I love your daughter and I hope we can start a life together."

Lord Winsley grew silent. "I was afraid you were going to say that."

Unsure of why Lord Winsley was even conversing with him, Stephen decided it would be best to ask, "What is it that you want?"

With a sigh, Lord Winsley replied, "I don't want to leave this world without reconciling with Gemma, but I am at a loss as to what I should do."

Stephen could hear the sincerity in his voice, but he had a few questions of his own. "If that is the case, why aren't you attempting to speak to Gemma?"

"She won't see me," Lord Winsley said with a frown on his lips. "I went by her townhouse earlier and the butler informed me that she would no longer receive me."

"Why not speak to your sister, Lady Montfort, for assistance?"

"I could, but I do believe that I have a greater chance of Gemma listening to you," Lord Winsley responded.

Stephen tightened his hold on his glass. He had no intention of making this easy on Lord Winsley. "You said some awful things to Gemma last night. Why should she speak to you ever again?"

"I may have overreacted."

"May have?" Stephen asked. "You threatened to disown her."

"I did, but I was just angry."

"You should learn to control your temper, then," Stephen countered. "You were out of line with Gemma."

Lord Winsley glanced over his shoulder before asking, "May I speak frankly?"

"I would prefer it."

"I don't like you, and I do not think you are worthy of my daughter," Lord Winsley said. "You are far below her station and will be an utter stain on our family's reputation."

Stephen took a sip of his drink, preferring to remain silent. He already knew how Lord Winsley felt about him and arguing with him would do little good about it. Besides, Lord Winsley had already done a good enough job of tainting his own reputation.

"But…" Lord Winsley paused, "Gemma wants you in her life, and I will need to come to terms with that."

"That is most generous of you," Stephen said dryly, "but Gemma has made it clear that she doesn't want you in her life anymore."

"I know, but I was hoping you could convince her otherwise."

"And why would I do that?" Stephen asked. "You have shown me nothing but contempt."

Lord Winsley nodded. "That is fair, but I am dying."

"You can't use your death as a way to manipulate your daughter, or me, for that matter," Stephen said, shoving back his chair. "Good day."

"Wait!" Lord Winsley shouted, his voice rising in panic. "I do not intend to manipulate anyone. I just want to make amends."

Stephen hesitated before pulling the chair back to the table. "What of Lady Winsley's role in Gemma's abduction?"

"What am I to do?" Lord Winsley asked, tossing his hands up in the air. "She is my wife."

"And Gemma is your daughter."

Lord Winsley shook his head. "Kitty swore to me that she never wished any harm upon Gemma."

"Lord Hawkinge abducted Gemma and tried to kill her," Stephen said. "Kitty played a role in that, no matter how small, and you should not be blinded by her so easily."

"I can't forsake my wife."

"I'm not asking you to, but I want you to sympathize with the terrible ordeal that Gemma went through."

"I do, but—"

Stephen cut him off. "Stop making excuses," he commanded. "What Lady Winsley did was wrong, and she should be held accountable for her actions."

"Are you implying that I turn her over to the magistrate?" Lord Winsley asked, aghast.

"No. But I suggest you have a frank conversation with her. Make her understand that her actions were inconceivable."

Lord Winsley caught the eye of a passing servant and indicated he wished for a drink. Then he asked, "What then?"

"That is entirely up to you."

"I don't have much more time to play the games of my temperamental daughter," Lord Winsley said.

Stephen lifted his brow. "You don't know your daughter very well if you think this is a game to her."

Lord Winsley's shoulders slumped slightly. "That is the thing- I don't know her very well. I never have. But I do love her."

"Pardon me for saying so, but you have a funny way of showing it."

"That is fair," Lord Winsley said. "Will you talk to her?"

Stephen took a sip of his drink, delaying his response. Why should he help Lord Winsley? After all, Gemma had made it clear how she felt about her father. Would it upset her if he spoke to her about a reconciliation? It was a chance that he didn't really want to take, especially since he wanted to offer for her today.

Lord Winsley leaned forward in his seat and said in a low voice, "You have every right to turn me down, but I pray that you don't. Please."

At that last word, Stephen knew that Lord Winsley was in earnest. He didn't think he would ever hear Lord Winsley utter such a word.

A server approached the table and placed a glass of brandy in front of Lord Winsley. Then he asked, "Will there be anything else, my lord?"

Lord Winsley's gruff voice returned. "Not at this time," he said with a dismissive wave of his hand.

Stephen took a sip of his drink as he considered Lord Winsley. He could easily send him on his way, refusing his request, but he couldn't seem to convince himself to do so. Something was holding him back. Perhaps it wouldn't be a terrible thing if he spoke to Gemma about her father. But he would not press the issue.

"I will help you." He put his hand up. "But I will not force Gemma to do anything she doesn't feel comfortable with."

Lord Winsley brought a smile to his lips, but it appeared more like a grimace. "I can agree to that, but that still doesn't mean I approve of you."

Stephen lifted his glass in the air. "I can live with that."

Lord Hawthorne walked towards the table with a bemused look on his face. "Am I interrupting something?" he asked, coming to a stop next to Stephen.

"No," Lord Winsley replied before he tossed back his drink. "I was just leaving."

"Hopefully, not on my account," Hawthorne said.

Lord Winsley pushed back his chair and rose. "Don't flatter yourself, Hawthorne."

As Lord Winsley walked away, Hawthorne pulled out a chair and sat down. "Do you want to explain what that was all about?"

"Winsley wants to make amends with his daughter, and he wants me to speak to her," Stephen shared.

"He came to you for help?" Hawthorne asked incredulously.

Stephen grinned. "I was just as surprised as you are."

"What did you say?"

"I told him I would speak to her, but I couldn't make any promises," Stephen replied. "Quite frankly, I don't know how Gemma will react."

"I heard that you and Winsley nearly came to blows last night."

"That is true, but I managed to show some restraint since Gemma was present," Stephen said. "I grew tired of his pompous attitude, and I just reacted."

Hawthorne leaned in and lowered his voice. "Did you have a chance to read the newssheets this morning?"

"I have not."

"Lord Hawkinge's death made front page news," Hawthorne said. "His body was found drifting in the River Thames and the magistrate has no leads on the cause of the death."

Stephen gave him a curious look. "How did you manage to cover up the events of his death, considering he was shot?"

"The coroner in that district owed me a favor."

"How did you…" Stephen stopped speaking. "I am not even going to ask how since I don't want to know."

Hawthorne smirked. "Furthermore, the captain of the merchant ship was paid handsomely to set sail at once and forget about last night."

"I assume you paid him off."

"It was the least I could do since Gemma is family," he said. "If the truth was ever leaked to the morning newspapers, the scandal would tarnish her reputation forever. She would be forced to retire to the countryside."

Stephen tipped his head in approval. "You are a good

cousin."

"I did it for you, too. I wouldn't want that scandal weighing over your head either once you marry my cousin."

"That is assuming she will accept my offer."

"She will."

"I wish I had your optimism, but I do fear that she will find me lacking."

Hawthorne leaned back in his seat. "I do believe it is a good thing to be somewhat fearful when offering for the woman you love."

"Why do you say that?"

"It makes you vulnerable."

Stephen took a sip of his drink, then said, "I do not like being vulnerable. It makes me feel uncomfortable."

"Most men would agree with you, but it is different when you are speaking from the heart," Hawthorne stated.

Lord Hugh arrived at the table and sat down. "Marielle sent me to tell you that Gemma is awake and it is a good time to propose."

Stephen groaned. "I hope that Marielle didn't tell Gemma that."

"Of course not," Hugh responded. "But I would be remiss if I didn't tell you that my mother is planning a celebratory dinner this evening in honor of your engagement."

"I suppose I should get this over with," Stephen said, rising.

"That's the spirit," Hugh joked.

---

"I would have killed Lord Hawkinge myself if he wasn't already dead," Marielle declared in a huff. "What he did to you was unforgiveable."

Gemma nodded. "I won't disagree with you there."

Her aunt spoke up. "It is a good thing that Nathaniel and Lord Haddington went with Mr. Wycomb to rescue you on that ship."

"It was," Gemma agreed.

As she reached for her cup of tea, her aunt said, "Well, I am glad that you are home, where you belong."

"I am grateful for that, as well," Gemma responded. "But now that I know I have an income, it changes everything."

"In what way?" her aunt pressed.

"I am in a position to live my life on my terms," Gemma said. "I am not a poor relation anymore."

"You must know that we never saw you that way," her aunt stated.

"I know, which makes me even more grateful for everything you have done for me," Gemma said.

Her aunt took a sip of her tea. "What do you intend to do with your newfound freedom?"

"I don't rightly know," Gemma replied.

Marielle perked up and encouraged, "You could always marry my brother."

Gemma laughed. "Need I remind you that he hasn't asked."

"You could always ask him," Marielle suggested.

Her aunt gasped. "Dear heavens!" she exclaimed. "What a ridiculous notion. A woman does not ask a gentleman to marry her."

Marielle reached for a biscuit on the tray. "It is progressive, but not unfathomable."

"In our circles it is," her aunt said.

Dinah stepped into the room and went to sit down next to Marielle on the settee. "What did I miss?"

Marielle spoke up. "We are trying to convince Gemma to offer for Stephen."

"It would be about time," Dinah responded.

Balfour stepped into the room and met Gemma's gaze.

"Mr. Wycomb has come to call, my lady," he informed her. "Are you available for callers?"

She felt a thrill of excitement course through her at the thought of seeing him. "I am. Please send him in," she said as she attempted to keep the eagerness out of her voice.

The butler nodded his head and departed from the room.

Dinah reached for her cup of tea and brought it to her lips. She made a face and placed it back onto the tray. "Well, I now get to add tea to the list of things that smell revolting while I'm increasing."

"You poor thing," her aunt cooed. "I promise it will get better."

Dinah didn't look convinced. "We shall see."

Stephen stepped into the room and smiled at her, causing her heart to skip a beat. She wished she could explain how every time she was with him she felt so complete.

He bowed. "My ladies," he greeted politely.

Gemma rose from her seat and dropped into a curtsy. "Mr. Wycomb," she said. "What a pleasure it is to see you this morning."

"I hope I did not call too early," Stephen said.

"Not at all."

Stephen held her gaze and she could see an intensity inside his eyes that she hadn't seen before. "Would you care to take a turn around the gardens with me?" he asked.

Gemma bobbed her head. "That sounds delightful."

He stepped closer and offered his arm. "Shall we?"

As he led her towards the rear of the townhouse, neither of them spoke and she found herself growing increasingly nervous. Which was ridiculous. She had no reason to be nervous around Stephen. She loved him. What pained her the most was that she didn't know if he loved her in return.

A footman opened the door for them and then followed them onto the veranda.

They started walking down the path in the gardens and

Gemma withdrew her hand. She clasped her hands in front of her to keep them from fidgeting.

Stephen cleared his throat. "Your father visited me at the club this morning," he shared.

"I'm sorry," Gemma said. "I can't imagine that was pleasant for you."

"It wasn't as terrible as I perceived it to be."

Gemma gave him a curious look. "How can that be?" she asked. "My father has been nothing but cruel to you."

"True, but it was different today."

"How so?"

Stephen grew quiet. "He wants to speak to you about making amends."

Gemma stopped on the path and turned to face him. "You cannot be in earnest," she said, her voice rising. "I want nothing to do with my father."

"Then so be it."

Gemma let out a disbelieving huff. "I can't believe my father would stoop so low as to try to recruit you to help him."

"He seemed sincere."

"He is a good actor," Gemma said.

Stephen offered her an encouraging smile. "You don't have to do anything that you don't want to do."

"Thank you." Gemma turned to start walking down the path but stopped short. "My father is unbelievable!" she remarked. "He has some nerve to even approach you and ask for your help."

"It seemed like a bold move on his part."

With a shake of her head, Gemma said, "No, I do not want to make amends with my father."

"That is your choice."

Gemma felt her resolve slipping and she asked, "Do you think I should, even after all the terrible things he said last night?"

"I don't know the right answer to that," he said. "Quite

frankly, I don't know if there is even a right answer."

Gemma wrapped her arms around her waist. "I don't know if I can trust him enough to let him in."

Stephen took a step closer to her. "You will know what the right thing to do is."

"How do you know that?"

"Because you are brilliant, my dear."

Gemma dropped her arms to her sides. "I daresay that I have managed to fool you into believing that."

"You did no such thing," Stephen said. "You are the most extraordinary person that I know."

Gemma's lips twitched. "You must not know very many people then," she joked.

Stephen reached for her hand and held her gaze for a long moment. Then when he finally spoke, his words were soft, intimate, even. "I love you, Gemma. You must know that."

Her breath caught in her throat. "I was hoping, but I dared not believe you loved me."

"I can't lose you," Stephen breathed. "Because if I ever did, I'd have lost my smile, my laugh, my everything."

Gemma lifted their intwined hands to her heart. "I love you, too," she admitted. "I never thought I would be fortunate enough to fall in love twice."

"Please put me out of my misery and agree to be my wife," Stephen said. "You have occupied my thoughts unceasingly since the moment we first met."

"I have been burdened, as well."

Stephen smiled down upon her. "Then let us marry and we will never have to be apart."

Gemma felt tears forming in her eyes as she said, "I will marry you, today, tomorrow or any day after that."

"I am relieved to hear you say that because you are the first person I want to see when I wake up in the morning and the only person I want to kiss goodnight," Stephen said, his voice hoarse. "My heart was made to love you."

Gemma felt a tear rolling down her cheek, but she felt no need to wipe it away. These were happy tears.

Stephen cupped her face gently in his hands, holding it in place. Her breathing hitched as he leaned in to press his lips against hers. The softness of his lips caressed hers as he explored her mouth, never deepening the kiss. It was as if he were trying to memorize every detail and the tenderness of it all made her heart ache, wishing it would never end.

He broke the kiss and leaned back slightly, his warm breath mingling with hers. "That was far better than I could have ever imagined."

"I wouldn't mind another kiss," she said brazenly.

He chuckled. "I will kiss you every minute, every hour, every day, if you will let me," he declared. "I will never tire of kissing you."

"Promises, promises," Gemma whispered as she kissed him on the lips.

After a long moment, Stephen broke the kiss and asked, "Should we tell our families the good news?"

"I am sure they deduced what is going on since I have little doubt that they are watching us from the window."

"Most likely, but I fear that your cousins will challenge me to a duel if we continue on as we have been," Stephen said, making no attempt to create more distance.

"That is a fair assumption."

"And I have seen Hawthorne shoot now."

"He is quite the marksman," Gemma agreed.

"But..." Stephen's voice trailed off, "it would be a shame to not kiss at least one more time before we go inside."

Gemma smiled. "I wholeheartedly agree."

As their lips met, Gemma knew that everything was just the way it should be. All her choices, her heartbreaks, her regrets, had led her to Stephen. And she would never take that for granted. She couldn't. She was all too aware of how precious love was.

## Epilogue

Three weeks later…

It was the best of days because Stephen was to be married today. He had longed for this moment since he had first offered for Gemma. His love grew for her every day that they were together. He knew in his heart that he would never tire of being in her presence. She silenced all of his worries and fears with her gentle touch and devotion. Gemma was everything that he'd ever wanted in a woman, and more.

Not even the pile of work on his desk could dampen his mood. He had been working on it all morning as he tried to keep busy. If he had his way, they would have already eloped to Gretna Green, but Gemma thought it was best that they posted the banns. She didn't want to start off their marriage with a scandal. Which was fair, but he just couldn't wait to start a life with Gemma.

Stephen signed his name on the document that was in front of him. He needed to focus on the task at hand, but he couldn't stop his wayward thoughts.

His butler stepped into the room with labored breathing.

"Lord Winsley would like a moment of your time," he said in between breaths.

Stephen looked up from his desk. "Where is Mr. Brown?"

"He is downstairs becoming acquainted with the household staff," his butler informed him. "Would you care to speak to him?"

"That won't be necessary, but I would prefer if you were resting."

His butler visibly stiffened. "I do not need to rest," he said. "I am perfectly capable of performing my duties."

"Regardless, Mr. Brown is the underbutler and should help relieve you of some of your tasks, freeing you up to oversee the new staff that I hired."

"Very good, sir," the butler said.

His words had just left his mouth when Lord Winsley stepped into the room with an annoyed look on his face. "I grew tired of waiting," he declared.

Stephen didn't even bother to exchange pleasantries with the infuriating lord. "What is it that you want?"

Lord Winsley didn't answer his question, but instead watched the butler's retreating figure before saying, "Why do you have a walking relic as a butler?"

"He is a good man and I do not dare turn him away," Stephen replied. "But I did hire new household staff to get this townhouse up to snuff for your daughter."

Lord Winsley huffed. "This hovel?"

"It is hardly a 'hovel'," Stephen argued.

"You should just burn it to the ground and start over."

Stephen knew there was no use in arguing with Lord Winsley since he saw fault in everything. "Why are you here?"

Lord Winsley reached into his jacket pocket and pulled out a piece of paper. "I received an invitation for the luncheon after the wedding, but I did not receive one for the ceremony," he said. "I assume that it was a mistake."

"It was not a mistake," Stephen said. "Gemma wants only close friends and family for the ceremony."

Lord Winsley puffed out his chest. "But I am her father."

"You two are still somewhat estranged."

"True, but she has started receiving me when I come to call."

"Regardless, it was Gemma's decision, not mine."

Lord Winsley walked over to the mantel that hung over the fireplace and picked up a small vase. "You could try to convince her to invite me."

"Why would I do that?"

"Because it is the right thing to do."

Stephen leaned back in his chair. "I do not think you wish to speak to me about what is right or wrong."

Lord Winsley placed the vase down and said, "I do not know why Gemma is holding my past against me."

"You can't run from the consequences of your past choices."

"So I made a few mistakes…"

Stephen cleared his throat. "You made many, many mistakes with Gemma, and I must side with my betrothed."

"Her mother was much more understanding," Lord Winsley muttered.

"Be that as it may be, you must respect Gemma's decision to not have you at the ceremony."

Lord Winsley frowned. "This is rubbish," he said.

"Come to the luncheon and celebrate our union," Stephen encouraged, rising. "Prove to Gemma that you are the man you claim to be, but do not dare bring Lady Winsley along. She is not welcome, and she will be turned away, as will you. I will not have Gemma's day ruined by that woman."

For a brief moment, it appeared as if Lord Winsley intended to argue with him, but instead he tipped his head in acknowledgement. "I understand."

The butler stepped into the room and announced, "Lord Hugh and Lord Hawthorne have come to call, sir."

"Do send them in." Stephen turned his attention back towards Lord Winsley. "Are we done here?"

Lord Winsley scowled. "I still do not see what Gemma sees in you."

Not wishing to engage Lord Winsley any further, he said, "Good day to you."

To his surprise, Lord Winsley approached him and held his hand out. "I do not think you are in any way worthy of my daughter, but I do hope you will take care of her."

Stephen reached out and shook his hand. "I will do whatever it takes to ensure that Gemma is happy."

Lord Winsley nodded. "I won't always be here, and it gives me great comfort to know she will be cared for."

"I love your daughter, and she won't lack for anything. I can promise you that."

"Thank you," Lord Winsley said, his voice cracking with emotion. "I shall see you at the luncheon, then."

Lord Winsley withdrew his hand and departed from the study without saying another word. A moment later, Hugh and Hawthorne stepped into the room.

Hugh gave him a curious look. "Why was Lord Winsley here?"

"He was complaining about how he wasn't invited to the wedding ceremony," Stephen explained.

"Why wasn't he?" Hawthorne asked.

"It was Gemma's decision, but she said she wanted to be surrounded by her loved ones," Stephen said. "Not that I am complaining, but why are you here? I thought we were meeting at White's for a drink."

Hugh grinned. "Marielle sent us," he replied. "She wanted to ensure that you were prepared for your upcoming nuptials."

"Why wouldn't I be?" Stephen asked.

Hugh shrugged one shoulder. "You know your sister," he

said. "She is just so excited to have Gemma in the family, especially since she has always wanted a sister."

Stephen came around his desk. "Shall we depart for White's?" he asked as he walked towards the door.

"I brought our coach," Hugh said as he trailed after him. "I thought you might want to make use of it after the wedding ceremony."

"I already have a coach," Stephen said.

"But didn't we decide it was merely 'adequate'?" Hugh asked.

Stephen stepped outside of the townhouse and saw a fancy black coach that was being pulled by two magnificent horses. A liveried footman was holding the door open.

"I believe I shall take you up on your offer," Stephen said.

Hugh gave him a smug look. "I thought that might be the case."

Hawthorne spoke up from behind them. "We should hurry if we want to meet our friends on time."

After they stepped into the posh coach, it merged into traffic and drove the short distance to White's.

They exited the coach and Stephen followed Hawthorne and Hugh into the club. Once they arrived at the table in the corner, he saw Lord Grenton and Lord Graylocke sitting down with a drink in their hands.

Grenton raised his glass when he saw Stephen. "Wycomb!" he greeted enthusiastically. "You have arrived."

Stephen lifted his brow. "I see that you have already indulged in the port," he remarked good-naturedly as he pulled out a chair and sat down.

Grenton chuckled. "This is my first glass," he replied. "I am just happy that you are falling prey to the parson's mousetrap."

"Why is that?"

Leaning towards him, Grenton lowered his voice as he

said, "You will have no greater joy than having a loving woman by your side."

Graylocke interjected, "Grenton may spout a lot of nonsense, but he is right about this. I have never been so happy as I am with Beatrice."

Hawthorne raised his hand at a passing servant, indicating he wished for a drink. "I think we can all agree that marriage has changed us all for the better."

The men all murmured their agreement.

Haddington approached the table and pulled out a chair. "Did I miss anything?"

"We are all singing praises about marriage," Hawthorne replied.

With a bob of his head, Haddington said, "It was the best decision I have ever made, but it took some groveling on my part to convince Evie." He paused. "But at least I didn't show up drunk for my own wedding."

Graylocke let out a sigh. "Are you ever going to let me live that down?" he asked.

"Perhaps, one day," Haddington said with a smile.

A server placed drinks down onto the table and walked away.

Hugh picked up a glass and raised it in the air. "I would like to make a toast to Stephen," he said. "Despite our many, many, many—"

Stephen spoke over him. "I get the point."

Hugh smirked. "Despite our vast differences, I am happy that you are marrying my cousin, Gemma, and I wish you a lifetime of happiness."

"Thank you," Stephen said before he tapped Hugh's glass with his own.

Hugh lowered his glass. "Does anyone else wish to make a toast?"

Haddington pushed back his chair and rose. As he held his glass up, he met Stephen's gaze and said, "There was a time when just the thought of you would make my blood boil, but now it is more tepid."

"Is there a point to your gibberish?" Graylocke asked.

Haddington's lips twitched. "I have come to realize that Stephen is a good man, and I am fortunate to consider him my friend."

"Did Evie tell you to say that?" Hawthorne joked.

"Perhaps," Haddington responded as he sat down.

Stephen grinned. "Thank you," he said. "I am pleased that we have been able to put our differences aside."

Hawthorne removed the pocket watch from his waistcoat pocket and glanced down. "It is almost time to head to the church. Are you ready?"

Stephen pushed his nearly full glass away from him. "I have never been more ready," he said. "I have been counting down the moments until Gemma will become my wife."

"Remember to make every moment count when you are with Gemma," Hawthorne counseled.

Grenton bobbed his head. "Marriage is the greatest adventure."

Stephen pushed back his chair and rose. "Shall we depart for the church?" he asked. "I don't think I can wait one more minute."

As all the men rose from their seats, Stephen felt a smile come to his lips. He couldn't wait to stand up in front of the church and profess his love for Gemma. She was his future, and the feeling was even more wonderful than he ever imagined it could be.

The End

# Coming Soon

**Some secrets are never meant to see the light of day.**

Miss Lizette Kent's life is in shambles. Not only did her mother just pass away, but she has been left without the means to provide for herself. While she is contemplating her future, she encounters an unexpected and vexing man: Tristan Westcott, a man that mistakenly seems to believe that she is the daughter of an earl, despite her insistence that she is not.

Tristan does not have time for games, but Lady Lizette is playing a maddening one with him. Lord Ashington assigned him to retrieve his granddaughter so that she may take her rightful place in Society. When their first meeting goes awry, he is forced to wait until she accepts the truth and allows him to escort her to London.

As two proud hearts negotiate a ceasefire, they reluctantly discover that they enjoy the other's company and begin to rely on one another. But as truths are unraveled, Lizette realizes that her future- and her heart- are in danger of being shattered.

# Also by Laura Beers

**Proper Regency Matchmakers**

Saving Lord Berkshire

Reforming the Duke

Loving Lord Egleton

Redeeming the Marquess

Engaging Lord Charles

Refining Lord Preston

**Regency Spies & Secrets**

A Dangerous Pursuit

A Dangerous Game

A Dangerous Lord

A Dangerous Scheme

**Regency Brides: A Promise of Love**

A Clever Alliance

The Reluctant Guardian

A Noble Pursuit

The Earl's Daughter

A Foolish Game

**The Beckett Files**

Saving Shadow

A Peculiar Courtship

To Love a Spy

# About the Author

Laura Beers is an award-winning author. She attended Brigham Young University, earning a Bachelor of Science degree in Construction Management. She can't sing, doesn't dance and loves naps.

Besides being a full-time homemaker to her three kids, she loves waterskiing, hiking, and drinking Dr Pepper. She was born and raised in Southern California, but she now resides in Utah.